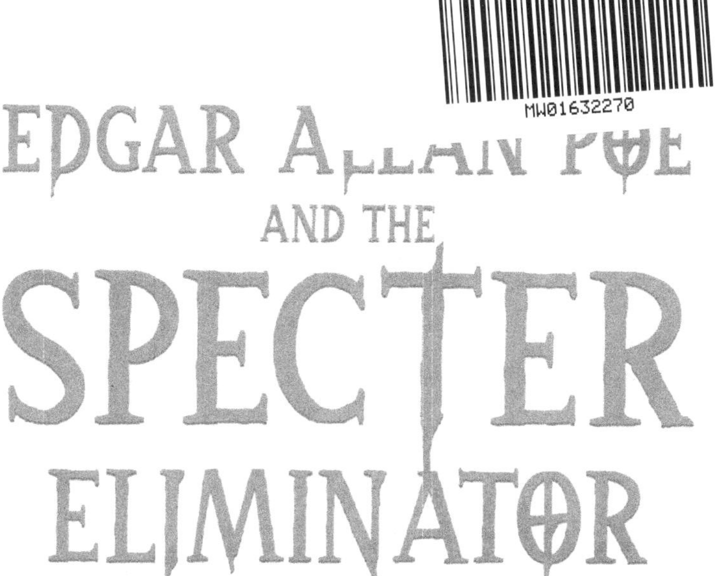

KEITH GOUVEIA & MATT PETERS

ISBN 978-1-63789-067-7
Gordian Knot is an imprint of Crossroad Press Publishing

For information address Crossroad Press at 141 Brayden Dr., Hertford, NC 27944
www.crossroadpress.com

First Edition - 2024

SPIRITS OF THE DEAD

Thy soul shall find itself alone
'Mid dark thoughts of the grey tomb-stone;
Not one, of all the crowd, to pry
Into thine hour of secrecy.

Be silent in that solitude,
Which is not loneliness - for then
The spirits of the dead, who stood
In life before thee, are again
In death around thee, and their will
Shall overshadow thee; be still.

The night, though clear, shall frown,
And the stars shall not look down
From their high thrones in the Heaven
With light like hope to mortals given,
But their red orbs, without beam,
To thy weariness shall seem
As a burning and a fever
Which would cling to thee for ever.

Now are thoughts thou shalt not banish,
Now are visions ne'er to vanish;
From thy spirit shall they pass
No more, like dew-drop from the grass.

The breeze, the breath of God, is still,
And the mist upon the hill
Shadowy, shadowy, yet unbroken,
Is a symbol and a token.
How it hangs upon the trees,
A mystery of mysteries!

Edgar Allan Poe, 1829

CHAPTER I

Chains clicked over sprockets and gears whirred as Specter Eliminator came to life. Edgar released the stoker—its skull knob once his favorite paperweight. In a few, short seconds, the ethereal tincture within would boil and iodized bitter salts would vaporize. He gripped the nozzle lance with both hands.

"Ma'am, I'm going to have to ask you to step aside."

"He's my husband."

"Was," Edgar said. "And I've been contracted to remove him from the premises. This establishment is none too pleased with a phantom scaring off its patrons."

"I'm a patron," Mrs. Dupuis said, standing with dignity between Edgar and the specter. "What about what I want?"

"Yes...well...." He was formulating a logical retort based on the benefit of pleasing one customer against the benefit of balancing the financial accounts, arguably not his strong suite, when he was spared when a small puff of vapor leeched from the nozzle's tip and hung on the air.

Mrs. Dupuis' eyes widened, and her bosom heaved in a deep breath as he leveled the weapon at her. Behind her stood the diaphanous, non-corporeal image of a man dressed in his Sunday best.

Unlike other specters Edgar had eliminated over the years, this spirit appeared calm, almost depressed, not at all restless or violent. He wondered if he was making a mistake in this case. But he could not ignore the complaints levied against the spirit, moaning at all hours, visiting adjoining rooms, flaring the gas lamps, and banging upon doors. This specter was calm at the moment; that was all. And having spent the retainer fee on cardstock, fresh ink, and a fine bottle of cognac—Edgar had no choice but to finish the job.

If this specter wished to act timid by hiding behind his widow, it was easy money.

Edgar had startled both the living and the dead when he'd burst into the lavish suite. A puzzled shock had adorned the woman's face, as if surprised someone—anyone—could have figured out her modus operandi.

The puzzle had proven rudimentary, his analytical mind not only deciphering the ghost's identity, but its routine as well within thirty minutes of looking over the Rowes Wharf hotel's ledger. The answer was there, written in felt pen for any common eye to see. Despite having one of the more luxurious homes in Boston, every Thursday night, Mrs. Dupuis checked into room 1140. The very room where Mr. Dupuis had been found murdered, presumably by his mistress's husband who was still at large. Edgar wasn't sure what transpired when Mrs. Dupuis visited, the late husband and widow had been conversing as if in their own drawing room when he entered, but it was obvious she had a calming effect on the specter, for on those nights she was absent, Mr. Dupuis's spirit drove guests from the premise in a speedy fashion and, worst of all, had them asking for a refund from the front desk.

"I know what they say, but he hasn't harmed anyone," she said.

The specter nodded in agreement.

"That is a matter of perspective," Edgar said over the hissing and clanging of his machine as pressure built. "It would be a shame to ruin such a lovely dress. Wool, I presume," Edgar said to move things along. "Please, Ma'am, step away."

With her hands on her curvy hips, she defied him. "What do you intend to do with that infernal contraption?"

"I assure you, Madame, he will feel nothing."

Her brow wrinkled as her nostrils flared in outrage. "How could you possibly know that?"

"Well…I…" She had a point. Being of the mortal coil he could never *truly* know. Not until the day of his own passing, at least. And, because they were always agitated, he'd never considered if the specters' final howls were of pain instead of frustration as he'd assumed.

The machine whistled, signaling it was primed.

Edgar grabbed Mrs. Dupuis' slender wrist. "Forgive me. I have to insist."

He pulled her out of the way. Her husband's pale face twisted into a snarl before he lunged, hands outstretched for Edgar's throat.

Edgar did not flinch. The sudden change of demeanor allowed him to shed his doubt and do what was required. With one hand keeping Mrs. Dupuis at bay, and the other on the lance, his finger applied pressure to the trigger.

The vaporized ethereal salts roared out with such ferocity that the nozzle's lance whipped his right arm off target. The white vapor knocked over a lamp. Its porcelain base shattered upon impact with the floor.

Mrs. Dupuis screamed, shrill and guttural, as if being murdered.

The room filled with an acrid fog. The immense heat and moisture blistered the floral wallpaper in a sweeping arc across the far wall before Edgar brought the lance around and finally engulfed the specter. Mr. Dupuis's curled fingers were mere inches from Edgar's throat, but Edgar barely heard the specter's growl over the rushing steam.

By the time the room cooled, and the vapor cloud cleared, the remnants of Mr. Dupuis's spirit had dissipated.

The woman wrenched her arm free and stepped in front of Edgar, her gaze scanning the room. "Beauregard?"

She whirled around to face him, the skirt of her sea foam-colored dress danced in her sudden movement, exposing the silk underlining. "What have you done to him?"

Edgar busied himself with coiling the hose and clipping the lance in its rightful place on his machine. The universe functioned on mathematical and astronomical principles. Everything and everyone were infinite pieces of the primordial particle, and a soul is nothing more than a collection of particles electrically unified by the gravitation of the body. Once the body dies, the particles of the soul dissipate, or should dissipate, and reunify with that primordial particle. Edgar merely helped errant souls along the natural path. But he wasn't sure how he could explain it to her.

The woman stomped her foot. "Answer me!"

"I imagine he passed on to the next world as he should have when he died."

Edgar opened a small door held in place by a hook latch, removed a hardcover book from the compartment and handed it to the woman. "A prose poem on the material and spiritual universe will help you understand what transpired here."

Mrs. Dupuis's brow wrinkled in her confusion. With a shaky hand she accepted the copy of his masterwork, *Eureka*.

Edgar smiled as she thumbed through the pages of his greatest achievement. "Just a simple token to elevate myself above the other brutes in this business."

A single tear streaked down her rosy cheek. "What will I do now? I have nothing without my Beauregard."

"My dear lady, with the fortune your husband has left in your name you shall want for nothing."

"I want my husband," she said through clenched teeth.

The argument lost, Edgar closed the small door. "Might I suggest a hobby then? Gambling perhaps?"

"How insensitive!"

The pulsating vein in the center of her forehead was Edgar's signal to go. He tilted his machine upon its axle and pulled it behind him, its wheels squeaking in protest as he exited the hotel room.

"I will not soon forget this!" Mrs. Dupris said as he closed her door.

In the hallway, a rankled guest looked upon Edgar for an explanation for the racket.

Edgar was not ashamed of this sideline employment and offered the man an honest explanation, "Merely eliminating a restless spirit." He nodded down at the Specter Eliminator as proof.

"Poppycock," the guest scoffed and slammed the door at Edgar as if slapping his face. Edgar merely shook his head and made his way toward the elevator car. Most people wouldn't believe in ghosts until the specter had them by the neck.

Once inside the cramped elevator car, Edgar simply said, "Lobby." The operator closed the accordion door and eased the drive lever forward. As the cage descended, Edgar counted the floors and noted the rhythm. Confident he could halt the cage with the doorway level to the lobby floor, he was tempted to ask the operator if he could give it a go.

While attending the University of Virginia, Edgar had discovered a hidden passion for solving puzzles and tinkering. He had an uncanny ability to dissect a machine and reassemble it in new, more efficient ways. The skill was utilized during his time as an Artificer in the Army and refined once he enrolled at West Point, but he found the idea of his creations being used in such a destructive and deadly manner disheartening and sabotaged his military career. Now that military life was just one of the many ghosts that haunted his mind, albeit a minor one.

The night manager greeted Edgar when the elevator door opened, standing before him in a half-bow with his hands folded together, and a toothy grin stretched across his cheeks. "I hope it went well, Mister Poe," the night manager said.

"Very," Edgar replied as he stepped off the elevator. "I shall be paid now."

"Won't you grant me a moment to inspect the room myself?"

Edgar flicked his wrist and waved the man off. As the elevator doors closed, he said, "Do not make me wait too long. I have other matters to attend to this night."

"I shan't be a moment." With that, the elevator car disappeared into the ceiling.

Edgar sighed loudly through his nose, eager to get home and continue work on his latest creation.

The single patron in the lobby looked up from reading today's paper. He wore a fine black suit and top hat and sat cozy in a high-back chair. Waiting for his wife to return from the theater, no doubt.

"Excuse me," Edgar said to the gentleman.

The gentleman nodded to Edgar but did not return to his paper. He offered a friendly, almost conspiratorial, smile, inviting conversation.

Edgar walked to the far end of the lobby and gazed upon the lobby's finery.

I should have negotiated better terms, he thought as he took in the fine wood carvings and gold leaf details in the crown molding. A large, crystal chandelier hung from the center of the ceiling, its light illuminated out into the street. The hotel's ambiance tickled his muse; one could write a great novel in any of these spacious rooms. No, not just a great novel, but a great *American* novel.

The elevator's door creaked as it opened, and the mousy-looking night manager stepped off with his lips pursed and brow furrowed.

"Mrs. Dupuis has confirmed your triumph."

"Naturally."

"However," the night manager said, "the room has suffered for it."

"It couldn't be helped." Edgar shrugged his shoulders. "You have a fine establishment here. Might I suggest a copy of my collection *Tales* for every room? Or perhaps a subscription to my magazine, *The Stylus*? It would certainly add a—"

"No," the man said as he walked past, not bothering to look Edgar in the eye as a true gentleman would.

The night manager returned to his station and pressed a single button on the cash register. With the chime of a bell, its drawer opened, and the man's fingers went to work. He pulled out several bills and three coins and placed them down in front of him.

Edgar narrowed his eyes as he tried to decipher if this were a jest, but the man stood defiant, his features cold.

"This is not the price the owner and I agreed upon," he said.

"I'm afraid the damage to the room must be compensated." The night manager tapped his fingers upon the desk in a rhythmic symphony.

"We'll just see about that."

The night manager simply nodded as if it was no threat to him.

"I'll be taking it up with the owner on the morrow," Edgar added to let the man know just how serious he was.

"Of course, sir," the night manager said with a smile, as if Edgar was a willful child making demands. Then he nodded once again. "Good evening to you."

Given what the hotel charged per night, Edgar figured their losses around seventy-five dollars per week for that floor. If he could not dicker a few more coins out of the deal, he could always threaten to put the specter back. Not that he actually had the capability for such a thing, but he would not share that information with anyone.

Edgar scooped the loose bills and three silver dollars off the counter, pocketed them, and walked out of the hotel with his head high and machine trailing close behind.

The transaction reminded him of the humiliation at *Graham's Magazine* when he discovered that scoundrel George Graham had been paying him four dollars a page where all the others received twelve. This time would be different, though, and he would fight for fair compensation or refuse the employment. No longer having to care for Virginia, Edgar refused to allow anyone to take advantage of him ever again.

CHAPTER II

Outside, an autumn breeze kissed his cheek and teased the hairs at the nape of his neck. The stars shone in the heavens and the moon reflected off the harbor. Waves splashed against the pier as a ship traversed the channel and Edgar couldn't help but wonder if it were carrying even more immigrants into the bustling city.

The scene stirred a myriad of images in his mind's eye as the muse whispered in his ear. He fished the coins out of his pocket and rolled them over his knuckles. The metal would make a fine accent to his creation. Tonight, he would allow the muse to work through his hands rather than his words. His medium would be silver, gears and spindles and springs rather than paper and pen.

As he walked Boston's cobbled streets toward the elevated cable car, he admired the city's beauty and basked in flickering gaslight and silence. Even the Quincy market was quiet. From the King's Chapel to The Common, the city was alive with history and inspiration for his writings. Though he would always be connected to his birthplace, Edgar knew the time was near to move on. The Wellmans, for whom he was currently house sitting, would return from safari within the week. Since Virginia's cruel and untimely passing, no one place had felt like home, and he often traveled to wherever there was work, whether it be lecturing, editing, or ghost hunting.

Virginia… He looked past gas lights, past the stars, and deep into the darkness, wondering if her light shined down on him now.

Then he felt the urge to drink. Not to forget her, but to dull the pain. No amount of alcohol could wipe her soft complexion, warm smile, soft brown hair, youthful spirit, and loving heart from his memory. She was ingrained in every fiber of his body, and her loss was an unfillable void.

And to think you once passed notes between Mary Devereaux and me. What a fool I was. Your forgiveness was a blessing.

There had been other women since her death, a few fiancés, but he could never refrain from comparing them to Virginia. The women, of course, knew this. Some walked away when this was revealed, others thought they could either live with it or change him. They were wrong.

The cable car had arrived when he reached the station and, as he lugged the Specter Eliminator up the steps to the platform, his thoughts turned to how he could make the damnable machine weigh less. He wove his way through the few disembarking passengers and made it onto the car before the gripman set it on its way.

Settling onto a bench between two gentlemen, he noticed their eyes upon his machine, their brows wrinkled in curiosity. He took out a few chapbooks and made his pitch. "Might I interest you in the prose of a fellow Bostonian?"

They shook their heads and looked away.

Typical. Exactly why he hated acknowledging himself as a Bostonian and only did so when in New England.

Edgar's thoughts drifted back to his Virginia and lingered there until he disembarked at Beacon Hill.

As he stepped out into the street, his gaze fixed on the swinging pub sign. "There's time for one drink," he said to no one, and then walked East instead of West.

Few patrons remained in the Blue Terrier at such a late hour, and Edgar recognized none of the current clientele. With its lavishly decorated mirrors, tiled walls and mahogany accents, the pub catered to the higher social class. Or so Edgar thought.

Edgar straddled up to the bar and the barkeep was already in the midst of pouring his drink. *Oh Virginia, I promised, but without you here, I must.*

As the barkeep placed the low-ball glass of Cognac before him, he said, "Mind yourself."

Edgar nodded in understanding as he slid his recently acquired bills across the bar top.

A hand engulfed the top of his glass, and another slammed down on his hand with the money.

"I find it hard to believe you have money for such fine indulgences, Mister Poe, while I patiently wait for you to pay your debt."

To Edgar's right, Andrew Hugh grinned ear to ear. Edgar then looked left to size up the hired muscle. A longshoreman for sure. Or perhaps, two longshoremen in one boiler suit. With a stern look, the barkeep was sent away, and the longshoreman guided Edgar's head back toward Andrew.

"When last we spoke about the salary loan I gave you in good faith, I was under the impression you had a high-profile job. And you assured me I would see my money before your other debtors."

"I fulfilled the job," Edgar replied.

"And?"

Edgar's tongue wet his lips, as if searching for that drink to steel his nerves.

"I'm waiting," Andrew said, and a firm hand pressed into his shoulder.

"There was a botheration with my payment. I'm going back tomorrow to negotiate—"

"There always seems to be a...*botheration* with you. You give me their name and me and Lewis will settle it up."

"Lewis and I," Edgar corrected and the pressure on his shoulder increased threefold. He gave the name of the night manager.

"Seeing how you can't afford to drink, you should go home." Andrew tossed back the Cognac in a single gulp. "And if all goes smoothly tomorrow for Lewis and me, then this will conclude our business."

Edgar found the man's boorishness off putting and wondered why he had ever gone into a business arrangement with this glorified street thug. The answer came hard and swift. Necessity. He had taken one loan to pay off another. A common practice of his that had shortened his options.

Without argument, Edgar stood and turned to leave.

"Be careful on your way home, Mister Poe," Andrew said. "We wouldn't want anything to happen to our great poet."

"Thank you for your concern," he said without looking back.

Nothing more than an idle threat, but it reinforced his need for work, either writing or ghost hunting. If only he could launch *The Stylus*; the magazine would set him up for the remainder of his years.

Edgar walked West a block and a half to the modest residence of the Wellman family, a red-brick home with fine, lavish furnishings. Though he cared little for the nautical instruments and paintings of ships—both on and off the dock—adorning the walls, he thought as he walked the hall, *perhaps one day I'll re-visit Arthur Gordon Pym and write another sea-faring adventure.* Mr. Wellman's life was interesting, to say the least, one worthy of documentation. The owner of several ships used in trade and whaling, he was afforded every luxury and rubbed elbows with the city's elite. Edgar certainly appreciated the vast library with several literary works even he had yet to read.

He stopped abruptly at the study door, the scotch inside calling him.

No. He buried the need. The work he intended to accomplish would require a steady hand and sober mind. He walked on past and entered his sleeping chamber.

With fresh kindling in the fireplace, Edgar dragged the oak table toward the bedside. Upon it rested his latest creation. In its current condition, it was nothing more than a hollowed-out husk, but in Edgar's mind it was already a masterpiece. The various wheels, sprockets, chains, springs, and pallets that would animate it were organized upon the table by size and quality. On the end table, dormant and silent, lay the gutted corpse of Mr. Wellman's fine ship's chronometer. A serious house-sitting transgression, but the precision and quality of the springs, cogs, and escapements needed to keep a chronometer accurate under the harsh conditions aboard a merchant vessel at sea made them irresistible. He could rarely find such parts, let alone afford them, so Edgar had plundered the chronometer. He planned to restore it to working order, but the chronometer would be rebuilt using Edgar's inferior parts. By the time the man of the house realized Edgar's malefaction, he would be miles from Boston, and not even Edgar knew where the roads would lead him this time.

Edgar had always had a fascination with exotic birds, but the idea of droppings left upon his backside from a bird on his shoulder was not befitting a gentleman of his stature. Inspiration struck during one of his loneliest of moments. No species in the world could be more exotic than a clockwork bird. *The Raven* had been, and still was, his one poetic success. He considered it a trifling poem, one popular mainly with ladies' clubs, but a poem that had become his mark. And so, to perpetuate his literary reputation and capitalize on his most popular poem, Edgar crafted the bird in the likeness of a raven.

Over the course of the last two weeks, he'd gathered materials, engineered designs, and cast forms. The breast, wings, and legs were made of burnished copper. A silver key protruded from its nether region. The wing's manus, metacarpals, ulna, radius, and humerus were jointed and hinged to the body with the hope of threading black feathers to the frame. But what material to use for the bird's feet and beak? Rubies would be perfect for its eyes, but he'd have to settle for something far less expensive.

With a firm, steady hand, and the aid of his magnifying goggles and tweezers, Edgar laid in the gear train, then gingerly inserted the spring-detent escapement, attached the mainspring, and finally added a balance wheel. With the foundation in place, he wiped the sweat from his brow and then attached a cannon pinion to a gear reduction for each wing.

He exhaled a deep breath. "Tomorrow," he said to the mechanical bird as he pushed the worktable off to the side, "we'll see if the saddle maker has finished your breast plate."

He stripped off his suit and pants, slipped on his nightshirt, and climbed underneath the goose-down comforter.

CHAPTER III

Edgar stood alone upon the stage. His heart raced, and his stomach roiled with anxiety as visitors were ushered from the anteroom. The large, circular chamber was too spacious. He could never draw a crowd large enough to fill all its seats. The three galleries above the parquet were first to be filled, he estimated those seats at fifty cents apiece. Was that all these fine folks deemed him worthy of? The higher end seats in the dress circle and private boxes remained empty.

And why was he on display for the patrons as they took their seats? Wasn't he deserving of a proper introduction? Patrons stepped and shuffled into the rows before him, but he found not a single distinguishable feature. There were far too many stage lamps for a simple reading. The glare overwhelmed his eyes. All he could make out were the tiny flames dancing along the aisles, insuring no one tripped on the descending steps, and blank, emotionless faces—a mask of taut skin devoid of noses, mouths, and eyes.

Edgar's voice lodged in his throat.

Was this some sick joke—a hoax to rile the horror writer? He held his tongue and remained professional. The faceless men and women awaited his macabre words, so he cracked the spine on his copy of Tales *and read the Raven's opening stanza.*

Two patrons harrumphed and walked out after the first line. He read on in his melodious voice without missing a beat, inwardly chastising their crassness.

Upon the fourth line, another two patrons stood and stomped out. The lack of physical features, and therefore expressions, made it impossible for him to deduce their reasoning for leaving. Were they unaware that tonight's reading was one of art and poetry? Perhaps they expected him to sing, or dance? Surely some mistake on their part. After all, he was a respected poet and editor, who has received dozens of invitations to recite and lecture.

As six more patrons walked out, he interrupted himself and called, "How dare you show me such blatant disrespect!"

Another four stood, turned their backs on him, and left.

"Fine! Leave!"

The remaining patrons stood.

"I still get paid. So, in the end, who did you hurt?"

With the last of the faceless ones gone, Edgar's head slouched forward in defeat. He stood alone in the dark, feeling worthless as a writer and a man.

Edgar awoke as the sun's early light peeked through the silk curtains, and its warmth radiated his cheek. He rubbed his eyes in an effort to stimulate them and erase the remnants of his dream. His vision came into focus and his gaze locked on his newest creation.

Perhaps I spent too much time on you last night, he thought.

Though his body could have rested easily for another hour, his mind had already begun the day's planning. He tossed the heavy bedding aside and walked out of the bedroom and into the hall. In the midst of a yawn, he caught sight of a whale's tooth on a nearby table.

"A scrimshaw," he said as he picked it up. The blunt end revealed the tooth to be hollow, but the ivory itself thick enough, perfect for what he had in mind for the beak and talons.

He marveled over the intricate, incised design. A squaw dressed in heavy fur as if it were winter when the image was captured in the artist's eye. The edges of the picture were blackened as though it were scorched by fire. He rotated the tooth and inspected every inch, looking for a spot where he could carve off a chunk without it being too noticeable. All the while, the Indian woman's piercing gaze remained locked on him. The detail was so precise, Edgar could not shake the feeling she was staring directly at his soul.

"I bet you kept a sailor or two in high spirits."

He could hollow it out from the bottom. *They'll never know,* he thought, then pocketed the piece in his pajama pants and continued his way toward the kitchen.

After coffee and some toast and jam, Edgar washed and dressed, then headed out. The city was alive with pedestrians, carts, horses, and carriages. Everyone had somewhere to be. Passersby tipped their hats and wished him a good day, and in turn, being the gentleman he was, he reciprocated.

As he turned down the north slope of Beacon Hill and crossed the unmarked border into the neighborhood of free coloreds, a few people stopped and gawked at him, as if shocked by his audacity in breaking through the social barrier. Like two sides of a coin, Beacon Hill was completely different on its south face than its north. On the southern side, individual Federal-style family homes by Charles Bulfinch stood opposite the brick, four-story rowhouses of the northern district. The small townhomes of the tradesmen lacked the finer qualities such as brass knockers, hand-carved moldings, and decorative columns of elite's mansions on the northern side.

Edgar cared nothing for his social transgression; coloreds were beneath him for sure, but so also were most all of his own race-the workmen, laborers, and farmers. As a gentleman, he was within his rights to conduct business with whomever he wished and if that necessitated a walk through what was not-so-affectionately called 'Mount Whoredom' by the Bostonians, then so be it. He walked with his back straight and shoulders up; the glances drifted elsewhere.

A thumping pulsed in the air like a steadily beating heart as Edgar approached the saddler's shop. Edgar walked around toward the back, where he found Mr. Thomas tapping a weave pattern into a fine piece of red leather. He wore nothing more than a leather apron and chaps decorated with intricate foreign designs. Sweat glistened on his biceps with each strike of the mallet, relaying to Edgar he had been working on this particular piece for some time already.

"Good morning, Mister Thomas."

Mr. Thomas looked up and said, "Mornin,' sir," to acknowledge Edgar, but hit the stamp twice more to finish some small detail before laying it and the mallet upon the bench. Edgar respected his work and Mr. Thomas didn't need to kowtow or play the fool with him.

He wiped his hands on his apron as he stood and shook Edgar's hand. "You will be pleased to hear your piece is finished."

Edgar slapped his hands together. "Excellent!"

The saddle maker picked up a rag draped over the edge of his workbench and dragged it across his brow and shaven head. "Follow me."

Mr. Thomas led the way toward the front of the store, a small showroom where six of the finest looking horse saddles Edgar had ever seen were on display. The saddle bases were wrapped in cushioning for the horse's comfort. Each had a deep seat and high cantle, and leather of the highest quality. Silver studs decorated the outer perimeter on one of the saddles, and another had colorful glass beads.

"Your craftsmanship causes me to wish I owned a horse."

The giant of a man smiled. "Thank you." He walked around the counter and bent at the knees. When he came up, the tin breast plate seemed lost in his boulder-sized hands. "Did you bring the piece this is to be mounted too?"

"No, sir, I did not."

"Shame. Would've liked to've seen the finished product." Mr. Thomas placed the item on the counter for Edgar to inspect.

Wide eyed, Edgar picked up the clockwork raven's breastplate, his fingertips barely touching the edges. True, he'd come to Mr. Thomas for a lower price than he'd get at a silversmith, but he also hoped the man's native style would lend a more authentic feel to the piece. The details far exceeded Edgar's expectations and were superior to any he could have managed on his own. Instead of a uniform pattern of stamped feathers, Mr. Thomas set some askew and ruffled others slightly- the imperfections creating an impression that a raven's breast had been turned into tin rather than replicated in tin.

"Did you stamp or etch these feathers?" Edgar asked.

"A little of both, sir."

"Marvelous."

The saddle maker nodded his head, a toothy grin stretched across his cheeks.

Edgar placed the breastplate down on the counter and fished in his pants pocket for the three silver dollars he had earned the night before, then held them out. "I believe this will cover it."

"You are too kind."

Mr. Thomas held out his hand and Edgar dropped the coins into his palm.

"I'm curious," Mr. Thomas said.

"About what?" Edgar asked.

"This ghost hunting you do, is it lucrative?"

"No, not very," Edgar explained. "An individual hunt pays well, usually, but hunts themselves are few and far between."

"All right. Good." Mr. Thomas's shoulders relaxed, and he smiled. "So, not many ghosts to hunt, then," he said, more to himself than Edgar.

"No, I didn't mean to give you that idea" Edgar said. "It's just most people who require my services wish to keep their privacy, so referrals are scarce. Then there are those who need help but don't seek it. They rationalize the disturbance as a draft or some other such nonsense."

The indomitable man averted his gaze.

"All right then," Edgar said, not wanting to pry. He had seen the behavior enough to know arguing was frivolous, when someone was ready to accept the unacceptable, they came looking for him. He changed the subject to ease the man. "By any chance, would you happen to have any more of those colorful glass beads?" Edgar pointed toward the saddle that had caught his eye earlier.

"Do I!" Mr. Thomas squatted down once more, and this time came up with a wooden box heaped to the top with glass balls of various sizes. "Help yourself."

Edgar's fingers rummaged through the beads. He pushed aside the browns, greens, and blues. If he could not have rubies for the raven's eyes, he would at least have red glass. Though it took a few minutes to find two perfectly shaped red orbs, his search was not deterred, and his patience was rewarded.

Not exactly identical, but they'll do just fine, he thought, staring at the two he had selected. Both had an identical vibrant color, but one had been cut on one side giving it an almost crystal-like appearance. *That'll be the side I set into the socket.* He smiled at his own ingenuity.

"I'll take these," he said, displaying his newfound treasures. "What do I owe you?"

The saddle maker held his hand up. "No charge."

Edgar smiled. "Thank you kindly."

"You're most welcome."

Mr. Thomas returned to his work and Edgar scooped up his belongings and saw himself out.

He walked home with a longer stride, eager to get home and finish his raven. If any eyes were upon him, he did not notice nor did he care, his mind preoccupied with attaching the breastplate, installing the glass eyes, and carving a suitable beak and feet from the whale tooth.

As he walked up the stone path toward the Wellman home, a voice off to his right called to him.

"Mister Poe!"

He turned to see a city letter carrier bounding up the sidewalk.

"Mister Poe, good morning. I have a delivery for you." The man already had his hand in his satchel as he turned down the cobblestone path. By the time he reached Edgar, the letter was in his hand and held out before him.

"Thank you," Edgar said, taking the proffered letter.

"Good day, sir," said the letter carrier before turning around and heading off for his next destination.

Edgar looked over the envelope, reading the return address. "Portland," he mumbled.

He knew of no publishing house located in Portland, so it wasn't a rejection or acceptance letter, and since he had no time for fan mail, he dismissed it for the time being and retrieved the house keys from his pocket. Whatever it was, it could wait, for right now only one thought dominated his mind.

Once inside the house, he hung his jacket, tossed the unopened letter onto the table beside the door, and then headed straight for his sleeping chamber where he had left the clockwork raven.

"I need a knife," he said, putting the glass beads down beside the copper body of the raven. Before heading toward the kitchen, Edgar took a calming breath, realizing he was too anxious. He needed to keep his excitement in check, or else face making a crucial mistake and botching his hard work.

He chose the sharpest looking knife in the drawer and snatched up the scrimshaw.

In the sleeping chamber, he dug the knife's blade into the blunt end of the whale's tooth. He quietly asked for forgiveness as if Mr. Wellman were in the room watching him desecrate his possession. As the gum and sulfur mixture heated for the adhesive, he whittled a beak and talons from the shavings and polished them to a high sheen.

When the adhesive had vulcanized, Edgar was finally satisfied with his polishing. He brushed the elastic glue onto the base of the beak halves in a hatch pattern and held each firmly to the face. First the small lower beak, then the larger upper. He went over the beads for flaws once more and used the minute scratches he found as a gripping point for the adhesive. Once set on either side of the head as eyes, the beads appeared identical, the face symmetrical. He attached the talons to the feet, and then finally screwed on the breastplate.

As he admired his work, he sighed in disappointment. He found the sight of the raven's featherless wings humbling. "I was too fixated on what I had, I forgot what I didn't," he said to the raven as if it could understand him.

Still, the urge to wind the key and see his creation in motion was hard to resist. He had worked so hard, and even if it wasn't complete, he needed to see it work. With the clockwork raven upturned in his left hand, he inserted the key between its legs and gave it a couple of twists. Just enough to test the set of the gears.

But the clockwork bird was not to be a mere amusement, not a mechanical pet that wouldn't ruin finery. Edgar's creation was first and foremost an alarm — a tool that would detect spirits and alert him to their presence.

Barometers had long been used to detect ghosts, but on a job, Edgar couldn't spend his time watching for a minute fluctuation in air pressure to indicate a specter was about to suck the life from him. He needed to be alert and ready to act. In his daydreams, he'd theorized about attaching a small bellows to a modified bird call to give a mechanical bird a voice. Inspiration stuck when he pondered how to activate the mechanical voice. Could he link the bellows with a barometer to not only activate the voice, but give the voice a purpose as well? And with that, Edgar's desire to create a clockwork spirit detector in the form of a mechanized bird became monomaniacal. If his creation worked as designed, whenever Edgar came in proximity of a specter, his clockwork raven would caw out a warning — keeping him alive and alerting him to potential business.

Edgar stood it on the table and sat at the edge of the bed, slouched forward, hands on his knees like a boy watching a fire take.

He picked up a probe and inserted it under the left wing to trip the bellows. "Come on," he said as the gears inside the raven's breast whirred to life.

The wings were the first to move, and only acted as a reminder of his failure. The framework flapped upward, then enveloped the copper body as if in a shudder.

The beak opened and closed and "CAW! CAW!! CAW!!!" The raven sounded its alarm. The head turning right, then left with each call.

Edgar's hands shot to his ears as the alarm echoed in the room and throughout the house. "Almost perfect," he said, gaze fixated on his new pet as the device ran through its fixed series of actions.

The copper and tin raven flapped its wing frames and then, unable to fly, it hopped into Edgar's lap. The sight forced a smile on Edgar's face. An overwhelming sense of pride in his work warmed his heart. Not since before Virginia's death had he felt so joyful.

There had been many accomplishments since her passing, the creation of the Specter Eliminator engine, the sale of "The Poetic Principle" and "Eureka," but without her there to celebrate with him, they were next to meaningless.

He lifted his creation up with both hands, face to face, eye to glass eye. "Virginia would have loved you. She'd have thought you whimsical."

The raven wound down and all motor functions ceased.

With pursed lips and the nod of his head, he placed the raven down on the table, careful to make sure it did not tip over, then walked out of the bedroom and down the hall. As he took his jacket off the coat hanger, his gaze locked on the letter.

I should be able to find some loose feathers around the pier and at the common, he thought as he tossed his jacket over his shoulders. *I suppose I am not above killing a black bird and taking what I need.*

He exited through the front door, leaving the letter on the table unopened.

Edgar returned home with two black feathers in his possession. He had found several white gull feathers and a few brown, but he wasn't willing to compromise.

A rustle in the nearby bush distracted him just as he was about to insert the house key. He turned to see emerald, green eyes staring up at him.

Meow!

The cat leapt out from underneath the bush and darted down the walkway. The feral beast disappeared into the shadows, and Edgar looked back down at its hiding spot. He could have sworn he saw black feathers sticking out from the corner of its mouth. Edgar slouched forward, rested his hands on his knees for support, and found a poof of black feathers. A smile forced its way onto his face. He stood, peered over his shoulder, and shouted to the cat, "Thank you."

At least I didn't disturb its meal, he thought as he gathered the feathers. *Would've been a senseless death if I had.*

With the necessary feathers in hand, he entered the Wellman home. The envelope sitting on the table caught his eye.

Edgar dropped the pile of feathers onto the table, unsealed the envelope and pulled out a folded piece of paper. The handwriting was clean, and he knew then it came from someone educated, but it wasn't concerning a lecture or reading. This was about business.

Dear Mr. Poe,

I hope this letter finds you well. My name is Ellie Feller, and I was referred to you by Mr. George Darby of Boston who spoke very highly of your talent for removing spirits.

I have an unusual request. I fear my brother, John, has met an ill fate. Like you, his profession is in the removal of spirits. His most recent job was at the Portland Head Light at Cape Elizabeth, and I have received word that he has not come out in two days.

My brother is a brave and proud man, and if my intuition is wrong, he will most certainly be cross with me, but since the caretaker of the lighthouse refuses to step inside, I have no choice but to beg for your assistance. With our father gone and mother bedridden, John is our only lifeline in this world. Please, I beg you, bring him home.

I will most certainly compensate you for your time and trouble.

Miss Feller

To Edgar, it was most likely some fool amateur had gone and gotten himself killed. However, if there was the slightest chance that he could indeed save this man's life, then he needed to act. He could call on this Ellie Feller for more information, but without knowing if she had reached out to anyone else, he couldn't afford to stop off to gather more information. George was a good man, and a fine blacksmith and great source of work, but the odds were good he provided Miss Feller with a whole list of Ghost Hunters.

"I've already lost a day," he said, convincing himself. He looked at his pocket watch and wondered if it were too late to catch the train. "Worst case scenario, I sleep at the station."

Edgar packed with feverish fervor. His clothes shoved into his suitcase without being folded properly, a scribbled letter barely legible for the Wellmans explaining the situation, and a dash through the house making sure windows and doors were locked and everything was in its proper place.

Though the house would be empty for two days, Edgar knew there would be no suspicion if he weren't seen. The neighbors would assume he was caught up in the throes of writing. And to disturb him meant incurring the artist's wrath.

He exited the home with his suitcase in one hand and pulling the Specter Eliminator behind him. The clockwork raven clamped onto the handle as if it were its natural perch, and indeed it was to be.

He mentally plotted his course as he walked to the train station. He would use the Boston and Maine Railroad exit in Portland, and from there take a horse drawn carriage to Cape Elizabeth.

He prayed that he would arrive in time to be of some use.

CHAPTER IV

Though the salt air would wreak havoc on his inventions if he stayed too long, Edgar could not think of a finer example of New England's beauty than Cape Elizabeth.

The white, conical tower of the Portland Head Light stood a hundred and one feet above water, its beacon flame still fueled by whale oil. The sound of water breaking on the rocks soothed him and one look at the quaint cottage attached to the lighthouse set his imaginative gears whirring with possible plots.

Perhaps another time, he thought.

"You sure you know what you're getting yourself into?" asked the coach driver as they drew closer.

"Why? What *am* I getting myself into?"

"That last fellow went in four days ago and hasn't come out. Another came round, a gentleman much like yourself, but was too cowardly to even venture inside."

Edgar held his tongue at the hypocrisy of the man's last comment. "Well, they should have hired me as their first choice," he finally said, gaze fixated on the lighthouse.

"Perhaps," said the old man, "but you won't find many willing to venture inside. Especially at night."

"I'm surprised to hear of such cowardice. Two ships have already wrecked and lost their crew—"

"There's been more than that over the years."

"Does anyone know who the spirit is?"

"Speculation only, of course, but many believe it is the ghost of Jonathon Bryant."

"And who is he?" Edgar asked, and then corrected his tense. "Was he?"

"One of the masons hired to build it. He walked off the job when it was decided to make the lighthouse taller. He believed anything above fifty-eight feet would be a death trap. Whether he is making it true or not is up for debate, but many costly repairs have already been made. From leaks to faulty flooring, there's been problem after problem."

"Is the keeper still on the premises?"

"No. Shame, too, as those quarters are fairly new."

"Then I'm certain I'll be comfortable during my stay."

"Let's pray you don't become a permanent resident. Whoa, Chester." He pulled on the reins and the carriage stopped a good twenty feet from the keeper's house. "I'm afraid this is where we part."

"You won't even bring me to the door?"

The old man looked over his shoulder and narrowed his eyes. "This is as far as I go."

"It's not even dark yet. Didn't you say—?"

"Out!"

With a nasal sigh, Edgar stepped off the coach and then retrieved his belongings. "I still expect you to come back in the morning."

"Awfully sure of yourself, aren't you?"

"I am a professional."

"You'll find me right here on the morrow. Best of luck to you, Mister. He-yah!"

Chester reared up at the tug on his reins, and then bolted. The carriage tilted left and right, and Edgar wondered why the old driver couldn't have gotten him here as quickly as he was fleeing now.

He really wasn't surprised by the man's sudden departure. When he'd arrived in Portland, and inquired about traveling arrangements, none were eager to help.

Edgar walked over to the cliff's edge and stood above the rocky precipice. Down below, waves crashed against the deadly coastline and the lighthouse's significance was not lost on him. Regardless of the fact that he was not the first choice for the job, he knew he needed to put his pride aside and get it done.

He entered the keeper's cottage, and a pungent odor bombarded his senses—a combination of excrement and garbage. Tears pooled in his eyes as his left hand shot up to cover his mouth and nose. On the kitchen table, centered in the room, flies buzzed around a half-eaten chicken carcass and what Edgar could only imagine as boiled potatoes.

It would appear John was in the middle of a meal when he was attacked.

Leaving his suitcase by the door, afraid the god-awful smell would somehow seep into his clothes; he wheeled his eliminator into the abode, the clockwork raven wound and alert upon the handle.

Aside from the deplorable mess left, not too shabby, he thought as his gaze traveled around the vast open room in search of John's body. There was no doubt in his mind he was too late to save John Feller, but there was still a spirit to exterminate and a fee to collect.

What do we have here? His gaze locked on an open book; face up on the floor by the door to the adjoining lighthouse.

As he took a step toward it, the temperature in the room dropped, and a chill danced down Edgar's spine. The hairs on his arm stood rigid. A mechanical screech caused his body to flinch uncontrollably, and he turned to see the clockwork raven's wing frames jerk upward and its head spin completely around.

Edgar removed his three sets of refracting eyeglasses from his waistcoat pocket and searched for the energy trace of the specter. Each set of lenses had been designed to reveal a different level of spectral intensity. Even if the phantom wasn't manifested, Edgar should see it, no matter how weak its signature. None of the pairs revealed a single trace.

When the bird's wings returned to its sides, the chill dissipated. *He couldn't have been successful,* Edgar thought, finding it odd the spirit was not attacking him as it had John. He didn't expect the keeper's cottage to be infected. The specter was most likely confined to the lighthouse itself. And even if the specter did inhabit the cottage, it was still day. Perhaps the bird was so sensitive it was reacting to the mere proximity of the spirit. *Good work Engineer Poe,* he congratulated himself.

Or maybe it was just that the sea air was already affecting the raven's mechanisms, though that seemed unlikely, considering he'd built the thing from nautical grade parts. "I'll check for rust later," he told the bird, then bent at the knees, and picked up the book that had piqued his interest.

He turned it over as he stood; it was a Bible. *Figures*, he thought. John Feller was not, for lack of a better term, a ghost hunter like himself. The man was a spiritualist, relying on mysticism to transfer earth bound spirits to the ever after.

With the Bible in hand, he faced the white door. Images of blood-smeared walls and corruptions of the flesh flashed through his mind. Dark possibilities of what lay in wait behind the door.

It must be done. Edgar tossed the Bible down on the table, scattering the flies from their meal, and steeled his nerves. With a deep breath and his eyes closed, he reached for the door handle.

The hinges creaked as it opened and revealed a small puddle of congealed blood on the floor. A mixture of squeaks and chattering teeth echoed in the open space and Edgar looked up to find a body hanging from the underside of the spiral staircase. Edgar covered his mouth with the back of his hand at the sight of the body's skinless skull and fleshless hands. At least a dozen rats crawled on top of the brown suit in search of more fleshy delicacies.

Edgar made the sign of the cross and said a quick prayer for the departed, more out of respect than for protection.

Despite the sunlight still filtering down from the lighthouse head, Edgar felt vulnerable. He retrieved the Specter Eliminator, primed it, and dragged it slowly up the metallic, spiral staircase.

Once level with the body, he saw John's left hand was tucked under the rope and pressed against his neck. He changed his initial notion of suicide. John had struggled, that much was clear. Edgar scanned for traces of the malicious spirit but could find none. *Perhaps he managed to do enough damage to force the spirit into hiding while it gathers its strength.*

Confident in this assumption, he approached John with little trepidation, but he could not help taking the occasional nervous glance over his shoulder as he inspected the body. The notion of the spirit materializing and shoving him down the stairs was not one his mind was willing to disregard.

Though the sight would have sickened a lesser man, Edgar had been desensitized years before. John's eyes were completely eaten away, as well as his lips and cheeks exposing the partially chewed jawbones. Pieces of mangled flesh still clung to the skull in odd-shaped patches adorned with bloody, rodent footprints. Under the unbuttoned shirt, and down the length of John's arms, Edgar could have counted at least a hundred bite marks and one missing finger.

Poor bastard, Edgar thought. *Now, how to get you down?*

Edgar had kept the envelope with Ellie's return address and had already resolved to make certain a body was brought home for a proper burial if he discovered John dead. Though he could imagine the distraught woman's reaction to her brother's mutilated corpse, it was the right—respectful—thing to do, for both the living and the dead.

With his left hand gripped tightly on the rail, he stretched his right arm toward John, hoping to grab hold of his boot or the cuff of his pants, but came nowhere close. Edgar peered down to the bottom floor of the lighthouse and wondered how much more damage John's body would endure from such a fall.

Only as a last resort, he told himself as an image of the body liquefying upon impact with the stone floor from such a height flashed before his mind's eye.

Without a knife, or the desire to haul his machine down the spiral staircase to fetch one, Edgar climbed the stairs higher and went to work untying the knot holding the rope taut. Unfastening the knot under tension proved daunting, but with the knot finally undone, he let the slack out in the rope. A single rodent lost its footing as the body swayed. The rodent plummeted to its death. Edgar could have sworn the others looked on with saddened eyes and heavy hearts, but they were just animals, incapable of such remorse.

He let the body drop several inches. The rats scurried up the rope and across his arms. Gooseflesh rippled across his skin, small lacerations formed under his clothing as their sharp nails dug into him in their haste, and bile burned his esophagus at the thought of their mange-ridden bodies crawling all over him. Arms locked, eyes closed, and lips pursed, Edgar waited for the moment to pass, holding steadfast as the vermin ran up his shoulders and down his back, returning to the stairs.

With both hands on the rope, he let out more slack as he took a step down the stairs toward the body.

"All right, work with me now," he said as if John could understand, then paid out more line to lower the body to within reach.

Edgar nudged John's body and it rocked an inch, the process of swinging him closer began. By the time his body swung close enough to grab hold of, Edgar's arms no longer wanted to cooperate. His shoulders ached and his hands itched. He reached out to catch John as he approached, but with little strength left, John slipped from his single-handed grasp and the rope dragged through Edgar's palm. The bright flare of pain ignited in his hand, and he instinctively released the rope.

"Oh," Edgar grabbed for the tail end of the rope as it fell, but it was beyond his reach. John plummeted to the cold, unforgiving stone floor below.

Not good, he thought as he grabbed his machine and huffed down the stairs.

At the bottom, John's lifeless body lay face down, arms underneath, and the left leg twisted at an odd ninety-degree angle.

"Botched that, didn't I?" he said as he scratched the back of his head.

With the smell from the other room reminding him of the mess he had found himself in, Edgar was faced with two choices. Clean up or sleep outside. With the sun setting, the temperature outside falling to the mid-forties, and the air damp, Edgar's choice was made.

He left the Specter Eliminator primed and his refracting lenses on as he disposed of the food scraps, wrapped John's body in a sheet taken off the single bed, and gave the dishes and kitchen table a good washing. Though he knew the animals would be attracted to John's body if he left it outside, he simply could not bear to have it indoors with him. He couldn't shake the idea of the rats returning and then venturing toward him as he slept.

As he cleaned, Edgar could not shake the feeling of someone—something—watching him. He stole the occasional glance around the room, but each search confirmed he was alone with his inventions. A few times he heard foot falls but was unsure if they came from inside or out. Either way, his searches proved fruitless.

Exhausted, he threw himself upon the bed and succumbed to the night.

CHAPTER V

"I find it quite unseemly that you invited the dead. Why should we have to compete against them for your affections?"

"Wait...what?" Edgar sat at the head of a long, mahogany table in a large, open, dining room. To his left sat, Sarah Helen Whitman and Elmira Royster—two women he had been engaged to in the years that followed his wife's death; to his right, Francis Allan and his biological mother, Elizabeth, and opposite of him, his wife Virginia—the young woman he had given his heart, his soul to.

He found himself staring at her, lost for words.

"Excuse me," said Sarah, "I was waiting for an answer." She turned away from him to address the other women. "This is precisely the reason I called off our engagement."

"Typical," Elmira said, "even though he's sitting right next to you, he's miles away. Off in some dark corner of his mind, thinking God knows what."

"At least he appears sober," Sarah added.

"Ladies, please," said Elizabeth, "Edgar is a good boy."

"Agreed," said Francis. "With all the tragedy in his life, it's no wonder his thoughts remain with the past."

Sarah snickered. "His actions are self-destructive in order to reset the sorrow and lost love he started with."

"Exactly," Elmira chimed, "he thrives off tragedy."

Edgar stood and slammed the palms of his hands on the table. "I do not have to sit here and listen to this character assassination."

His foster mother looked up at him with her left eye narrowed. "Sit down."

As Edgar took his seat, a hard fact was made painfully obvious to him. The realization that he had an affection toward a certain type of woman. Having each of these ladies before him at the same time, their similarity was undeniable. Shoulder-length, black hair framed soft complexions and rosy cheeks, petite noses and plump lips, and wide, sorrowful brown eyes.

"These are fine women, Son," Elizabeth said. "Why couldn't you have been a fine man?"

Edgar ignored the question and looked directly at Virginia. "I've missed you," he said.

In return, she cracked a half-smile as if he had informed her of something she was already privy to.

"Are you going to say anything?" he asked Virginia. "I've longed to hear your voice again."

"Can't you see she's ashamed of you?"

Edgar gave Sarah a sideways glance, too gentlemanly to tell her to stuff it. He turned back to Virginia. "Please."

Virginia broke eye contact with him, looking to her right. "Ah, dinner is ready."

Edgar found his wife's voice cold and flat, lacking the warmth and life he had been so fond of.

A well-dressed servant stepped out of the shadows and placed a dome-covered silver platter in the center of the table. "Bon appétit," he said, removing the cover and revealing Edgar's head with an apple stuffed in his mouth. One look into his own, glossed, dead eyes was enough to stifle his appetite.

When he did not move to serve the main fare, his ladies took up their silverware and beat the handles upon the table in unison like the rude, impatient boys at school used to.

Edgar awoke to the *click-clack* of Chester's hooves. Without checking himself in a mirror, he leapt from the bed and headed outside to greet the coach, afraid of the crotchety old man leaving prematurely out of fear.

The driver smiled upon seeing him, then pulled on the reins. "Good to see you alive."

"Good to see you're a man of honor," Edgar said.

"I presume you were successful!"

"Not exactly." Edgar stroked Chester's forehead, brushing the horse's black mane back behind its ear.

"What about the other guy?" asked the driver.

"I was too late to be of any use to him." Edgar turned away from the horse and peered over at the wrapped body. It appeared to be as he had left it.

"Shame," said the old man. "So, what now?

"I'd like to spend one more night. Will you come back tomorrow?"

The old man broke eye contact with Edgar and peered off toward the horizon. "I don't know. This concluded our business—"

"I'll pay you." Edgar removed a single bill from his pocket and offered it up.

The driver scratched his chin, still refusing to look Edgar in the eye.

"Fine," Edgar said, retrieving another bill.

"Same time tomorrow then?" he asked, snatching the money before Edgar could change his mind.

"Please."

"You have enough provisions to get you through?"

The mention of food brought a quick rumble from his stomach, a reminder that any food left behind was either spoiled or on the cusp of turning.

"I'll tell you what…." Edgar fished out three more bills, "You take me and Mister Feller to town, then return me, and this is all yours."

"Deal." The old man snatched the money. "But I ain't touching him." He pointed to the body.

"Fine."

Once John's body was loaded on the back of the coach, Edgar stepped inside and gave the go-ahead to the driver. He felt uneasy leaving his inventions at the lighthouse but knew the fear and ignorance of the neighboring people would keep them safe.

Though the road was riddled with bumps and missing stones, the ride was pleasant thanks to the plush padding. Along the way, Edgar's thoughts drifted to the poor girl to whom he would have to deliver such terrible news to. He knew all too well the emotional turmoil caused by the loss of a loved one, and though he could not relate to sitting by the bedside of a parent, waiting for their death, he imagined it, too, was a bitter pill.

An image of his foster father slouched in an armchair flashed through his mind. Unable to lie down in the comfort of his bed, John Allan had died in his favorite chair. Despite their strained relationship, Edgar had immediately returned to the Allan house upon word of his foster father's illness only to be chastised once more. The image of John threatening to strike him down with his cane where he stood still haunted him. John's swollen legs and bulbous abdomen from the accumulation of fluid were still vivid in his mind. Out of spite for the refusal of his aid, or the welcoming of his forgiveness, Edgar had passed on the funeral. A decision he had yet to lose sleep over.

One of these days I should at least visit his tombstone, he thought, before pushing the matter from his mind entirely.

The coach stopped and Edgar pulled the white curtain back to peer out the window. *Must be the coffin maker's,* Edgar thought, seeing the shack-like structure with the variety of coffins chained together in a row, ranging in size and material propped against the weathered boards.

As Edgar stepped from the carriage, the front door creaked open, and a homely looking man stepped out to greet them. He wore a gray suit, the shirt underneath an odd yellow as if it were stained with sweat and or other bodily fluids, and though the man did not appear elderly, white hair jetted out from underneath the hat's rim.

"Good day, gentleman," said the coffin maker.

"Good day, sir," Edgar replied, trying not to stare at the jagged scar running down the full length of his face on the left side.

"What can I do for you today?"

"I am in need of your services. I must travel with a corpse and I'm afraid a sheet simply won't do."

"Come," said the man, extending his arms and inviting Edgar inside to peruse his wares. "I have many fine coffins to choose from."

Once inside the shop, Edgar lowered his voice and confided, "Also, if it's possible, the body is in… disorder."

"No worries, sir. I have a few tricks up my sleeve," the coffin maker assured him with a confident nod. "Now, what kind of wood can I interest you in?"

Edgar gave a quick glance over the coffins and crude contraptions designed to alert the living that their loved ones were buried alive. He settled on a plain pine box. "This one will do."

"Would you like me to line it with velvet? Perhaps a nice—"

"No thank you," Edgar said, "My funds are limited, and I will have to be reimbursed for the purchase by the family."

"I see. Very well."

The man's head hung low, and Edgar wished he could do more for him, but it simply was not possible. He knew the chances of being reimbursed were slim, given the letter's claim, and he could not afford to be out of pocket for such an expense.

"If you would just bring the body inside. I'll make the preparations."

"Thank you," Edgar said as the man returned inside.

"Don't look at me," said the coach driver. "I ain't touching no body."

"Fine." Edgar approached the backside of the carriage and then hoisted the sheet covered body up onto his shoulder without hesitation. As he walked toward the shack, John's arm slipped out from under the sheet and Edgar swore he heard the old man gasp.

"I'd like to make it home for dinner."

Edgar narrowed his eyes at the driver. "Could you at least get the door?"

The old man nodded his head and jumped down from his perch.

I'll have to kill that man…, he thought, *fictionally speaking of course.* The idea put a smile on Edgar's face.

"Christ it stinks in here!" said the coach driver as he pinched his nose.

As Edgar entered the place of business, the coffin maker pointed to a metal slab in the center of the single room. Edgar laid John's body atop it and took a step back.

As the coffin maker unfolded the sheet, Edgar asked, "Any recent murders or child deaths in the area?"

"What the hell kinda question is that?" asked the coach driver, his brow wrinkled with disgust.

The coffin maker stopped what he was doing and turned to Edgar, wide-eyed and slack jaw.

"I meant no offense," Edgar said, surprised he had offended a man of his profession. "It's just that…those are the ones who need my…services."

The old coachman crossed his arms and let loose a nasal sigh while the coffin maker returned to removing John from the sheet.

"And how did you say this happened?" he asked upon seeing the state of the body.

Edgar knew the question was rhetorical, a simple snide remark from a man most would find odd. In fact, Edgar was certain the scar on the man's face came from either a distraught customer or a bully.

The old coachman's cheeks puffed out and his hand shot toward his mouth at the sight of John. In a flash, he bolted out of the shack and Edgar could not help the smile that forced its way onto his face.

"I take it he didn't know about this," said the coffin maker, a grin adorning his face as well.

"Not a clue," Edgar said.

"I can fix this. Maybe take some skin from the backside of another body. Wouldn't take me more than a day."

"That won't be necessary."

"Suit yourself. Quick and dirty it is. Shouldn't be more than an hour." The coffin maker turned away from Edgar and fiddled with the tools sprawled out across his table. "Come back then."

"Thank you," Edgar said, not knowing what else to say. He feared he may have offended the man. Though he respected the fact he was a simple businessman, Edgar just could not justify such an expense.

He walked out of the shack to find the old man giving water to his horse.

At least he loves something.

"Ready?" asked the driver.

"Not exactly," Edgar said. "We have an hour to waste."

"Plenty of time to get into town and fetch provisions." The old man gave Chester one last stroke across his muzzle, then climbed up into the driver's seat.

Edgar stepped onto the coach and glanced back at the row of coffins before they were off.

As they traveled to town, Edgar could not help but feel sympathetic toward the coffin maker. The man was alone, much like himself, segregated to the outskirts of town, and by the looks of his scar, subjugated as well.

And here I am taking away what little joy he manages to eke out of this existence by turning his offers of service down.

Though he still felt the work unnecessary, Edgar would buy the gentleman a fine bottle of cognac as a consolation.

In town, the driver took Edgar to the market and the butcher shop for needed supplies before returning to retrieve John's body.

CHAPTER VI

After dinner, and with no sign of the murderous spirit since nightfall, Edgar set out to thread the black feathers he had collected onto the clockwork-raven's frame.

Curious, he thought, when he picked it up and noticed one of the glass eyes had lost its luster. *In my haste, did I not seal it properly?* He wondered if moisture had crept in behind the glass.

"First things first," he said as he wound the key. "Don't want your gears to rust tight." Once the key was wound to its maximum, he then placed the raven down on the table to fetch his satchel of tools.

With tweezers in hand, he grabbed his creation and went to pluck the bead from the socket. The raven let loose a high-pitched screech and spun its head around, putting the offending eye on the opposite side.

The act gave Edgar pause, but still he persisted.

Just as the tweezer's tips were about to pinch the bead, the raven jerked free from Edgar's grasp and stabbed him in the hand—just above the thumb—with its whale-bone beak.

"What the devil!" Edgar brought his right hand toward his mouth and encased the wound with his lips, sucking the rising blood.

The raven crashed to the floor but sprang upright and hopped underneath the table.

With the pain ebbing, Edgar dropped to all fours and looked straight at his infernal contraption. "Come out here you!"

In response, the mechanical bird hopped backward, further away from his extending reach.

"Fine! I'll come in after you." Edgar crawled across the floor like a cat ready to pounce.

The sound of metal grinding gave him pause, and he turned, wide-eyed, as his mechanical creation flapped its featherless wings and took flight.

"I'll be damned," he said, then back tracked out from under the table. He stood, half-disgusted and half-elated with his creation. Never could he have imagined the mechanical bird capable of flight. It wasn't meant to fly, only to flap in mimicry of flight.

The raven perched itself on the rafters above and glared down at him. Edgar could have sworn it was mocking him.

"Come down here this instant."

A metallic *Caw* echoed in the cottage in response. Not something in its routine of repetitive actions. It was as if the damnable thing was thinking for itself.

He pointed a shaky finger at the raven and spoke to it as if he were scolding a child, "You'll be sorry if you wind down and you're stuck up there. Or worse, fall and smash into itty-bitty pieces."

The bird turned its metallic head to the left as if in a snub at Edgar's words.

How rude!

He breathed deeply through his nose, counted to ten, and calmed himself. "I'll just work on something else."

Since his arrival at the lighthouse, the muse had been kind, whispering inspiration into his ear. Along with the food supplies, Edgar purchased a new, crisp notebook in order to pen the percolating tale.

He sat down at the table with pen and paper, took one last look at his disobedient companion, and then summoned forth the words.

Jan 1 — 1796.

This day — my first on the light-house — I make this entry in my Diary, as agreed on with De Grät. As regularly as I can keep the journal, I will — but there is no telling what may happen to a man all alone as I am — I may get sick, or worse ….

Edgar wrote and exorcised his fears into the journal. He wrote entries for January second and January third and had just started on an entry for January fourth, a strong start for a new story, when the clockwork raven released an ear-splitting screech.

"CAW! CAW!! CAW!!!"

"What the…?" Edgar flinched, dropping his pen.

The table he was using shook, and the nearby cabinet doors opened and slammed shut in a morbid rhythm. The loud banging echoed off the plastered walls. Dishes fell from their resting spots and shattered on the floor.

Finally, Edgar thought, making a move toward his machine.

A punch in his solar plexus stole the air from his lungs and sent him hurling backwards. He hit the ground hard and wheezed for breath.

Foolish, he cursed himself, realizing he had left himself vulnerable to the attack.

As he retrieved the pair of highest strength lenses from his waistcoat pocket, a tight grip around his throat, and he was forced back to his feet by an unseen assailant. Struggling to breathe as if seized by a sudden asthmatic attack, he slipped the glass frames over his face and locked gazes with the dead eye of an unrecognizable man.

Half the spirit's face was missing, the edges willowy like smoke on a summer's breeze. The other half screwed up in a twisted snarl as it continued to apply pressure.

John was partially successful, Edgar thought. *He just needed more time.*

Sparkles of light danced in Edgar's vision as the tightness in his chest increased and an icy sensation spread over his mind.

This is it. This is how I die.

The clockwork raven screeched, then spread its featherless wings, and dove off the rafters above. With uncanny grace, it swooped down and passed through the murderous spirit, dissipating it.

Edgar dropped to his knees as he took a deep breath. He looked around the room but found no trace of the ghost. *It interrupted the spirit's energy. I'm brilliant!*

Though he doubted any of his calculations or random choice of scavenged materials had anything to do with the unexpected benefit, he was grateful, nonetheless.

The raven circled back and landed on the table.

Caw!

The raven faced Edgar's machine and leaned forward as if pointing at it.

"Right," he said, realizing his creation was telling him to get moving.

Edgar lunged for the skull handle and shoved the stoke lever in and out, turning the machine on. The Specter Eliminator burst into life. In a few short minutes, the tincture inside would be brought to a boil, and the iodized bitter salts would be ready. He just had to survive until then.

The raven called out another warning and Edgar whipped around to face his attacker. The specter hovered before him, its legs missing from the knees down. Before it could strike Edgar, the raven flew straight forward.

With a grunt, the ghost drifted to the right and dodged. The raven circled around as if determined to protect its creator. A high-pitched whistle signaled the machine was ready and Edgar snatched up the lance and pointed it at the spirit.

His raven was relentless in its aerial assault and Edgar refrained from unleashing the hot vapor, afraid of ruining its mechanical parts.

"Out of the way!" He waved his hand in hopes of catching the raven's attention.

Focused on the raven, the ghost followed its movement. The moment his mechanical companion was out of harm's way, Edgar depressed the trigger and let loose a cloud of scalding vapor that engulfed the distracted spirit.

With an animalistic roar, the specter froze. The decayed edges of its torso and arms dissolved and rapidly collapsed upon itself until there was nothing left but the half a face. Then that, too, faded from view. The malevolent spirit had been sent to the hereafter, and the lighthouse was free from its tyranny.

Edgar's gaze fixated on the clockwork raven perched on the back of the chair. It stood proud with its head up, wings tucked back, and breast plate out.

"Thank you, my friend."

The raven bowed.

"You understand me, don't you?"

A nod signaled its response.

"I truly am a genius." Edgar smiled, but then noticed the dead eye staring at him and his train of thought derailed. He made a move toward his creation in hopes of rectifying the imperfection. "Now if you'll just let me—"

But the raven screeched and leapt into the air.

"No…don't…"

The raven flew back to the rafters above.

"Come down here this instant!"

Caw!

"Your key will wind down soon enough. Then we'll see about adjusting that disposition of yours." Frustrated, Edgar turned off his Specter Eliminator, scooped up his scribblings, and mumbled, "I hope your joints freeze up there."

Edgar awoke to the metallic tinging of a bell. His eyes fluttered open to inky blackness. The tone hung in the air and faded away as if lingering from his dream. He rubbed his eyes in order to speed up the adjustment to the dark.

Probably just the raven winding down, he thought as he turned to his left side. His gaze fell upon the clockwork bird perched on the back of the chair. The odd angle of its cocked head was the proof Edgar needed that it had indeed wound down.

"Serves you right," he said with a smile.

In his peripheral, shadows moved, and he asked, "Who's there?"

The front door slammed closed, and he swung his legs over the edge of the bed. He darted toward the door, bumping his thigh into the table's corner.

"Bloody Blazes," he said, still moving toward the door.

With reckless abandon, he opened the door and ventured into the night barefoot. The silhouette of a man in a tall hat and long coat rounded behind the rocks at the front of the property. The cool night air washed over him as Edgar peered into the darkness for some stranger. *Who would prowl around here at night? It was hard enough to get anyone to come here during the daylight hours.*

Through the howling wind and the rustling of the bushes at the tree line, a horse whinnied. *Had Miss Feller hired another ghost hunter? And why wouldn't the man announce himself? I'm going to have to have a talk with George about his referral process.*

His thigh throbbed from its impact with the table, and he closed the front door.

This development would keep him up well into morning, so Edgar put on the kettle and sat down at the table to finally clean the smog from behind the glass eye and to sew the feathers onto the frame of his mechanical wonder.

CHAPTER VII

"What do you mean you 'won't be paying for my services'?"

Edgar stood before the mayor of Portland, put off by the man's folded arms and pursed lips. Edgar's fists clenched, ready to grab the high collar of the mayor's jacket, ruffle his poofy bowtie, and smack the smug look off his bearded face.

"Since there is no proof of your claim—"

"You want proof?" Edgar slammed his palms on the edge of the mahogany desk. "Easy. Spend the night."

The mayor's eyes went wide at the suggestion. "I think not."

"The fact that I'm alive and have the body of the man you originally contracted with, is proof enough. Ask the old man outside."

"Ah," the man waved his hand dismissing the notion. "Charles Hill never met a rumor he didn't like."

"Fine." Edgar stood straight and grabbed hold of his jacket lapels in an effort to calm himself. "How about I write an essay on the Portland Head Light haunting and send it to every newspaper and magazine in circulation. It would certainly shed some light on those mysterious crashes."

"You're bluffing," said the mayor.

"Regardless of my good deed, ships wouldn't feel safe coming into the harbor," Edgar continued, ignoring the statement. "What do you think that would do for the local economy? I'm betting it would hurt far more than my paltry fee. The way I see it," he scratched his chin, "whether it's by the newspapers or you, either way I get paid."

The mayor narrowed his eyes and Edgar imagined rusted gears straining behind those brown irises.

"Very well," he said, opening his desk drawer.

The mayor filled out a bank note in Edgar's name, tore the slip from the pad and held it out. But when Edgar reached for it, the mayor pulled it back.

"You breathe a word of this to anyone and I'll hunt you down personally."

With a nod, Edgar reached further across the desk and snatched the slip. He checked the figures written out and once satisfied, he turned away.

"Good day, Mister Poe."

"In the future," Edgar glanced over his shoulder and narrowed his eyes at the pompous man, "I hope I'll be your first and only choice. Else you'll be the one delivering the sad news to a distraught family. Good day."

Edgar stood before the Feller's front door; his gaze fixated on the young woman who had greeted him.

"Can I help you?" she asked again.

Despite his grief, and her patch-worked dress and grime-smeared cheeks, Ellie Feller's beauty was not lost on Edgar. She stood with one hand against the door frame and the other wrapped around the door's edge. Her breasts filling out the top of her dress, strands of her honey hair jetted out from under a tattered bonnet, and faint freckles sprayed across the bridge of her nose and under her deep blue eyes that Edgar found as inviting as the ocean.

Charles, the carriage driver, nudged his elbow into Edgar's side.

"I received your letter," he blurted out, his mind jumbled with the why and how of his coming here. Warmth spread in his cheeks, and he hoped his face wasn't crimson.

"Ah," her mouth and eyes went wide at the realization of who he was, "You must be Mister Poe." she said, looking into his eyes and adding to his discomfort. "Any word on my brother?"

"Please, call me Edgar." He glanced back at the cart. "I only wish I brought happier news."

She looked past him at the coffin in the cart. Tears pooled and soon cascaded down her rosy cheeks.

Fool, Edgar scolded himself. *So much for tact.*

"It's as I feared then," Ellie wiped a fresh tear. "You brought him home. That's more than I could ever ask for." She paused, then added. "George said you were a gentleman. And the best…"

"Did he?" Edgar asked. "Well, I don't know…." But she wasn't listening.

She stole a glance over her shoulder. "How will I break the news to mother?" she mumbled.

"If you wish, I could do it," Edgar said.

"No, that's all right. Tell me," She took Edgar's hand in hers, "did he suffer?"

Edgar bowed his head and held still his tongue.

"Oh!" In the midst's of a sob, Ellie threw her arms around Edgar's neck and leaned in, hugging him.

"Eh-hem!" The cart driver cleared his throat, a not-so-subtle signal for Edgar.

Without knowing any other way of asking, he blurted the driver's question. "I've taken the liberty of having your brother's remains placed inside a coffin. Where shall we leave him?"

A deep, heavy sob turned into an all-out cry. "It's my fault. I shouldn't have let him go on his own."

Edgar's crisp white shirt dampened from her tears. "There's no way you could have known."

She pulled back. "He was so stubborn. He insisted he'd be all right."

"This is all very touching," said the cart driver, "but our business is concluded, and I'd like to be on my way."

Edgar pursed his lips at the man's insensitivity and wondered why on Earth he had paid up front. Though the man did have a nearly two-hour ride ahead of him, it was no excuse for his rudeness to Miss Feller.

Without uttering a word, he placed his hands upon Ellie's shoulders and eased her away from him, then walked up to the backside of the cart and grabbed the foot of the coffin. He rested it on the ground, then lowered the head of the coffin. Then, he grabbed his machine and personal belongings, and placed them by the door.

"Off with you," he ordered.

"Fine. Good night miss." The old man dipped his head. "Sorry for your loss."

Ellie did not respond. Instead, she angled her head upward and looked away while crossing her arms.

The carriage fell out of sight, and Edgar would have to walk to find lodgings for the night.

"Won't you come in?" asked Ellie.

"But of course. What shall I do with…?"

"Help me bring him inside." Ellie bent at the knees and grabbed hold of the foot of the coffin.

Edgar nodded and followed suit.

He was surprised at the strength in her small frame. Ellie had her end of the coffin in the air and situated before he could follow suit, and not once did she ask for a break as they carried it through three rooms of the house.

CHAPTER VIII

John Feller's body was returned to his bedroom until preparations could be made. The room was small—barely fitting a twin-sized bed, an armoire, and dresser—and told Edgar little of the man. No work bench. No half-built contraptions. No devices upon the walls or shelf. Only a bible, crucifix, and religious iconography.

"You should know, he was almost successful," Edgar said as Ellie looked upon the pine box sheltering her from the horrors befallen her brother. "When the spirit finally showed itself to me…it wasn't whole."

"Thank you, but that only adds to my guilt. Had I been there, I could have given him the needed time to finish."

"How so?" He meant no disrespect, and he hoped it hadn't come across as such to her ears, but he simply could not fathom how she could have helped in any way.

"Follow me," she said, exiting the room.

She led him to another smallish bedroom down the hall. The only distinctive difference between the two rooms was the pink bedding. Ellie went straight toward the armoire, and upon opening it, retrieved a large metal pole.

"Is that a lightning rod?"

"A magnetized one," she said, turning to face him.

"That must have taken some doing." He scratched his chin in wonderment. "How do you keep from getting electrocuted?"

"For starters, I don't do this in a thunderstorm," she said, holding it straight up in the air. A smile stretched across her cheeks. "And I wear these." Ellie held up a pair of thick, leather Blacksmith gloves.

Her smile was infectious, but still, he could not understand the lightning rod's purpose. The effort involved in creating a magnetic field to magnetize the iron and in maintaining the magnetic domain of the material for whatever its function hardly seemed worth the trouble.

"Think of it as a sword," she offered. "One that disrupts the spirit's flow of energy. They break apart for a brief minute. When they reform, I swing again."

"Did George Darby fabricate that for you?" Edgar asked.

She nodded.

"He's becoming quite the metaphysical weapons smith," Edgar joked.

She chuckled at this and said, "Yes. It always buys John the necessary time to complete the prayer." Her head hung low as fresh tears surfaced. "Bought him."

"I'm sorry." Edgar placed a comforting hand upon her shoulder, not knowing what else to do or say.

He could now understand the logic; however, he feared such a weapon provided a false sense of security. One missed swing and a sharp blow could knock the magnetic domain out of alignment and render the weapon useless.

Just as he was about to warn her of the dangers, a frail voice called from the neighboring room.

"Ellie."

"Yes, mother, I'm coming. Excuse me," she said as she walked past him.

Edgar followed but stayed in the doorway to the largest of the bedrooms.

Inside, an aging woman lay in a four-post bed, the down comforter pulled up to her chin. The woman's pale skin and sunken cheeks moistened with sweat.

Ellie approached the bedside, then placed the back of her hand to her mother's wrinkled brow. "You're burning up."

"Is there anything I can do?" Edgar asked.

Ellie gave a half-smile looking appreciative of the offer. "Fetch a basin of water and a washcloth?"

"Of course." He nodded to Mrs. Feller.

"Who is this man, Ellie?" she asked.

"My name is Edgar Allan Poe."

A hint of life sparked in her eyes as a trace of a smile appeared. "Did you find my son?" she asked.

Edgar lowered his head, wishing he had better news for the woman who seemed to be more concerned with her son's wellbeing than of her own.

Ellie took her mom's hand and answered for him, "John didn't make it, Mother."

The woman's lower lip trembled as the weight of the words fell upon her, extinguishing the hope that had clearly swelled in her heart. She tilted her head upward and said, "He belongs to you now, Lord. Watch over him and tell him his mother loves him with all her heart."

Edgar walked toward the kitchen to fetch the basin, the display of emotion too much for his hardened heart. Memories of Frances Allan danced in his mind. Though not his true mother, she'd provided him with enough love and affection to offset his foster father's disdain. For him, the world was a darker place without her in it, and he knew those same thoughts were going through Ellie Feller's mind right now.

He recalled seeing a water pump outside on the way in, and with the basin in hand, walked outside and filled it. As he worked the handle, his mind wandered, thoughts of the shattered family's future tormenting his already troubled soul.

There's no way they'll be able to support themselves, he thought as water poured forth from the pump's mouth. *I can only imagine the mounting medical bills.*

When he returned to Mrs. Feller's room, Ellie stood at her mother's bedside holding a glass of water. The frail woman sipped from the proffered glass, while a trickle ran down her chin. At the sight of him, Mrs. Feller stopped drinking and leaned back.

"Did my John suffer?" she asked.

"Ma'am I—"

"Tell me!"

The level of authority in her voice caught Edgar by surprise. "He was hung and left for the rats."

Mrs. Feller let out a whimper that was silenced when she pinched her lip between her teeth. Her head turned to the side as fresh tears pooled.

"I brought the basin," Edgar said to Ellie, "but I couldn't find a fresh cloth."

"I'll get one," Ellie said.

"No," Mrs. Feller interjected, "leave me. I wish to be alone."

"But—?"

"Mind your mother," the old woman demanded.

Ellie nodded and walked out with her gaze locked on the floor. Edgar followed.

"It's hard losing a loved one. I'm sure she's not angry with you."

With a sniffle, Ellie turned toward him. "I know. Thank you."

"If you'll be all right, I should be getting off. I need to find lodgings for the night."

"Nonsense, you'll stay here tonight. I insist."

"Where?" Edgar asked. "We put your brother in his room."

Only after he blurted his thought did he realize how self-centered and insensitive it was. "Sorry. That didn't come out right."

Ellie smiled, looking as though she found his awkwardness appealing. "We have a bed set up in the cellar. You'll have privacy there."

"That would do nicely," he said, unable to resist the smile stretching across his cheeks. Even in the darkest of moments, the young woman found something to lift her spirits, and Edgar admired that.

"I can help you with your belongings."

Edgar held his hand up, palm out. "That won't be necessary. I can manage."

Ellie's smile faded. "I could use the distraction."

He nodded. "Understandable."

They walked nearly side-by-side toward the front door where Edgar's bag and machine had been left. Upon seeing the clockwork raven, Ellie's eyes went wide.

"You tinker?" she asked, her hands reaching for his creation. She stopped just before grabbing it and turned to him. "May I?"

"Go ahead."

Ellie picked up the clockwork raven with childish glee and went to wind the key but paused. "That is a rather peculiar placement of the key," she said, blushing.

"Oh, well, I didn't think of… You see…" Edgar paused and took a breath. "If the key is upon its back, when removed, the mechanism is exposed. And well, I was concerned with detritus and debris and, with the current placement, gravity aids with the removal of…"

She'd been grinning at his embarrassment, but now let it loose with a laugh. "It is perfectly fine and logical Mister Poe."

He nodded, but continued, "It just seemed the natural place…"

One more short snicker escaped her before she turned her attention to winding the bird. It came alive with a screech. The rhythmic *clinkety-clank* sound echoed in the room as it craned its neck to look upon the young beauty.

It really is of my making, Edgar thought.

"Wonderful," Ellie said as the bird worked its newly, feathered wings. They flapped up and down in a rhythm that gave its creator the impression it was happy.

The clockwork raven jumped out of Ellie's hands and landed on the table, it twirled around and chirped as if in a dance.

"How did you program it to do that? You must be brilliant with punch cards."

"I honestly have no idea how it can do some of the things it does. It can fly."

"Really?"

"Yes."

"Amazing. Too bad about that eye though," she said, and though Edgar knew she meant no harm, the words stung like those from his harshest critic.

"I admit I didn't use the best materials, but I plan on rectifying that at the first chance I get. I thought it was moisture built up behind the glass, but when I removed it from the socket, I found there was a flaw in the bead. Funds simply won't allow me to rectify the embellishment."

"I'm sure you were paid handsomely for the Portland Head Light job," she said, the smile gone and a hint of malice in her tone.

"Speaking of which." Edgar pulled out the wad of money and handed it over to her, not bothering to pull out a single bill for his time and effort.

Ellie's jaw hung open as her fingers wrapped around the tightly banded bundle of money. Edgar could almost see the desire in her eyes to shun her responsibilities and spend it all on lavish clothing and sweetmeats.

"I can't." She shoved the money back into his hands. "You earned it. Right is right."

Their hands still touching, he pushed the bills toward her. "I want you to have it. With your brother gone, you'll need it more than I."

She took the money, gaze fixated on the artistic details. "You're a good man, Mister Poe," she said without looking at him.

"Well don't go spreading that around." He half-laughed. "It would tarnish my image."

The mechanical bird leapt from the table, circled around them, and then landed on Edgar's shoulder. It rubbed its head against Edgar's cheek, the metal cold and rough against his delicate skin, but the gesture was appreciated.

"You finally coming 'round to me?" he asked as he went to stroke its neck.

The raven let loose a *caw* and was airborne.

As the stubborn creation circled in the air, Edgar said, "I swear, that blasted contraption has the devil in him."

"I don't think so," Ellie said as it left the room and headed down the hallway. "It's just misunderstood."

"And how do you feel about it pestering your mother?" Edgar asked, watching it turn the corner toward the master bedroom.

"What?" Ellie dashed after it.

CAW!

"You get down from there this instant!" Ellie's voice held a commanding tone.

I wonder if I can re-use the parts, he thought, picturing Ellie bashing the raven with a broom or some sort of make-shift weapon. And what could her Lightning Rod do to it? With his hands in his pockets and a short stride, Edgar followed after them.

He walked into the room to the raven perched atop a wooden acorn adorning the right, headboard post, and Ellie jumping up to reach it. Her elderly mother lay still with a devilish grin breaking the wrinkles on her face.

"It's all right dear," said Mrs. Feller. "I take kindly to it."

"Are you sure, Mother?"

"Yes," she said, looking up at the bird who in turn looked down upon her. "There's something oddly comforting about it. Perhaps it just may be my guardian angel."

"All right then. We'll let you rest." Ellie walked up to Edgar, hooked her arm under his, and escorted him out.

Edgar stole a glance over his shoulder at his creation. *Peculiar.*

"It's getting late. Are you tired, Mister Poe? I can have your bed ready in a few minutes."

"I'm not tired in the least. I have quite odd sleeping habits. Occupational hazard I suppose."

She smiled at his joke.

"How about a nice cup of tea then?"

"That would be lovely," he said.

As he sat at the table, and Ellie put the kettle upon the stove, the two conversed. The range of topics jumped from her fond memories of her brother's playful teasing, politics, his departed wife Virginia, and back to her brother and the means he had used to thwart spirits.

Ellie placed a mug before him, then sat down. With both hands on the cup, allowing the heat to radiate her palms, she sipped the hot brew. Her neck slouched into her shoulders as her eyes closed and her lips pursed.

"Just what the doctor ordered?" he asked, already knowing the answer.

"Yes," Ellie said, drawing closer. "I hate to pry, but I have to ask, where does your darkness come from?"

As if he had been asked the question a thousand times, Edgar answered, "From the brooding over my losses, imaginative and figurative."

Ellie leaned back with a puzzled look, a slight crook in her neck and narrowed eyes.

"Death has been a constant companion in my life. It's only natural I explore that relationship in my writing. You know that old adage, write what you know." He smiled, adding a bit of brevity to the heavy turn of the conversation. "Look at the time. Perhaps we should call it a night before dawn breaks."

"Do you need any help?"

Edgar couldn't help but wonder—even hope—that there was an underlying meaning in her question. The odd chance of a romantic encounter, but the idea of her sickly mother right upstairs and in possible need of care while they were in the throes of passion prevented him from inquiring.

"I can manage."

She smiled that large, infectious smile. "Good night then."

"Good night, Miss Ellie."

She walked to her room, the sashay of her skirt hypnotizing.

Another time, he thought, then ventured downstairs to his sleeping quarters.

"Thank you very much. Good day." Ellie closed the door on the postal worker, a letter in her hand.

"What time is it?" Edgar pulled a chair out from the table and sat. "How long did I sleep?"

"It's almost noon," she said. "You do keep odd hours."

"Any coffee?"

She put the letter on the table in front of him and crossed her arms. "You just received a letter from a Mister Tomlinson Bulloch of Georgia."

"I did?"

She narrowed her eyes and her voiced hardened as she said, "Awfully presumptuous of you to give our address."

"I assure you; I have not given this address to a soul."

She harrumphed and turned to the stove.

"Perhaps George Darby assumed I could be reached through you," he offered.

"And what of my brother?" she asked without turning around and busied herself with the kettle and coffee press.

Edgar held his tongue and opened the letter.

Once the coffee was steeping, Ellie asked, "What is it?"

"Mister Bulloch has a haunted property near Dawsonville, Georgia and can't seem to sell it. He is in immediate need of my services."

Ellie merely nodded.

"Yes, there have been complaints of ear-shattering wailing and crying. Apparently, a young woman killed herself after her fiancée ran off with her sister. The mother and father didn't have the heart to excise her, so they simply up and moved away."

Ellie bobbed her head as she gave it thought. Then said, "The parents' sudden departure probably made it worse. You'll take it?"

"Mister Bulloch included an open train ticket in the envelope."

"He is presumptuous," she scoffed. "Shall I write him back and inform him you're on the way?"

Edgar stood, not catching her sarcasm. "No need. Let me freshen up and I can leave immediately."

"Well, at least have some break—…lunch first."

Edgar nodded, took his seat again, and prayed Ellie could brew a decent cup of coffee.

CHAPTER IX

Edgar stepped into the train compartment. He plopped himself into the center of the bench, glad to have it all to himself. He bounced a couple of times, testing the cushion's softness and found it more than adequate for an overnight trip.

He wriggled down into the seat and nestled his head against the backing, then closed his eyes and embraced the silence. His mind called forth an image of Ellie beside her mother's bedside and his clockwork creation perched defiantly on the corner post. He wished not to leave the raven with them, but the damnable bird had refused to leave the mother's headboard — viciously pecking at Edgar's hand and digging its talons into the wood with such force that Edgar feared the ivory talons would splinter and snap off. When he approached it with a sack, it flew aloft, and Edgar did not want to make a great scene in the mother's bed chamber. So, it remained behind while he performed this assignment for Ellie. Just one more reason to see her again. He could certainly use the money himself, and for The Stylus, but he knew all too well how it could serve Ellie better in her hour of need.

The Stylus. After a decade, his ambition of running his own monthly literary journal was close to fruition. Of course, there were highs and lows, but dreams were meant to be difficult to build character. No longer would he toil for someone else's glory. Since Virginia's death, he had been working tirelessly on raising the funds. Once he did, he could afford to pay professional rates to the youngest and brightest of the literary world. The doors he would open with The Stylus, the heights he would elevate modern literature, the accolades he would receive.

A sharp whistle signaled the train was ready for departure and the compartment door opened. Edgar lifted his head as a well-dressed man in a black suit and top hat stepped inside.

"This is a private compartment," Edgar said, full of self-importance.

"Oh, I am aware Mr. Poe," the gentleman said, a wide, toothy grin blazing from his face. "I booked it for us." The man's smile could have swallowed the entire train.

"Excuse me?" Edgar said. The man was dressed as a gentleman but did have the ruffled edges of a traveler. *Did the Bullochs send out a request to him as well?* He didn't need competition right now. The man did not carry any equipment, unless it all fit in his small valise. Just enough room for a bible and crucifix.

"Where are my manors?" The man extended his right hand, smiling as if he intended to devour Edgar. "My name's James Laurent."

Edgar accepted the gesture, taking notice of the dainty ring squeezing his pinky. A size too small, even for the littlest finger, the ring was too feminine for a man of his stature. An eccentric gentleman - *what a nuisance,* he thought. "Nice to meet you," he finally said.

"The pleasure is all mine," James said, still shaking his hand.

Edgar dropped his polite countenance and let his hand go limp.

"Oh... my apologies." James released his tight hold on Edgar's hand and placed his valise under the plush bench seat.

Once James was settled in and the train was underway, Edgar cleared his throat and asked, "What did you mean, you booked this compartment? Are you employed by Mister Bulloch?"

"Oh no. No." James laughed at Edgar's confusion, annoying Edgar further. "I'm a ghost hunter like yourself."

Poe nodded; this James Laurent was indeed competition.

"I arranged all this," James indicated the compartment, and seemingly, the entire train, "because I have a proposition for you."

"For me?"

"Yes," James said, smoothing his lapels and slacks, preparing to give his pitch.

"Have I met you before?" Edgar asked, sensing something familiar about the man.

James chuckled. "I think I'd recall meeting the great poet, Edgar Allan Poe."

Edgar nodded, flattered. While he desired to be America's greatest writer, he knew his fame hardly extended beyond the poetic circles. Unless this man had studied him thoroughly, it was unlikely that a fellow ghost hunter would also know him as a poet and writer.

"Have you been to Cape Elizabeth recently? In Maine."

"You are a quick one Mr. Poe," James said, his smile confession enough. "As I was saying, I have a proposition for you and before I go into business with anyone, I always do my research."

"Business?"

"Yes, Mr. Poe," James said with a too friendly, almost conspiratorial, smile and Edgar recognized him as the man with the newspaper from the Rowes Wharf Hotel in Boston. "We should join together, you and me. With your fortitude and imagination, and my connections and mind for business, we'd make quite the team. Cooperate. Incorporate. Share our knowledge and experience. Advertise. Establish contracts and terms. No more unreliable jobs here and there as they come along. No more haggling with clients."

Edgar nodded and waved for him to stop his pitch. "I'm afraid my ambitions lay elsewhere."

James leaned back and gestured for Edgar to explain.

"Literature is my true calling. Publishing. This is all just a way to make a living until the first edition of my magazine is published." Edgar launched into his own pitch, "Might I suggest a subscription to The Stylus? It would certainly inform and entertain a gentleman of your intellect. Subscriptions are five dollars."

"Man alive! Publishing Mr. Poe? Literature?" James seemed genuinely shocked and for the first time since he entered the compartment, he was not smiling. "You cannot honestly believe that scribbling poems and stories to scare women compares to ridding the land of malicious spirits?"

"My dear sir. Literature is the heart and soul of culture. Of society itself," Edgar said, trying to keep from yelling. "Without it, there is no reason for life to exist."

"And ghosts are its biggest threat!" James said. "They defy the natural order. The longer they spurn Heaven, the more corrupted and dangerous they become. You saw what became of Mr. Johnathan Feller at the lighthouse. The thing capable of doing that was no longer the soul of a man."

When Edgar offered no retort, James fixed him with a pensive continence.

Edgar was unsure if he was judging him or studying him. Either way, he did not appreciate it. "So, are you to work this job as well?"

James's smile returned to his face. "I am, in a way."

"How so?"

"I've been hired to observe your work and verify your results."

"Observe and verify?" Edgar liked this man less and less with each sentence he uttered.

"Please don't view me as an adversary," James said. "This is what I was trying to explain. I've convinced Mister Bulloch to hire us both for the same job as a team, at our regular rates. We both win here. And there are banks and private lenders all over the country with haunted properties. Think of the possibilities."

Now it was Edgar's turn to smile. "Are you interested in ridding the land of malicious spirits or making your fortune?"

"The former," James said, then leaned forward and whispered, "But why not do both?" He then reached for the Specter Eliminator. "So, this eradicates ghosts?"

"Yes." Edgar pulled it back against his bench.

"Darby's work?" James's gaze dissected it.

"No, mine," Edgar said and hoped James would catch that his short and concise answers were a subtle attempt at ending the conversation. However, James's troubling grin signaled to Edgar the man was nowhere near finished.

"Excellent, you tinker, too."

"I do." He was glad that damnable raven had refused to come along.

"I could never imagine we'd have so much in common."

"Indeed."

Edgar removed his jacket to ease the stuffiness in the compartment.

James let loose a chuckle and pointed at Edgar's vest. "How many pairs do you need?"

"Come again?"

"Do you lose your glasses often?" James pointed at Edgar's refracting lenses in his jacket flap. "You have three pairs."

"No. These are refracting lenses that enable me to see the spirits," Edgar answered smugly. "Each pair is stronger than the other."

"Oh! You need something like these." James took out what appeared to be chemist's goggles with four jeweler's loupes mounted off each side. He slipped them over his head and, with the flick of his lanky finger, slid a loupe with what Edgar assumed to be a refracting lens over the base glass. He then did the same for the remaining three lenses, compounding them. "At this strength, no ghost can escape my sight." He smiled that toothy grin. "No matter how weak or crafty they are."

Conceding how brilliant the device was, Edgar cursed himself for not thinking of it on his own. At least this James Laurent was a man of science, like himself. And, while he feared the answer, he needed to ask the question, "And what is your method of hunting?" Edgar indicated James's bag, which he still hoped held a crucifix and bible.

"Oh, I don't have any of my hunting tools with me. These are just my personal effects," he answered without answering. "I'm just observing on this job."

"As you said," Edgar grumbled. "But which method do you prefer?" he pressed on.

"So inquisitive Mr. Poe," James evaded again. "Nothing as fancy as yours, I assure you. Don't worry about me stealing your thunder."

Edgar nodded in capitulation and dropped the subject. Whatever James's method of eradicating ghosts was, it must not have been very impressive, or effective. Edgar would guard his methods and tools.

The two conversed as the train chugged southward through the night. James kept the focus of the conversation on Edgar, bringing up every tragic event in his life that shaped the man before him. They discussed the loss of his mother and truest love. Though Edgar was put off by James's knowledge of his life and eagerness to dredge up so many painful memories, it was not all that uncommon for him. Enthusiasts of his prose were often an eclectic bunch, thirsting for any sordid detail about the man behind the curtain. Lack of privacy, imitation, and the critics razor, those were the ugly side of fame and Edgar had made his peace with that years ago.

Most of the information on Edgar's life James had knowledge of could have been pieced together from newspaper articles, interviews, and author biographies, but some could have only come from the Virginia hall of records.

Every attempt to shift the flow toward James's personal life or even his methods of ghost hunting was foiled with a sideways glance or single word response and the subject redirected back upon himself. And James's ceaseless grin was as disingenuous as a politician's; the man smiled with his mouth, but not his eyes. Much like his gentlemen's clothing- easy to put on, but it didn't change what was beneath. The man had clearly done his research and was definitely some fashion of dangerous competition.

The only breaks Edgar received from James's non-stop chatter during the fourteen-hour trip were when he excused himself to use the facilities. Each time upon his return to the train car, Edgar prayed James had tuckered himself out, or grown hoarse, but there was no such luck.

When the train arrived in Dawsonville, Edgar gathered his belongings, eager to both get away from the man, and beat him to the job.

"One moment, Mr. Poe," James said as Edgar exited the train car. "We can share a coach to Mister Bulloch's."

Edgar looked over his shoulder to respond. "I would like that," he lied with a forced smile, "but I really should get cleaned up first."

"I as well," James said, then added. "I'll hire the coach on my own account."

This man had certainly done his research and Edgar desperately wished he had the funds to decline.

"If you insist," Edgar said, his tone dull and flat.

CHAPTER X

"Good afternoon gentlemen," a bulbous man dressed to the nines greeted them on the platform. From his crisp brown suit, Edgar knew he must be someone of importance. The man offered a warm smile and a stern handshake.

"Mister Bulloch, I presume," James said, stepping forward and taking the man's hand. "James Laurent."

"Yes, yes. Misters Laurent, and Poe?"

"Pleased to meet you," Edgar nodded and shook Mr. Bulloch's hand.

"Good. Good. Mister Poe, how fine of you to take the time to come. Your reputation precedes you."

"Thank you," Edgar said, releasing his hand. "But I wonder why I wasn't your first, and only choice."

"My apologies. We had no idea of your current whereabouts, and I'm afraid, time is of the essence. There have been threats."

"Threats?" Edgar asked. "From the spirit?"

Edgar noticed James's posture stiffen and that the man took a half-step back. Threatening spirits accounted for most of the business. You had to expect danger. Perhaps this man was all bravado and no courage.

"Oh, no. Not from Julia," Mr. Bulloch said, shaking his head. "Poor girl just howls and cries incessantly. Protests from the neighbors. They're threatening to burn the house to restore the peace."

"Oh my," James said with a nervous laugh.

"Shall we go straight to the house then?" Edgar asked, and turned to James, "Unless Mister Laurent needs time to prepare himself."

"Not I," James answered, steadier now, and burned by the insult.

"Good," Edgar said, not showing any remorse for the slight. "The sooner it's done, the sooner I can collect my fee and be on my way."

"Excellent," Mr. Bulloch said, oblivious, and gestured through the depot. "My buggy is right this way."

"How fortunate you were here then, Mr. Bulloch. You've saved us the trouble of finding a carriage."

"And the expense," Edgar said under his breath.

James gave him a raised eyebrow as Mr. Bulloch remained oblivious.

Without further back talk, Edgar followed the men to the street, pulling the Specter Eliminator behind him.

Outside, Edgar's breath lodged in his throat at the sight of a gleaming white, steam-powered buggy. It appeared to be a standard four-wheeled, single bench, open vehicle, but without the driving harness and with the addition of a large boiler behind the bench seat. The body was painted a glossed white with a bright crimson fine line striping. The bench was finished off with crimson tufted upholstery. The lamps, brake handle, and steering shaft were of polished brass. The wheel rims and spokes were also crimson and the wheels themselves appeared to be bonded with thick black rubber.

Edgar took a shaky step toward the magnificent contraption. "I've only read journals.... Never would I have.... You're definitely a gentleman of wealth and fine taste."

James offered no compliment, but his eyes were wide with envy and desire.

Edgar knew he was grinning like a schoolboy, but he could not resist. "I can't wait to see it operate."

"Then climb on up," said Mr. Bulloch as he planted his shoe firmly on the step mounted under the chassis. He then gripped the steering wheel and heaved his bulk onto the seat. As Edgar and James secured their luggage, Mr. Bulloch scooped coals from a wicker basket and tossed them into the firebox enclosed within the boiler.

Edgar wedged the Spector Eliminator in the back and insulated it against the boiler with his valise. Once confident it was safe, he climbed onto the bench seat. James followed and squeezed Edgar between himself and Mr. Bulloch.

The moment the first puff of steam burst forth, Mr. Bulloch released the parking brake, and they were off, put-putting down the cobblestone road. Though the ride was bumpy, the bench cramped, and the padding on the seat insufficient, Edgar could not have been happier.

As they made their way through the city, many pedestrians stopped to gaze upon the steam-powered marvel, the envy in their eyes apparent. This lifestyle was what he'd always envisioned for himself and Virginia, to be looked upon by the masses with both gratitude and jealousy.

"So, what do you think?" asked Mr. Bulloch.

"A work of genius."

"Yes," James agreed, "Though it needs an enclosure to protect its passengers from the elements."

"One would think that," Mr. Bulloch acknowledged, "but one underestimates the fair Georgian climate."

Spanish moss hung from the trees, yellow jasmine blossomed on shrubs, and the saw palmettos gave the region a tropical aura. Once out of the city center, Edgar caught sight of a white-tailed deer before it bolted off into the underbrush as they approached, the loud sound of the roadster startling it.

"Quite the scandal around these parts," Mr. Bulloch explained the house's history, shouting over the engine's racket. "Julia Lucas and Charles Collins were engaged almost from the moment of her debut. Mister and Missus Lucas approved, and Mister Lucas had brought Charles into the family's business. The week of the wedding, Julia's younger sister Lydia goes missing. In the family's distress, it took them a few days to realize Charles Collins hadn't joined in the search or offered his support. It comes out that Charles and Lydia had eloped to Savannah. To make matters worse, Lydia had not debuted in society. Mister Lucas, and some gentlemen from the club, went down to Savannah and convinced the scoundrel to marry the girl. The marriage allowed the Lucas family to preserve some appearance of decorum, but Charles being her brother-in-law instead of her husband must have been too much for poor Julia. She hung herself a month later. They've all moved to Baldwin County since the haunting started."

Outside of town, the houses were large, unlike the tenement homes Edgar had grown accustomed to in the cities, and it was apparent that the gold discovered in the north Georgia mountains had provided a healthy economy.

"Here we are," said Mr. Bulloch as he slipped the parking brake into gear.

A black wrought iron fence surrounded the property. Large windows flanked the paneled front door capped with a crown. Decorative moldings and dentil work embellished the cornices, and it had a side gabled roof with double chimneys.

"The Lucas family must have been wealthy to simply walk away from such a beautiful mansion," Edgar said as he examined the white, two-story home.

"They were…are. I bought it for a jar of picayunes," he said. "But now cannot sell it in order to make my profit. So, I'm stuck with the little end of the horn."

"Don't you fret about that," James told Mr. Bulloch. "We are going to rid you of this abomination."

This spirit's cries must be quite obnoxious, Edgar thought. By his calculations, the houses had almost an acre between them.

"Julia, the ghost that is," Mr. Bulloch said, "usually keeps quiet during the daylight hours, so you'll have to wait until nightfall."

"Of course," Edgar said, grabbing hold of the Specter Eliminator and valise. Sunlight disrupts their ethereal energy, making spirits lethargic."

"Oh?" Mr. Bulloch asked. "Is that the science behind it? Fascinating."

James appeared interested in this trivia as well and Edgar might have overplayed his hand.

Edgar shrugged his shoulders. "I don't quite understand the science of it myself," he exaggerated to Mr. Bulloch and turned to address James. "Perhaps Mister Laurent can enlighten us."

"Me?" James asked but recovered himself. "Oh no. It's just one of the mysteries of the business."

"It certainly is," Edgar mused.

"Well, Mister Bulloch," James said, changing the subject by taking charge again. "If you would be so kind as to give us the key, we should be all set."

Mr. Bulloch fished in his coat pocket and pulled out the singular key. As he handed it over, he said, "Shall I come back tonight to fetch you? Say, nine o'clock."

As James took the key, Edgar said, "That won't be necessary. Just another night in a strange place. Story of my life." Edgar noticed James fidgeting with his coat sleeves but held back his smile. The man was surveying the house nervously. "Unless, of course, Mr. Laurent takes issue with remaining in the house?"

"Certainly not," James protested. "If you are as good as you boast, there should be no problem."

"Very well. There is a tavern back up the road a way." Mr. Bulloch released the break and waved them goodbye. "Happy hunting."

James unlocked the door and opened it, but then motioned for Edgar to take the lead.

"Thank you," Edgar said entering, his mind focused on the job.

The furnishings were just what Edgar had expected. A cherry, elliptical staircase and a crystal chandelier immediately caught his eye. Bearing left, and leaving the foyer, they entered the sitting room.

The focal point of the room was the fireplace, its dark-stained wood spanning nearly the entire outer wall. Black marble with veins of gold surrounded the pit, with two pillars acting as guardians against the raging fires, and quatrefoil carvings running along the mantle. The pointed arches of the windows were duplicated in the tall backs of the chairs with vertical rope molding running up the straight legs and repeated ornamental foliation with trefoils carved into the splats. The red fabric was embellished with three-lobed leaf tracery. A large table, which Edgar assumed was walnut, was centered in the room. Squatting foxes ready to pounce were carved into the table skirt.

A man could get used to this, he thought as he basked in the excessive luxury.

Edgar wheeled his machine into the room, then dropped himself onto the single sofa. He leaned back into the arm and rested his head, his body weary from travel.

I can't remember the last sleep-filled night, he thought and wished he'd forced his clockwork raven to come along. The alarm was crucial if the spirit turned out to be malicious.

His gaze fixated on the family portrait centered above the sofa. Sitting in front of their mother and father, the two sisters smiled wide, unaware of the betrayal that would destroy their family. He wondered which sister had been engaged and which was the seductress.

Tragic.

Edgar knew no one could hurt a person like family. It was a hard lesson to learn, and it was obvious to him not everyone could deal with such a reality.

The man who had raised him—who he had looked up to—had never seen fit to adopt him, to make him a legal heir. Thinking back on it now, he supposed the conflict was only natural as both were independent of mind and a little more than stubborn.

Considered a self-made man, John Allan worked hard to afford the luxuries provided to his family without the superior education Edgar desired. Edgar knew the disdain his foster father held toward paying his tuition, and still he pushed. Only now, of sober mind, could he see it was unfair to have begged for more than the allowance given to him.

Edgar tilted his head up toward the plastered ceiling, but he saw through it, into the sky and beyond. *Why did you push me away in the end?*

No matter how much he thought about it, he could not find an answer. Though the desire to write to his brother, Henry, to inquire his opinion on the matter often took him, he suppressed it, and tossed any scribbling into the trash bin.

"You're awfully quiet all of a sudden," said James.

"I'm fine, nothing a little rest won't cure. Would you mind?"

"By all means," James said. "I'll see what we have in the pantry for later. Rest up." With that, James left the room.

Depressed and weary, Edgar closed his eyes and let sleep take him.

John Allan slept. Despite the subtle green tint to his sweat glistened skin and balloon shaped lump in his throat giving him a toad-like appearance, the man's swollen features weren't enough to prevent Edgar from recognizing his foster father. There had been a time he both loved and admired the man, but those days had long been since forgotten.

As if sensing Edgar's presence, John's eyes fluttered open.

"Hello, Pa," Edgar said as John collected his thoughts.

With a raspy wheeze, John said, "I suppose you need money?"

Now that he had mentioned it, Edgar looked around the room, wondering how he had gotten there. "No," he said, knowing that couldn't have been the reason. "I know you'd just as soon give to a stranger's needs than my own."

"Then why are you here?" John's voice sounded cold and laced with disdain. "I told you to never return."

The walls around them expanded. The room grew larger. Believing it to be a trick of his over-active imagination, Edgar answered John's question, "To be honest…I'm not sure why I'm here."

"Then you should leave. I don't want you here. Go back to your great adventure and leave me be."

Edgar, no longer looking down upon John, but rather at eye level, took the man's hand in his own and said, "I can't do that." He found John's skin cold and clammy to the touch, but he wasn't repulsed. "You're dying. Perhaps I'm here to thank you properly for—"

With pursed lips and furrowed brow, John pulled his hand away. "Don't touch me. Everything you touch turns to disease. It's no wonder your father abandoned you."

"Please don't say that."

"You disgust me," John snarled.

As if every belittling remark from his foster father chopped him down in size, Edgar now looked up at John, who in turn looked down on him.

"What did I ever do to deserve so hard a fate?" Edgar asked, his voice sounding childish to himself, but unable to prevent it. "I have admitted to both you and to God my follies, and still you carry such hatred toward me."

John's chuckle turned to a cough. When the fit ended, he said, "You took my forbearance for granted, squandered every penny bestowed upon you. You brought shame upon this house with your dreams of grandeur."

"My greatest sin was wanting you to be proud of me. You could have helped in my writing career, but you could not be bothered. How many letters to you went unanswered?"

"You call those letters? More like insipid cries of a child." John steepled his hands and batted his eyelids. "I've fallen on hardship, need money. Ad nauseam."

Edgar could not argue and the truth in John's words made him feel smaller still.

"You, always with your hand out… with your sense of entitlement."

"You're right," Edgar said, "but all boys seek the approval of their fathers, and that was something you withheld from me. Whether I was fulfilling your wishes or not."

John leaned forward and said in a soft voice, "There's a reason for that. I'm not your father. And thank God for small miracles."

Edgar looked upon his scolding father figure with glossy eyes, too hurt to say anything else.

CHAPTER XI

Crying roused Edgar from sleep, putting an abrupt end to his unwelcome nightmare. His eyes fluttered open, and he looked around the room blindly, unable to pinpoint the whereabouts of the spirit or his unwanted partner. The cries were so loud, they encompassed the entire estate.

Time to go to work, he thought as he pulled out his weakest lenses and slipped them on. The haunting was still fairly new, and he should be able to spot her without them, but it was best to have them ready, just in case. He stoked the Specter Eliminator to life and searched through the home room by room.

The first floor being devoid of spirits, he ventured upstairs to the bedrooms. *Always upstairs,* he thought as he lugged the machine up step by step. *Perhaps I could wear it as a knapsack, mounted to some sort of a frame.*

Deep, lonesome moans turned to pain-filled wails as Edgar reached the landing. He estimated that it came from the second bedroom on the right. As he entered, he saw her. The spirit sat on the floor, her feet sticking out from the bottom of her dress. From behind, her petite frame reminded him of Virginia, and the dark, curly locks draped over her shoulders brought images of, Eliza, his mother. With a deep sob, the young maiden craned her neck and peered over her shoulder. She looked at him with the same wide, saddened eyes his mother always had.

Edgar pointed the lance at her, but something inside him didn't want to do this. His hands shook as his emotions struggled against his rational mind.

A keening shriek vibrated the glass in the window and Edgar feared it would shatter. He dropped the lance and covered his ears. Though the ghost remained on the floor, the sound grew louder, driving him to his knees. Cold sweat coated his arms.

This is how I am to die? he thought as the pain became unbearable.

The shriek ended abruptly, and the spirit turned her back on him.

He eyed his machine; he could obliterate her now. Should. But for reasons unknown to him, she spared his life. Her shriek, though painful, had merely been a warning.

"I'm not going to hurt you, Julia," he said, surprising even himself. Steeling his nerves, he reached out and placed his hand on her shoulder.

The young woman reached up lightning fast to grasp it. The movement appeared violent, and his breath lodged in his throat, but he refused to flinch. He would face his fear head on just as he had his harshest critic.

With a deep sob and sniffle, the crying came to an end. She looked up at him with tear-swollen eyes and a furrowed brow. Her touch was cool and gentle.

She was far too young to have her candle snuffed out; much like his dearest Virginia. The reminder of his own loss should have angered him, but looking into her eyes, for once he was at peace.

"It's going to be all right," he said, though he didn't know why the words passed over his lips.

A smile found its way onto her pale face and in that moment she was beautiful.

The all-too-familiar sound of his machine boiling the water within caught him off guard and caused Edgar to turn around. There, behind him with the lance leveled on the ghostly young woman, was James Laurent finally out from his hiding spot.

"No. Don't!" Edgar lunged to intercept James.

James side-stepped his advance and a burst of scalding vapor spewed forth.

With one final pain-filled moan, the spirit dissolved from Edgar's sight.

"What have you done?" Edgar asked.

James pushed his refracting goggles up upon his forehead. "I wanted to see your machine in action. You did come here to do a job didn't you?"

"Yes, but I—"

"Then what's the problem?"

"Where were you just now?" he asked.

"I merely stepped outside for some fresh air. Luckily for you I returned, else you would have botched the job." James returned the lance to its holding fixture on the machine and then walked to the spot where the woman had just been only seconds before.

Edgar could not be certain if James was truly a coward or if he was being played. Either way, he did not trust this man.

"I'll see if we got her or not?" From within his great coat, James removed a device. "A spirit detector," he said with his disingenuous smile and held it up for Edgar to view. "My own design."

Only slightly larger than James's hand, the copper box had only three features upon its face — a meter above a knob above a thumb-sized crystal. A black metal rod was mounted to each side and looked almost like a set of tuning forks.

With the twist of a knob, gears ticked, and the number dial spun. Two tuning forks at the machine's sides lifted away from the copper housing and came sharply together. After they struck, a metallic Ting! reverberated and the tone faded as the tuning forks retreated from one another until they were one-hundred-and-eighty-degrees apart, all the while spinning in a counter-clockwise direction.

That sound, Edgar thought. The tone was familiar. *High B? Low A?*

He tried to identify the note but had never been very good with music. He couldn't recall when and where he may have heard that particular ring and was too curious about the Spirit Detector to concentrate upon it for long. A small spec of fog appeared in the crystal's center and caught Edgar's eye. The blotch expanded as the tone rang until it consumed the entire crystal. With a mechanical chime, the meter's needle stopped near the number 140.

"The house is clear."

"What happened to the crystal?" Edgar asked.

"Don't worry, it's normal," James said as he removed the crystal from its housing. "All the negative energy corrupts it." James pocketed the now dull crystal.

"Why not just throw it away?" Edgar asked.

"It still has some value," he replied as he fixed a new—clear—crystal into the detector.

"I see," Edgar said so as not to appear dazzled by the man's brilliance. "So, why were you skulking in the shadows?"

"You're a very interesting man, Mister Poe. And I could not pass up the opportunity to see how the competition works. I must say, I'm not impressed."

"Luckily for me, I could care less," Edgar said, straightening his back and puffing out his chest. "There was something different about her. She seemed...passive. Unlike many of the others I've crossed paths with, save for one other. I can't help but think we've made a mistake. Lately I've pondered the reasoning behind—"

"Nonsense." James's tone was harsh, his constant smile gone now. "Why some choose to remain on this plane rather than venture on? What does it matter? They don't belong here. This world is for the living, not the dead."

"Who are we too—?"

"My father died of Cholera when I was very young. Instead of passing on to the next world, he remained."

"A noble gesture," Edgar said.

James's eyes narrowed. "It doesn't matter if my father stayed behind out of some righteous commitment to me and my mother or not. Ultimately, after years spent outside of protection of Heaven and God's grace, his innate depravity overwhelmed and corrupted him. As it does all of them."

Though Edgar could have used the tidbit to mount a rebuttal—that there was hope for his father's spirit before he became corrupted—the conviction in the man's eyes was enough for him to realize he would not dissuade him this night.

"No longer the good man my mother swore him to be," James continued, "his noxious spirit murdered her in a prideful and envious rage." James stroked the ring upon his pinky and Edgar assumed its significance. "Choked the life right out of her before my very eyes."

Edgar nodded in commiseration, having watched his own mother die. But he could only imagine young James's horror at watching his mother murdered by a specter. "Did your father turn on you as well?"

James's expression hardened into a glare hard enough to intimidate Medusa. "I did not give him the opportunity."

"Oh?" Poe considered, but disregarded the possibility that a young James dispelled the spirit. What could a young boy, even an untrained young man, do? "You fled?"

"No." James did not seem to take his question as an insult, but held his gaze a moment before confessing, "I lit the house."

"I apologize for losing my temper."

"You're over thinking it," James said, his disingenuous smile returning. "Best you put it out of your mind and focus on something more lucrative."

Edgar nodded. "Speaking of which, since you used *my* machine."

"Yes, you may be the one to collect the bounty. I'll see myself out."

"Good night then," Edgar said as the man left. *And good riddance.*

CHAPTER XII

Unable to sleep with the unanswered questions left by James's actions and the guilt of not doing more for the ghostly woman, Edgar found the nearest tavern Dawsonville had to offer.

"Scotch," he said as he sat down at the bar.

The bartender poured the swill his establishment passed off as fine alcohol. Before the man could assist another patron, Edgar tossed it back and tapped the rim of the glass. The bartender obliged and poured another, then Edgar let him be.

He raised the glass and sloshed the amber fluid around, staring deep into the whirlpool. Despite what many said about him, Edgar was not an alcoholic. He simply had a disposition to alcohol, and it didn't take much to inebriate him.

"You're plum crazy," said a man at a nearby table.

Edgar peered over his shoulder. Two men leaned into the table behind him as if trying to have a private conversation, with no idea how loud they actually were.

"I know what I heard," said a rotund man dressed in a workman's bibbed trousers.

"Bah," said his companion, a bearded man who looked to be a hack driver. "Them savages call it the trail-where-we-cried. So why in tar'nation would their dead be laughing?"

"I know what I heard, and I heard children laughing," the workman said. "Ask Spears. He'll tell ya!"

"Spears's a crazy old coot. No one would believe 'im. And I ain't gonna believe you."

The Indian Removal began around these parts, and the *trail where we cried* extended from Georgia all the way to the Indian Territories west of the Mississippi. Edgar left his empty glass at the bar and slid off the stool. Work would be a more suitable distraction. "Excuse me gentlemen, but I couldn't help but overhear." He looked at the rotund workman who was making the claims and asked, "Am I to understand that you saw ghosts?"

"Well, no," the workman said as he lowered his head, not wanting to admit to believing in such things to a stranger. "I didn't see no ghost…" His bearded friend smiled at this admission, so the man saved face by adding, "But I heard 'em."

"You're certain?" Edgar asked.

"Yes sir," he said, smiling at Edgar's attention. "Spears and I were collecting timbers from them Cherokee buildings most of the afternoon. Weren't no one else around, nor any children playin' around there, but we both couldn't shake the feeling something was eyeing us. And right at dusk, I'm tellin' ya, I heard 'em. Gave me the shivers."

"Them two were probably drunk," the bearded hack driver told Edgar. "If those were my kin, I'd tan their hides for being out that way at all."

"That ain't got nothin' to do with it."

"So you was drinking?"

"Ah," the workman waved his hand and dismissed the other.

Edgar found the soirée comical; the two grown men argued like an old married couple. "Where was this that you say you heard them?"

"New Echota," said the workman as if Edger were dull for not knowing. "Off Chatsworth Road."

"My apologies," Edgar said, "but I'm not familiar with the area. How far is that?"

"I'd say almost four miles east of here," the bearded hack driver said. "Just before the Coosawattee meets the Conasauga River."

"New Echota was that Cherokee town," the workman said with disgust. "You can't miss it."

"Excellent," Edgar said. He could walk the distance in under an hour. "I thank you fine gentlemen for your time," he added, withdrawing several bills from his pants' pocket. He tossed them onto the round table. "Next round's on me."

"Thank you kindly," the hack driver said, then signaled the waitress with a raised hand and snap of his fingers.

"You be careful out there, Mister," the workman said. "Ain't just ghosts you gotta watch out for in them there woods."

"Thank you for the warning. Good evening gentlemen." Edgar turned and walked out of the bar.

Outside, he peered up into the night sky to gather his bearings, then proceeded to head in the north easterly direction. The cool air forced him to walk with his hands in his pockets and a slight slouch in his posture, his chin tucked against his chest so that the collar sheltered his exposed neck.

Edgar should retrieve his Specter Eliminator from the mansion, but, though the men had been frightened, they were not harmed. If they were indeed the spirits of children, and they were laughing, then reason suggested they were merely playing with the men and had no ill-intention. This might be the perfect opportunity to put new theories to the test.

Was it possible for an earth-bound spirit to be inoffensive? To serve a greater purpose? Certainly, if Edgar were to find a positive answer to those questions, it would be with children.

He followed the pine lined road east, walking under the light of the full moon; the stillness and silence of the night comforting him like an old friend.

After over an hour of walking, Edgar came upon a few dark and empty buildings set back from Chatsworth Road. The largest building was a two-story structure which might have been a church or courthouse. The porch railings and front door were missing, and the interior was empty of furniture. Even the shutters had been taken. Several heavy timbers had been cut from the side of the buildings. Surely the work of the rotund workman and his friend *Spears*.

He walked through the still, silent village. What looked to have been a store, due to its large gallery, sagged under the weight of Jessamine and Passion vines consuming it. The front windows of the store were absent of their glass and the entire structure leaned off to the right side.

Due to the overgrowth, Edgar literally stumbled upon several mortared-stone foundations where cottages or workshops had once stood. It was similar to every other small town and village he'd ever visited or passed through. Perhaps the buildings were a little more spaced out, and maybe there was more space dedicated to the town square, but there was nothing strikingly "Cherokee" about the place.

At the far end of the village was the cemetery, but he didn't expect to find the ghosts of children there. Contrary to superstitions, spirits didn't often haunt cemeteries because people didn't usually die in the cemeteries. Cemeteries were ritualistic grounds for burial, of peace, no matter the religion. Spirits, ghosts, and specters were attached to significant locations from their lives. But on the edge of the cemetery, a single white rose grew where a trail led into the woods. He bent at the knees for a closer inspection. *The Cherokee Rose*.

The Cherokees believed the rose blossomed through the prayers of their chiefs and the tears of the grieving mothers of their people. With its gold center and seven pedals, no other symbol could ever represent the suffering of those people better.

Putting faith in the Cherokee belief, Edgar ventured into the wood.

His heart hammered in his chest. The stillness of the night was awkward, and the lack of wildlife disheartening. No field mice scampered through the leaf litter, no deer frolicked through the underbrush, and no owls asked their inquisitive question from their perches.

Spooked by specters? he wondered.

As he passed a small cropping of Cherokee Roses, youthful laughter carried on the wind, confirming he was on the right path.

The laughter grew louder, and Edgar withdrew a pair of his refracting lenses and slipped them on.

He whirled at a giggle behind him.

Where are you? he wondered.

He was nudged from behind and stumbled a step forward but remained upright.

"The devil?" he exclaimed as a child's laughter mocked him. He dared not spin around and inadvertently startle the playful spirit again.

"I take it I am it," he said with whimsy. "Shall I count then?"

Nothing but the rustling of leaves in the wind.

"All right." Edgar raised his left arm and covered his eyes with his hand. "One…Two…Three…."

The giggling returned and he counted six distinct octaves before the laughter faded. That lost potential weighed heavy on him. Only now, years too late, did he wish he had been more involved in Indian Sovereignty. He could have written to President Taylor or, at the very least, a Georgia congressman, provided essays to magazines in order to heighten awareness, anything other than ignore the issue and be complacent as an entire people were persecuted.

"Ready or not," he said, taking the abrupt stop to the laughter as a sign. "Here I come."

When he pulled his hand away from his eyes, three or four children darted into the trees ahead of him. Edgar left the path, entering the trees after them. They cut and wove between the trees like a swarm of bees, laughing as they crisscrossed each other's paths. Definitely six of them, possibly eight; the boys in blouses and Kentucky jeans, the girls in homespun dresses.

"Oh, there you are," he said, dashing forward toward the middle of the bunch where the spirits crossed paths. "I've got you now."

When he broke into a clearing, the laughing stopped.

He walked to the middle of the moonlit clearing and called, "Hello. Children?"

They had led him to this place and now it seemed the game was over.

A lonesome howl broke the silence and sent a ripple of gooseflesh down his spine. The hairs on his arms stood as if charged by static electricity.

Wolves.

A twig snapped behind him and he turned around, coming face to face with a gray wolf. The beast arched its back and lowered its head. A low, guttural growl emanated deep from within its throat, the fur on the back of its neck bristled.

He stole a glance to his left and then his right. Another wolf appeared before him from out of the underbrush. It growled with a toothy grin, as if acknowledging the trap Edgar had fallen into.

"Oh, children," he said to himself. "I meant you no harm. I just wanted to—"

The wolf stepped toward him and barked, flashing its large, sharp teeth, and snapping its jaw shut as if it'd bitten a piece out of the night.

"Easy, easy," Edgar said to the wolf as if it was simply a domesticated dog.

A voice called out from the darkness, asking, "Then why are you here in the middle of the night?"

It was not a child's voice. Not even a specter's voice. It was a man's voice. And it came from the tree line.

Edgar turned to try and make out who was there. "Who is there?"

"Perhaps you just wished to plunder a few graves," a different man's voice insinuated.

"No. I, I just wanted to—"

But the beast took another step toward him. and Edgar's attention locked onto it. He stepped backward and withdrew his pen knife from his vest pocket and opened it to hold off the wolves. With the mother-of-pearl handle and two-inch steel blade, it was an impressive blade in a publisher's office or a fashionable barroom, but rather pathetic in the wilderness.

A third wolf leapt upon a rock. Teeth bared, saliva stretching between its gums.

"Damn it all," Edgar cursed, holding the little blade of his penknife against the wolves.

"Why else would you be here in the middle of the night?" the man's voice asked.

Edgar sidestepped to the right, but his feet slipped on the uneven ground, and he stumbled a bit. He slammed his palm against the cold, damp earth to halt himself.

"You don't belong here," the second voice said.

"Research. Inquiry. I'm a ghost—" Edgar said but stopped himself before saying the word "hunter". It wouldn't have cast him in a favorable light. "I, I am interested in ghosts. I study, them," he said, regretting that this made him sound like a spiritualist loon, not respectable or professional at all. "I'm a ghost, inspector," he tried, but didn't even believe it himself.

"These aren't your spirits," the second voice said.

Not his spirits? Were these men Cherokee? They didn't sound like savages.

"Do tell," Edgar exclaimed, but before he could ask for clarification, the wolves closed in, leaving nowhere to run. One to the left and the right of him, the other directly in front of him, eyes burning with rage.

Edgar closed his eyes and imagined his dear, sweet Virginia standing before him with open arms. How lovely it would be to see her again.

A gentle breeze kissed his cheek as a bark rang in his ears, followed by a yelp and a thud. Then soft footfalls treading away.

Edgar opened his eyes. Two of the wolves had run off; the other was dead on the ground, an arrow piercing its heart.

A tall man and his companion stepped out of the dark tree line and into the clearing. Both were dressed in linen shirts, cotton trousers, single breasted waistcoats, and frock coats as any other self-respecting southern gentleman would be. Except the taller one carried a bow and both of them wore pistols at their waists.

Edgar held his ground; if they wanted him dead, he would be. That much he knew. "Are you Cherokee?" Edgar asked.

The two glanced at each other before the taller of the two asked, "Why are you in these woods alone?"

The shorter one placed a tin lantern he'd been carrying on the ground and opened it. He lit the small taper by means of a phosphorus match and then held the lantern up to better reveal Edgar to their eyes.

However, this served the same purpose for Edgar. He removed his refracting eyeglasses and looked them over.

Their hair was black, and their skin was tanned like that of workmen, so they could be Indians. However, they weren't dressed in bright-colored, free-hanging calico shirts and rough leggings made of stroud or deerskin. But being here, and their ability to use the bow, who else would be out here?

"Why are you in these woods?" the taller of the two asked again.

"I've received word of ghosts in the area. I came to investigate the claim." Edgar told them only as much truth as was needed, seeing no point in mentioning his personal perturbation.

The man who held the bow stepped toward him, eyes narrowed, and brow furrowed. "For what purpose?" he asked.

"For the purpose of research. I mean no harm. I am but a mere writer," Edgar said offering the least threatening representation of himself. "My name is Poe. Edgar Poe. You've likely never heard of me, but I assure you, I am a poet and composer of stories."

The two men looked toward one another and as if sharing the same thought. Their bearing relaxed. They turned to him, their faces bright with smiles, and both asked questions at the same time.

"Edgar Allan Poe?"

"The critic and editor?"

"Well, yes," Edgar said, placing his palm on the nearest tree trunk to stabilize himself. "You are aware of me?"

The shorter of the two stepped forward and took his hand, shaking it vigorously. "Professor Ramsey at Middlebury is a great admirer of yours. He often expounded upon your *Philosophy of Composition*."

"Middlebury?" Edgar asked, reclaiming his hand.

"Middlebury College. In Vermont," he clarified, then introduced himself. "My name is Andrew. Andrew Walker."

Edgar nodded in acknowledgement.

"And I'm William," the Cherokee with the bow and arrow followed. "I've read you in *Southern Literary Messenger*."

"Did you attend Middlebury as well?" Edgar asked.

"No. I studied in Maryland, at Washington College."

"Oh, yes. Washington," Edgar said, nodding. "Fine school. Very fine."

"Yes," William said and shifted from one foot to the other.

"Professor Ramsey at Middlebury. I will have to make his acquaintance," Edgar mused. "Perhaps a lecture could be arranged."

The three men glanced from one to the other, but no one spoke. All aware they had been conversing and exchanging greetings as if in a city salon, but were in fact, in a dark clearing, miles outside of town, and in the dead of night.

"Right," William said to Edgar. "Let us leave these woods." He then glanced to Andrew and nodded his head toward the fresh kill. Andrew nodded in agreement, handed the lantern to William, and approached the dead wolf.

Edgar cleared his throat. "I suppose I owe my life to you fine gentlemen," Edgar said, "Thank you, else my more delicate parts would be traveling an unpleasant journey through the bellies of those wretched beasts."

"Hungry, not wretched," Andrew said with a firm hand on the wolf's abdomen. He gripped the arrow and pulled it free. A trail of crimson splashed across the earth. He handed the arrow back to William and hoisted the carcass up and over his shoulder.

"You're taking it?" Edgar asked, unable to hide the disgust in his voice.

"To waste the kill would be to disrespect the animal," he explained to Edgar as he took back his lantern.

William notched the bloody arrow as Andrew raised the lantern before him. When Edgar hesitated, Andrew said, "Come," and lead them down the path Edgar had followed in from the abandoned village.

"With the state of the village," Edgar said, "I didn't believe anyone remained here. May I be so bold as to ask why you are about here?" Edgar asked.

Andrew and William stopped on the path and looked back at him.

"Mind you," Edgar stammered, "I'm very grateful that you were."

The Cherokee looked at one another, the weight of their purpose evident on both of them. Looking back to Edgar, William said, "Interestingly enough, you might be just the man to understand."

"William," Andrew said to cut him off and shut him up.

William turned back to Andrew and asked, "Who better?"

Andrew didn't speak, but kept his eyes fixed on William, not relenting.

"Ross said to be patient and wait for a blessing of opportunity," William said. "Finding a writer and editor in New Echota doesn't strike you as an opportune blessing?"

"Gentlemen," Edgar interrupted. "I don't mean to instigate a quarrel."

They looked to Edgar for a moment before Andrew nodded his consensus to William.

Andrew took a deep breath and let it out as if he was preparing to jump from a bridge. He stepped up to Edgar and asked, "Are you familiar with *The Cherokee Phoenix*?"

"Of course," Edgar answered, a little insulted and confused to be asked such an elementary question. "The phoenix is best known as a being of Greek mythology but has equivalents in other traditions. It is typically a red bird associated with fire, the sun, and rebirth. Therefore, I would assume the *Cherokee* phoenix would be—"

Andrew held his palm up and shook his head to stop Edgar. "My apologies," he said. "*The Cherokee Phoenix* was a newspaper."

Edgar stared at Andrew with mouth still open from being interrupted. He had never heard of such a thing. He blinked and his mouth closed and opened a few times before he asked, "A newspaper?"

"Our newspaper."

"A newspaper!"

"In Cherokee," William added.

Edgar guffawed and shook his head. "Incredible. Now I must offer my apologies. I was not aware of this publication."

Andrew waved off Edgar's apology, saying, "It was not widely distributed and only of interest to Cherokee."

"When we were forced out of our homes," William broke in, "our Chief, John Ross, hid the main component of our printing press."

"We've returned to retrieve it," Andrew said as if this explained everything.

"But why go to such lengths?" Edgar asked. "Simply remake the component."

The confusion must have been evident on his face for Andrew explained further, "This is a special component, of a unique design. A type-engine if you will. There is no other mechanism like this anywhere in the world, let alone in Indian Territory."

"I see," Edgar said. "And the inventor of this type-engine?"

"Dead."

"Of course," Edgar said, nodding that he was familiar with how the universe functioned. "Why would anyone leave such an item behind?" Edgar asked.

"It would have been confiscated," William said. "Years before removal, the Georgia Guard seized our first printing press and destroyed the sets of Cherokee type to keep Chief Ross from educating and organizing our people. He knew that if any of the Georgia Guard or federal soldiers discovered the new printing device, it too would be confiscated and destroyed. So, it was hidden and left behind."

"But to re-establish *The Cherokee Phoenix* in Tahlequah, we now need this component."

Edgar nodded that he understood. And he did. Aside from spreading the literary arts, a regular periodical informed and united communities. To destroy something of such value was nothing short of barbarism.

The Cherokee nodded, their lips pursed, and their heads held low as if holding back a wave of emotions threatening to consume them.

"So, what do you need from me?" Edgar asked.

"We need you to retrieve it for us," William said.

Edgar understood while the exchange of land and the relocation to Indian Territory was ostensibly voluntary, the Cherokee had essentially been exiled and for William and Andrew to show their faces in town would raise suspicion if not hostility.

Edgar nodded. "It's the least I could do I suppose," Edgar said. "Where is it?"

"In Worcester's old missionary house," answered William.

"I see," Edgar said.

"Which is now occupied by the brother of Colonel Bishop," William added.

"Oh dear..."

"It is not too far," offered William.

"Come, follow us," said Andrew.

As they walked, William shared their story with the wordsmith.

"We adapted to the white ways and got along peacefully enough with the Georgians, but when gold was discovered in the hills, speculators trespassed on our lands seeking their fortune. As we defended our lands, pressure mounted on the Georgia government to deal with the *Indian problem*. Governor Gilmer used the legislature to *appropriate* our land, claiming the gold was the property of the Georgian State.

We brought several legal suits against the state of Georgia and the U.S. Government itself, but those long court battles ended when the U.S. Supreme Court supported Georgia's claim to the Cherokee lands in 1830. Congress and President Jackson then passed the Indian Removal Act which exchanged all Indian lands in the East for unsettled lands west of the Mississippi River. We did not recognize the Act and refused to leave our ancestral lands. So, in the middle of winter, the federal government forced us from our homes at gunpoint, stripped us of our possessions, confined us in large stockade camps, and finally sent us a thousand miles to the west—by foot. Nearly four thousands of our people died of starvation and disease in the camps and then of the elements and disease and murder on that journey."

Upon hearing this, all Edgar could do was offer an apology that felt too little, too impersonal, and then silence befell the trio.

CHAPTER XIII

Edgar followed William and Andrew through the Georgia foothills until they came upon a tucked away, two-storey, rectangular silhouette home. From the outside, the missionary looked quite spacious with its steep roof and centralized door and if Edgar hadn't known better, he would have described it as a true Cape-Cod style house.

"You're sure you can do this?" asked William.

"Yes," Edgar replied. The hour was late, and Edgar knew whoever the occupant was, surely they'd be well in the throes of slumber.

He approached nervously, mentally running the possible explanations for his presence. If he was caught in the act, he could claim he was hunting ghosts… or play the part of the drunken fool having entered the wrong house. He turned back, his nerves on edge. From the tree line, the two Cherokee waved him on.

This is for the best, he reiterated to himself. If he were caught, worst case scenario, he'd be tossed into a cell for the night and pay a fine. The experience could prove useful in future literary works. However, should William and Andrew be caught trespassing in a white man's house in the middle of the night, they'd surely be hung at the gallows, left on display for all to see and the crows to feast upon their rotting corpses.

And the best approach would be to tell the truth within the lie.

Taking the front steps two at a time, he breathed deeply and then wrapped his knuckles upon the front door. After he allowed a minute to pass, he tried again.

Finally, after a third attempt, a man opened the door. Despite the hour, the man proved himself a true southern gentleman when he asked, "How may I help you?"

"I apologize for the intrusion at such an ungodly hour," Edgar said, pushing a calling card into the man's hand, "but I come to you with a matter of dire importance."

"And you are?" The man asked as he peered at the card, pulling it back and drawing it closer to make out the text.

"The one and only," Edgar cut him off. "Author of the macabre and hunter of specters, I am, Edgar Allan Poe." Though he felt foolish hamming it up for the man standing before him in his ruffled, floor-length night robe, he needed to put the man at ease and gain his trust.

"And in what capacity are you here this night?" asked the man.

"Unfortunately for all of us, I am on the hunt. Two men were accosted by spirits near New Echota."

"Injun spirits?" the man asked.

"Indeed," Edgar replied. "I am sorry to say, I have inadvertently chased one into your home and for that, I am truly sorry."

The man's eyes went wide as the levity of Edgar's lie weighed on him. "I'll wake my wife and we'll head over to the Jackson's estate. Please help us."

Pushing his guilt aside, Edgar replied, "You can count on me." Though the man did not question how Edgar was to remove the spirit, he felt the need to cover all aspects to prevent future doubt. "But I do have one request."

"Name it," the man said with more enthusiasm Edgar could have expected.

"Do you have a Bible I may borrow?" Edgar asked, knowing a proper southern gentleman would have a gospel of his Lord.

The fear in the man's eyes dissipated and was replaced with ire from the indignation of such a question. "You'll find one in just about every room of this house," he finally replied.

"Thank you. Again... my apologies for this inconvenience."

With a nod, the man of the house dashed up the central staircase to fetch his wife.

Edgar's gaze followed the man, and when he dipped out of sight, he looked around the spacious open room. William had told him they often gathered around the fireplace in front of him and that there was a bedroom on the other side of that wall, with four more upstairs.

"A modest home," he mumbled.

"What do you mean we have a ghost?" a woman's voice shrieked, and Edgar could only assume it was the lady of the house. "Who's here?"

Edgar did his best not to listen in on the one-sided conversation, but the woman's tone and his natural curiosity were against him. The misses was clearly skeptical, and it took every ounce of restraint on his part to keep from storming up to the bedrooms and turning on his charm.

Finally, the couple came down the stairs. "The house is yours. Please see to this problem," said the man.

The wife gave a harrumph, rightfully holding on to her doubt.

Edgar gave a nod and said, "You have my word."

"Come along dear," her husband said as he pulled her out the front door and she allowed it without further protest.

"Now then," Edgar said as he moved to complete his task. Knife in hand, he knelt and slid the blade between the floorboards under the tread and popped it free.

Reduced to a common thief, he thought with a smile as he removed the wood and revealed the carpet bag Andrew told him about. He gripped each end and lifted the type-engine out of the cubbyhole. "Umph," he muttered, not expecting the weight. Feeling off balance, Edgar rested the bag upon his knees.

He opened the sack and slid back the cloth to have a peek. "Exquisite," he said as the filtering moonlight refracted off the brass fittings and polished wood.

He removed the device from the sack to reveal a hexagonal cylinder about a foot and a half long with openings on each end. A circular aperture with cap on the left end and a rectangular slot on the right end. The panels of the hexagon contained an assortment of levers, valves, and even a crank; but the main panel was covered in a hundred ivory keys, most of them glyphs, or rather letters, he was unfamiliar with.

I absolutely must meet this Samuel Worcester, he thought. The possibilities of such a conversation teased his muse.

Realizing he was wasting precious time, Edgar returned the type engine to the carpet bag. Upon standing, he proceeded to flip a chair over, tilt a family portrait, and knock over an expensive looking vase to give the impression of a struggle. Satisfied, he then left the former missionary with his gaze locked on the forest's edge. The Indians were nowhere to be seen, but Edgar knew them to be close.

A torch light in the neighboring estate's window caught his eye. Though Edgar knew the couple he had displaced eagerly awaited the opportunity to return home, he felt it was in everyone's best interest if he returned the type engine to its people and send them on their way.

"You have it," Andrew said as Edgar approached.

"I do." He handed the prize over, and overwhelming pride coursed through him at the idea of returning the valuable device to its rightful owners.

"My people thank you," said Andrew before accepting the proffered device. The man took the weight of the device as though it were a newborn babe. In that moment, Edgar could not fathom anyone calling this gentle giant a savage.

"Should you find yourself in Tahlequah, pay us a visit. Our *Oukah* will surely want to thank you with a feast in your honor," William said.

"That is mighty kind." Edgar bowed his head out of respect for their customs. He reached into the inner pocket of his jacket and pulled out one of his chapbooks of poetry. "May it keep you company on your long trip home—er—back to your people."

William and Andrew's smile did little to ease the guilt swelling in Edgar's heart. He cursed himself for stumbling on such a sensitive topic. How could they call a place not of their choosing anything other than a prison?

Afraid of insulting the men any further, Edgar extended his right hand. The two braves looked first at the gesture, then the other. With a wide smile, Andrew was the first to shake Edgar's hand, and William followed.

"It was a pleasure meeting the both of you," Edgar said.

"May *Yowa* see to it that our paths cross again," William said.

With a final nod of their heads, the two Cherokee warriors were on their way back to Tahlequah in Indian Territory.

Edgar gave the two men a few minutes before turning and looking back toward the torch-lit window. He hadn't even gotten the couples' names.

One more thing to apologize for I guess, he thought before beginning his walk.

CHAPTER XIV

Edgar awoke to the midday sun penetrating the bedroom curtains. With the back of his hand sheltering his eyes, he rolled over in hopes of falling back to sleep, but there were no shadows to escape to. The room was bathed in light from all directions.

"Fine," he mumbled, his mouth sticky and dry. As he sat up, he had no recollection of the hour in which he had returned to the estate.

"James?" he called out, the silence in the house unnerving him. "James!"

Fearing his supposed partner had run off to claim glory and payment for himself, Edgar whipped the satin sheets aside and jumped out of bed. Frantically, he called James's name repeatedly as he moved from room to room in nothing more than his night shirt.

Perhaps I can still get to Tomlinson Bulloch's estate before James has an opportunity to run off, he thought. With that minutia of hope, he then proceeded to dress in a mad dash. Though he needed a bath after running through the woods last night, time would not permit. Instead, he used an extra helping of cologne to mask his musk.

Not forgetting his manners, once dressed, Edgar made the bed he slept in and proceeded to the door. Upon opening it, he found Tomlinson Bulloch standing before him, his right hand balled into a fist ready to knock.

"Good morning Mr. Poe." A large smile formed on the man's portly face.

"Are you here to toss me out?" Edgar asked, immediately assuming the worst.

Mr. Bulloch's eyes went wide as a look of shock and disappointment nestled on his face. "Not in the least, Mr. Poe." With his left hand, Tomlinson tugged on the lapel of his jacket and with his right, he reached into his inside pocket. Withdrawing an envelope, he said, "I've merely come to honor our agreement." Tomlinson held out the envelope. "Here is your payment. In full."

For the first time in a long time, Edgar found himself speechless.

"Go on," the man said, nudging the envelope closer to Edgar. "You may count it if you wish."

"No. No." Edgar shook his head as he accepted the proffered envelope. "That won't be necessary."

"Mr. Laurent credited you completely with the capture and disposal of young, Miss Julia Lucas."

"He did what?" Edgar could not believe what he was hearing. Had he been wrong about the man all along?

Tomlinson smiled a wide, toothy grin and his portly belly reverberated as he laughed. "He said you might be modest. Such a gentleman you are, Mr. Poe. To show my appreciation, you may stay here for as long as you'd like."

"That's kind of you," Edgar said, feigning a smile, "but as generous as the offer is, I should be on my way."

"I understand," Tomlinson said with a hint of dissatisfaction in his voice.

Looking at the steam-powered buggy behind Mr. Bulloch, Edgar brazenly said, "However, I would not decline an offer of riding in that wonderful buggy of yours one more time. Perhaps you could take me to the train station?"

"It would be my pleasure."

With his payment in his pocket, Edgar stood at the train station contemplating his next move.

Either I return to Portland immediately, or I can make a few important stops.

He could wire Ellie's share of the money to her. She sorely needed it, but he had to go back to see her anyway. Not just to retrieve his raven, but to see her angelic face one more time.

Edgar stepped up to the ticket counter, money in hand. *It shouldn't take me too long,* he rationalized. *Besides, I could sell some books along the way.*

"May I help you?" asked the young man on the other side of the glass.

The embroidered B&O logo on the ticket seller's cheaply made denim cap seemed out of place and tacky to Edgar, considering the fellow was clean shaven and cozily buttoned in his navy-blue jacket.

Edgar returned the young man's smile and said, "One ticket to Martinsburg please."

"Business or pleasure, sir?" he asked, a polite gesture as he filled out the ticket.

"Little of both, actually."

"Very good, sir." He lifted his head up and looked Edgar in the eyes. "Here you go."

Edgar placed his index finger upon the ticket's edge and slid it out from underneath the glass partition.

"Will you be needing any assistance with your bags?"

"No, I'll manage, thank you."

"Good day to you," said the young man as Edgar walked away. "Next!"

As he passed a newsstand, he placed his valise down on the ground beside his portable machine and plucked a copy of *Scientific American* from the shelf.

He had sent an essay to the publication months back and had checked each magazine since. Travelling as much as he did, mail was slow to find him, and he'd probably see it in print well before ever receiving an acceptance or rejection letter. In his mind, the only logical reasoning they would have to not run the piece was dependent on their convictions toward Newton's teachings. The article centered on praising Johann Wolfgang von Goethe's Theory of Colors for it was his thoughts on the indivisibility of light that led Edgar to the creation of his refracting lenses.

And apparently James Laurent as well, Edgar thought.

On the cover of the magazine was a sketch of what looked to be a steam-powered locomotive that did not require the use of tracks to travel. The brief write-up underneath the image claimed the machine could pull plows and threshing machines without the aid of a horse or oxen. However, to Edgar's keen eye, the front, treadless wheels looked incapable of moving through soil given the heavy bulk of the bin and boiler.

He flipped through the pages with no intent on purchasing the magazine and when he found his article absent, he placed the rag back upon the shelf and continued on his way.

Large puffs of smoke periodically exhaled from the locomotive's stack as he approached. The familiar sound of the hissing vapor soothed him. Fortunately, there was no one Edgar had to share the train car with this go around. Without the obligation of idle chit-chat, he enjoyed the quiet and allowed his mind to wander for the eight-hour trip.

His thoughts bounced between James's treachery against Julia Lucas's spirit, and his generosity in allowing Edgar the reward money for the cleansing. Despite James's best efforts, Edgar could not bring himself to trust the man. There was something wrong about him that Edgar could not place his finger on. An arrogance beyond his own perhaps. Edgar turned toward his machine, and the young woman whose grief had consumed her even in death, returned to the forefront of his mind.

In the end, was she in pain? Am I destroying them, or setting them free?

Edgar had crossed paths with a gunslinger a year back that used blessed salt shot and holy water. The man was a nomad, a drifter from state to state in search of work. They volleyed for the same job—a textile worker haunting the cotton press that was responsible for taking his life. One look at the outlaw's unshaven face, grime coated cheeks, yellowed teeth and drab clothing, and Edgar had felt sorry for him. He'd stepped aside and allowed him the bounty as the man had referred to it. The violence of that particular cleansing had committed itself to Edgar's memory.

Sometime during the ride, Edgar fell asleep. When the train pulled into the B&O Roundhouse and Station Complex, the car attendant gently shook his shoulder and said, "Sir, I believe this is your stop."

Rubbing his eyes, he looked out the window to verify. "Thank you."

The man nodded, then moved toward the next car.

Rotten luck, he thought as he yawned. He had missed the mountain view as the train passed through the gaps. The fruit trees along Apple Pie Ridge always provided an intoxicating aroma that stirred fond childhood memories of Frances Allan baking in the kitchen on a Sunday morning.

Gathering his things, Edgar made his way off the train.

Located in Northern Virginia, Martinsburg was a city on the rise. Ground was broken on a north to south toll road expected to run from Courthouse Square Shopping Center to the Potomac River, one that would make traveling to Randolph's Shop of Curiosities easier, albeit at a cost.

Mark Randolph was as brilliant as he was strange, and the cramped shop a reflection of his extraordinary taste and thirst for knowledge. Along the outer walls, bookcases stretched from floor to ceiling. Most housed volumes on subjects from demonology to herbal medicine, while a few displayed skeletal remains, crystal balls, and short, jewel crusted daggers. Glass curio cabinets with a variety of pestles and mortars, ancient scrolls, jarred fetuses and mummified animals, incense and blessed candles, created an elaborate maze on the shop's floor. Edgar had often teased that the only thing missing was a mythical, minotaur guardian.

One could spend an entire year sorting through Mark's wares and still not discover all the shop's secrets. Inspiration struck every time Edgar visited, and when the muse chose to be a fickle wench when he was under a tight deadline, he'd make an immediate detour to the shop and uncover some hidden gem that sparked his sense of wonder and infatuation with the macabre.

As Edgar stepped into the store, a bell chimed in the back. As always, he could not locate or identify the trigger. *One day, Mark,* Edgar thought. *One day.*

Mark looked up from the open book laid across his counter and smiled. "Edgar, good to see you."

"How's business old friend?" he asked as he walked up to him.

"Slow," he replied with a heavy sigh. Straightening his posture, he continued, "Seems people are moving away from mysticism and embracing science."

"Sorry for my part in that." Edgar leaned against the countertop and smiled. "Perhaps I can turn it around for you though."

"What do you need?"

"Some iodized bitter salts and…some information."

"Usual amount?"

Edgar nodded.

"And this information?" Mark asked.

"James Laurent, have you heard of him?"

With his hand rubbing his chin, Mark searched his memory bank. "Sorry, name doesn't ring a bell. But there was someone asking about you not that long ago."

"Who?"

"He didn't give his name. I didn't think anything of it at the time. It's not unusual a patron comes in and wants to know and or buy what the great Edgar Allan Poe can offer."

"Lanky, well-dressed with sunken features?" Edgar asked.

"Yeah." Mark's eyes went wide. "I didn't cause trouble for you, did I?"

With the smile gone and as much seriousness as he could muster, Edgar replied, "Damn near caused my death."

"I am *so* sorry. Had I known, I…"

The smile on Edgar's face must have warned Mark of his deceit.

With a shaky finger and a wide smile, Mark said, "You're a real bastard."

Edgar chuckled. "Lord knows why the man has shown so much interest in me, but I'm not concerned."

"Maybe you should be. I'll be right back with your order."

As Mark walked away, Edgar pondered the notion.

Just not enough to go on, he thought.

Unable to decipher if James was merely an overzealous fan or a threat out to steal work or to rob him of his writings, or his inventions, Edgar needed to dig further.

When Mark returned from the back room, Edgar said, "Since you were no help with this James character, perhaps you know of some work I could distract myself with."

"I do not," he said, then handed over a vial of yellowish granules.

"Pity." Edgar took the vial, pinching it between his thumb and index finger.

If he were in desperate need, Edgar could make his own—the substance nothing more than a magnesium, sulfur and oxygen compound coated with potassium iodate—but then he would be cheating himself the pleasure of these visits.

He pocketed the vial and handed over a single dollar bill. "Keep the change."

Mark furrowed his brow. "This is too much."

"Well," Edgar paused, "you could always repay the kindness by stocking a few copies of my latest poetry collection in your store."

Mark leaned back, hand on his chin again.

Edgar saw through his quizzical look. He knew his friend was only pretending to mull the idea over, but he played along and waited with bated breath.

"I suppose I could take a few copies."

"Excellent!" Edgar hunched over to retrieve a handful of his chapbooks.

"On consignment of course."

"Of course," he replied, handing over the stack.

Mark placed his hand on the top copy. "The usual twenty percent?"

Edgar nodded.

With the terms verbally agreed upon, Mark scooped up the books. A single copy was placed on a wrought iron stand inside the glass counter, and the others were given a home nestled between *The Count of Monte Cristo* by Alexandre Dumas and Mary Shelley's *Frankenstein* on a bookshelf labeled fiction.

In the brief moment in Mark's absence, Edgar's thoughts drifted to the young woman James had turned his machine on again. Along with Julia's image, the guilt of his failure returned as well.

"What's wrong?" Mark asked as he approached. "You look puzzled."

"I was just thinking…" Edgar asked, leaning in, anticipating Mark's words. "Given all the books you've collected on the subject, you might be about the only person who could answer this."

Mark moved closer, conspiring with him, and nodded for Edgar to ask.

"Do you think there's a better way to deal with spirits?"

"There is nothing more practical than your machine," Mark said, straightening his posture. "Sure, there are other effective means, but none as safe and efficient as yours. Where is this coming from?"

"I recently came across a young woman. A Miss Julia Lucas. She wasn't hurting anyone. Just grieving."

Mark nodded his head as if knowing where Edgar was going. "You thought about letting her be, didn't you?"

"Yes, but the choice was ultimately made for me."

Mark placed a comforting hand upon Edgar's shoulder.

Edgar continued, "The fact that she didn't attack has gotten me thinking that maybe they're not all bad. Maybe some need to be handled differently."

"So, she didn't attack you at that moment." Mark's grip tightened as if to emphasize his point. "But anything could have set her off. It was right to send her on her way."

"I suppose," Edgar said, but his heart still weighed heavy with guilt. "There was just something in her eyes that told me she meant no harm."

Mark removed his hand. "What's done is done. No sense dwelling on it."

"That's reassuring." Edgar turned to leave.

"Going all ready?" Mark asked.

"I figure since you're of little help today, I best go see Georgie. Perhaps he either knows this James Laurent or has a lead on work."

"Just like that?"

Edgar craned his neck. "Yeah."

With a hurt look, Mark's head bobbed. "Fine, tell twitchie I said hello. Safe travel."

"Will do." Edgar walked to the door, then stopped, feeling the need to make sure Mark knew he was teasing. "And I'll see to it some business comes your way."

"Go on," Mark said with a smile, "get out of here you royal pain."

With a chuckle, Edgar said, "Good day, old friend."

As the door closed behind him, Edgar wished it was as easy to visit George Darby as he made it sound—a simple carriage ride or brisk walk—but George's smithy was located just outside of Boston. With another long train ride in his immediate future, Edgar walked to the nearest tavern for a stiff drink and a hot meal.

CHAPTER XV

"Never thought I'd be back here so soon," Edgar mumbled as he stepped out of the train station. *Do I walk to the outskirts of town? But if anyone sees me…*

Edgar's guilt for how he abandoned his post at the Wellman's estate weighed heavy on his shoulders. With his abrupt departure and thievery, he knew he had pushed the boundaries of friendship. *And if my treachery were reported…*

Realizing it was best not to be seen, his decision was made. With his chin tucked against his chest, neck scrunched into his shoulders, and hands in his pockets, he walked in a north-westerly direction. He did his best to avoid passersby, crossing streets as pedestrians approached and pretending to stare off in the opposite direction as if something had his attention so as not to make eye contact with anyone, for he knew how recognizable he was. With his receding hair line, there was no mistaking his signature brow.

As he made his way toward George's smithy, his thoughts darted from the mysterious James Laurent to his unfinished short story, to the lovely Ellie and her sickly mother, then back to James.

No matter how hard he tried, or how deep he probed his memory bank for previous run-ins with the man, Edgar could not discern James's intentions. Was he a ghost hunter with designs on Edgar's more affluent clientele? Or an aspiring poet out to rob him of his writings? Or a merchant inventor after his inventions? One thing was sure, he was no gentleman. The single act of kindness given to him by James could have been nothing more than a rouse to throw Edgar off, but if that were the case, then James had made a grievous error in underestimating Edgar's cynicism.

He stepped through the underbrush and breathed a sigh of relief. *Finally.* The blacksmith's shop was a quaint log cabin with a single pitched roof located in an acre-wide clearing of Boston's surrounding wood. The thick, black smoke from the burning bituminous coal hovering over the treetops like a beacon signaled its location.

Edgar walked in on a negotiation. A young couple dressed in tattered, grime-stained clothes bartering for a few more coins for the ore presented to George.

"Take it or leave it." George's head cocked to the right, then straightened. "It's my best offer."

Edgar could not remember ever seeing the mousy-looking man behind the counter be so rude and flippant to his patrons before. Always the consummate professional, George Darby set aside his own beliefs and either built or lent a helping hand in the construction of elaborate machines designed to eliminate specters, something he himself did not believe in. "Work was work," he often said. The timid man with straggly, untamed hair kept his opinions to himself and never accosted anyone.

But for reasons unknown to Edgar, today was different. Edgar remained silent, afraid of incurring George's new-found wrath. Like it or not, he needed information and had to stay on the man's good side.

"Please, my wife is with child. Soon she won't be able to work, and we need—"

"I'm not buying tales of woe, only raw materials. Maybe he can help you." George pointed to Edgar and the couple turned to look upon him.

They gave him a once over and then turned back to George, relaying they did not recognize Edgar's significance.

With low pay and long hours, the miner's life was difficult, often forced to relocate to wherever there was work once a mine ran dry. If his pockets were lined heavier, Edgar certainly would have provided some charity. He'd survived on it so often himself. For now, all he could do was stand back and hope George's heart warmed to them.

George's shoulders twitched. "I've made my offer. As you can see, I have other customers. Make your decision and be off."

The couple looked upon one another and as if the two held a secret language, the husband slid the offered coins upon the counter into his open palm without uttering another word to George.

Edgar stepped to the side and let them pass. Their faces etched with worry and regret. Some of his earnings from the plantation job would ease their misery, but Ellie's mother needed it more.

George fixed his gaze on Edgar. "What do you want?"

His tone struck Edgar as unnecessarily harsh. He could think of no wrong he'd ever done George and always paid him a finder's fee for jobs. "Good to see you, too," Edgar replied sharply as he stepped up to the counter.

"The Wellman's are very angry with you for taking off."

"And they have every right, but that's neither here nor there. What injury have I done you?"

"I'm sorry," George said, shaking his head. "I am very busy."

"Not a problem," Edgar said as George walked out from behind the counter and headed toward his workshop.

Edgar followed and before he could chastise his friend's rudeness, his eye became attracted to a gold-toned metallic hand twice the size of his own sticking out from under a large white cloth.

George, tracing Edgar's gaze, spun around and tossed the fabric over the exposed appendage.

"What do you have under there?"

George's right shoulder convulsed. "Nothing for you."

Again, unnecessarily harsh, and as Edgar recomposed himself, an image flashed in his mind. One of a man broiled alive inside a powered suit of armor.

"You're building—"

George's hand slapped against Edgar's mouth and remained firmly in place, his lips pressed together with a soft whoosh of air escaping, *ssshhhh*.

Edgar grasped George's wrist in his fist to remove his hand by force, but George's eyes darted around the workshop like a mouse on alert for the cat—fear clouding the man's mind. Edgar peered around the open room but found no possible threats.

George leaned in close and whispered, "It isn't safe. Not in front of…." He motioned his head toward the mechanical oddity under the tarp as if it were alive and listening.

Edgar nodded, though he failed to see the immediate danger. George's hand fell away, and he then led Edgar into the other room and closed the door behind them.

"What is the meaning of this?"

"He told me I should expect you." George paced the room. "Should have kept the door locked."

"Is that what I think it is?" Edgar said, motioning toward the other room with his thumb over his shoulder.

He stopped his nervous shuffling and said, "Yes."

"That *thing* is the reason I left West Point." Though Edgar's tone was that of a scolding mother's, he kept the octave at a dull whisper.

Matching Edgar's tone and brashness, George replied, "Had I believed you'd show up here, I would have moved it out of sight all together. You must be desperate to run the risk of the Wellmans's wrath."

"Never mind that…. Do you have any idea the repercussions such a thing presents?"

"I cannot discuss this with you." George turned his back on him. "You're out of your league. These men are not to be trifled with, and he's not the only one you have to worry about."

"I know your motto, but why help them?" Even as he asked, the answer came to him as if heaven's split open and lightning struck him where he stood. "Where's Kimberley?"

A single tear ran down the left side of George's face. The only answer Edgar needed.

"I have resources at my disposal, let me help."

"The only thing that can help her is for me to finish that infernal contraption." George's hand trembled in the air.

"They took your daughter."

"Stay out of it."

"Fine," he said, seeing there was no discussing it with the man. He should have known those bastards would find someone else, someone with less scruples than he and something to lose.

While at The United States Military Academy at West Point, Edgar had been approached to join a team of military engineers. Word had gotten around about his tinkering, and they wanted him to help build something capable of protecting a soldier from harm, granting said soldier inhuman strength, and the capability to take the fight wherever need be. They wanted powered suits of armor.

The idea was visionary; however, after dissecting the blueprints, Edgar documented several design flaws and brought them before the board. Rather than address the risks of severed limbs from gears falling out of alignment; the obvious bull's-eye on the armor's back caused by the mounted steam engine; or the insufferable heat and weight such a device forced upon the pilot, the board dismissed his recommendations entirely. Just as he surmised, the prototypes proved too hot to wear for the duration of a battle and too cumbersome to maneuver if the steam engine failed. Several men died during testing, trapped, and cooked alive in the suits meant to protect them. Prying their bodies out of the thick steel gave Edgar the horrific impression that he was opening a can of preserved humans. Edgar made complaints and insisted the program be halted. When he took his objections up the chain of command and refused to continue his work, he was quickly and quietly dismissed from service.

"What did you come here for?" George asked, breaking the awkward silence that had befallen them.

"Information, and by the look of what's going on around here I suspect you have it."

"You should go. Forget what you saw," he said, his head shaking. George's right hand trembled, and it was a wonder to Edgar how the man could be such a precise machinist.

"After how long we have known each other," Edgar said, "I cannot simply walk away."

"Go. Forget it."

"George, please," he persisted, but George remained silent as a grave. "Fine," Edgar said, not letting the issue go, but changing subjects to give George a break and get him talking again. "I have my own troubles. Ever hear of a ghost hunter named James Laurent?"

Running his shaky hand over his forehead and pulling his hair back, George said, "You know I don't pay too much attention to things like that."

"True," Edgar said, "but—"

With his palm pressed to his forehead, George blurted, "He's after your machine."

"Who?" Edgar was taken aback. "James?"

"He's dangerous." George's body rocked as he spoke and whether Edgar believed him or not, there was no denying George believed the threat real. "Don't let him fool you."

"I don't understand. He had a chance to take it in Georgia."

George grabbed Edgar by the shoulders and gave him a light shake. "I'm positive. He wants it."

Edgar looked deep into the frightened man's wide, brown eyes and asked, "For what purpose?"

George lowered his head as if in shame, and Edgar knew then he was the one who filled James Laurent in on all of his personal details.

"Why does he want my machine, George?"

"I've said too much." George released his hold and took a step away.

"George, if you know, tell me."

"I'm sorry. I can't help you. Now, go. I have work to do."

"Is he the one who took Kimberly?"

George remained silent and with his back to Edgar.

Edgar could try to beat the information out of him. Or tie George to a chair and force him to watch Edgar dismantle the war machine until he broke down, but he was not capable of either approach. Besides, a young girl's life was now held in the balance.

"You might not believe in the metaphysical world of spirits, but something terrible is afoot. I think you can see that much."

George nodded but remained rooted to the spot and did not turn to face Edgar.

"Just so you know, I hold no ill will toward you. You're doing what you have to do." Edgar wrote down Ellie's address on a piece of paper and said, "This is where you'll find me if you change your mind. Write or send a telegram, I'll cover the charges." Edgar placed the address on the workbench next to George. He reached out but didn't take it. Just tapped it in place with his finger.

"Take care of yourself," Edgar said, opening the door. "And I pray this all works out for you as you hope."

"Edgar..." George turned to face him.

"Yes?"

"Be careful out there."

Edgar gave a polite nod, then turned, and left the shop.

As he walked back toward the train station, Edgar was left with more questions than he had answers. If James had wanted his machine, he'd had his chance to take it in Georgia. And why take a young girl from her father? Ghost hunting was a specialty business for sure, but also a small industry. Or was Edgar mistaken? Could there be that much money at stake?

With an image of West Point in his mind's eye, he probed his memory. The black and gray granite buildings were unforgettable in their design—a seamless blend of Gothic architecture with Medieval fortress size. As if he were taking a mental tour of the facilities, he focused on faces he passed by, men he shared classes with, and those he used to gamble with, but still came up with nothing.

At some point in time, our paths must have crossed.

He continued to dig deep into his psyche knowing the two shared so much in common that it only made sense they ran in the same circles, but the deeper he went, the more encompassing the darkness became.

CHAPTER XVI

Ellie opened the door to the third wrap of Edgar's knuckles.

"Mister Poe..." Fresh tears streamed down her reddened cheeks at the sight of him. With a deep, pain-filled sob, she threw her arms around him and cried into his shoulder.

"What's wrong? Is it your mother?" he asked, stroking the backside of her head.

"She passed...in her sleep," she said in between sobs.

"I'm so sorry. I should have come sooner."

She pulled away from him, sniffled, then pinched her nose, and wiped away the running mucous in one fluid motion. "There's nothing you could have done."

"I could have at least wired your money ahead. Maybe—"

Ellie took his hand in hers and shook her head. "It was her time. Money couldn't have changed that."

Edgar took a deep breath, the words doing little to ease his guilt over his selfish decision. At the least, he could have been here for moral support rather than leisurely traveling the countryside in search of information about a man he would rather never see again.

He forced a smile for Ellie's sake.

"Have you eaten?" she asked.

Caught by surprise by the question, Edgar's response was not immediate. "You don't have to do that."

"It's all right," she said, "I could use the distraction."

"Then I would like to offer my assistance," he said, still smiling.

"Why Mister Poe, I didn't know you could cook."

"Well, my dear, it's just another form of chemistry."

Ellie hooked her arm in his and escorted him to the kitchen.

The clockwork raven was perched on the back of a kitchen chair. It seemed to take notice of Edgar, so he tipped it a nod and asked Ellie, "Has it been working properly?"

Ellie was confused for a moment, but noticing Edgar was looking at the raven, she said, "Oh yes. If he didn't wind down so often, I'd think he was a real bird."

Edgar nodded in self-satisfaction and the raven gave a short, sharp caw at him.

While Ellie cracked some eggs, Edgar diced a ham steak. They worked side-by-side fixing their omelets and chopping ingredients. Their hands touched as they both reached for a knife and Edgar was surprised to feel warmth spread on his cheeks. Even at his age, and with all he had accomplished in his life thus far, this beautiful woman made him blush, and with the pinkish hue in her cheeks, the sentiment was reciprocated.

After breakfast, Edgar cleaned up the dishes allowing Ellie to relax for the first time since he had left. She had lost so much in the past week and yet still found the courage to smile. He admired her strength.

As he finished drying the last plate, a knock at the door sounded.

Ellie bounded out from the adjacent hallway and said, "Probably another neighbor passing on their condolences."

Letting her handle the door, Edgar toweled off the plate, and then returned it to the cupboard. By the time he had turned around to see who was at the door, Ellie had closed it and was fiddling with an envelope.

Her brow wrinkled as she read the letter. Once finished, she slapped her hands against her thighs and breathed a heavy sigh.

"What's wrong?" he asked.

Ellie sat down at the table, propped her elbows, and placed her head in her hands.

"Anything I can do?" Edgar pulled a chair out and sat down beside her.

Ellie lifted her head and looked upon him, fresh tears pooled at the base of her eyelids. "You've done enough. I couldn't..."

He placed a comforting hand on her shoulder. "Nonsense."

She sniffled and said, "Are you sure?"

"Of course. Tell me."

"I didn't tell you this before, because...well...it's embarrassing."

Edgar slid his hand down the length of her arm and took her hand in his. "You don't ever have to worry about that with me."

"Like you, my brother used a machine to exile spirits."

"Really?" Edgar withdrew his hand and perked up in his chair. "What kind?"

"If you're interested in seeing it, you can find it in the basement." Ellie's slack posture, pursed lips, and saddened eyes relayed her displeasure with his interruption.

Refocusing his attention on her, he said, "Please, continue."

With a breath, she carried on, "Last year, after countless jobs, we discovered the machine didn't work as well as we had thought. The spirits returned."

"How?"

"I don't know," she said. "I never understood the science. Originally it was my father's idea. John completed it after his death to honor him."

Edgar's gaze drifted down as his head dipped. Shame and regret weighing his thoughts. He had done nothing to honor the only father figure he had known. Though it was not too late to do so, his mind could not come up with a suitable homage, a testament to how little he knew John Allan, and that only compounded the guilt.

"After dozens of letters demanding a refund, we were left in a financial rut. It's one of the reasons we were ill prepared for our mother's sickness. And we just started to regain our reputation when the Portland Head Light job came up." Ellie's head lowered. A single tear splashed upon the oak table.

"Is that what came in the mail today?" he asked. "Another refund request?"

"Yes," she said, looking up at him. "The last job Johnny had used the machine on has finally come calling."

"Where abouts?"

"It's local, though. A short walk down the road and onto Shady Lane."

"That's good. Leave it to me, but first, I'd like to see your brother's machine."

She faked a smile. "Go ahead. But take a candle."

Edgar nodded and pushed his chair away from the table. On his way out of the kitchen, he grabbed a candle from a shelf and lit it. Then ventured down the narrow stairwell into the basement, the soft glow of the tiny flame provided enough light to reveal any immediate obstacles in his path but did little to recede the inky darkness.

"Where should I look?" he called.

"On my father's desk."

He shook his head, not knowing where her father's desk might be and hoped it was the only one down here.

So much clutter, he thought as he weaved between rows of boxes. Edgar walked past a stack of chairs four high, a curio cabinet, and a porcelain tub full of books. If his mind hadn't been preoccupied with fiddling with a new toy, he would have rescued each and every one of them from the cold, dank basement right then and there. Finally, he happened upon a desk and his gaze locked on the wooden box sitting at the center of it.

Taking the device out of the box, Edgar was unable to resist taking it apart in order to see its inner workings. The faulty machine was comprised of a large, metal sphere attached to a glass tube and mounted on a base plate alongside a smaller, silver ball that appeared to operate like a pendulum. A seam ran across the midsection of the larger sphere and Edgar delicately applied pressure upon it. The upper half came away with a *pop* and revealed a comb of metal teeth pressed against a silk belt as it passed over a roller. The silk belt ran around a second, smaller roller, with its own metal comb, at the base of the glass tube.

Edgar rotated the roller and as the belt passed between the combs it transferred a static charge to the large metal sphere. When the spheres collided with one another, the transfer of power ionized the moisture in the air. The cause of its malfunction was either due to the polarity or frequency being reversed.

A solid attempt, he thought as he re-sealed the sphere and returned the device to its box.

With his curiosity sated, Edgar returned upstairs, determined to right the situation.

CHAPTER XVII

Edgar looked down at the envelope and verified the address. The house before him, old and decrepit, and he doubted anyone had lived there in years. The wooden clapboard warped and rotted, the shingles hung lopsided from rusted hinges, the shrubs leafless, and the lawn browned and crisp.

With a shrug, he grabbed the tarnished knocker; it broke off in his hand. He frowned at the chunk of metal, wondering why. Located inland, the house was nowhere near the corrosive, salty sea-air. As he raised his balled fist to knock, the door opened.

"You're not John." A stout woman with a stern expression greeted him, the only color in her face were the dark circles under her eyes.

"No ma'am," Edgar replied, "John Feller has passed away."

"Caw!" the raven interrupted, causing Edgar to flinch away from the thing on his own shoulder.

Edgar looked at the bird, but it was not sounding its alarm, merely being vexatious, so he continued, "I am here to resolve his debt to you. Mrs. Collins, I presume?"

"Yes." The woman's hard gaze softened, and she stepped to the side. "Come in."

Edgar stepped inside, his machine trailing behind him.

"Hopefully, *that* contraption works," she said, eyeing his device.

"I assure you, ma'am," he said, not bothering to mask his disdain with her lack of faith, "it does."

Inside the home, Edgar found a similar level of decay as the outside. Cracked and peeled wallpaper, broken picture-frame glass, and mold.

"CAW!!! CAW!!! CAW!!!" the clockwork raven released its ear-splitting alarm.

Flinching again, his hand bolted up to still the bird before he was conscious of the need for action.

With the alarm silenced, he withdrew his strongest refracting lenses from his breast pocket and slipped them on.

"What in God's name…?"

"What's wrong?" asked Mrs. Collins.

Edgar remained silent, unable to answer her question. All around the living area, phantasmal blotches radiated on the walls. He dipped his chin and peered over the glass's rim, but the blotches could not be seen with the naked eye.

"Is this where Mister Feller operated his machine?" he finally asked.

"Yes," she said, her look of concern morphing back to one of animosity. "I mean no disrespect to the dead, but he was a bloody swindler. Things were good for a while, the banging, sudden drops in temperature, and the moans all stopped. But then, everything seemed to go to pot. Did you see my prize rose bushes?"

"I did," he said, though he would never have guessed the barren shrubs had once been show piece worthy.

Mrs. Collins lowered her head. "It's as if the house itself is dying."

"And Mister Collins…is he—"

"Heavens no," she said as if reading Edgar's mind. "My husband is out of town on business. He asked me to go with him. I should have. Don't know why I stayed. Each passing hour I feel weaker and weaker."

"Let's see what we can do about that," Edgar said as he flipped on his machine.

The engine putted to life as the gears turned and the pistons pumped. A small vapor cloud leeched from the nozzle and hung in the air.

Letting his curiosity get the better of him, Edgar walked up to the nearest blotch and lifted his finger to touch it. The gelatinous fluid pulsated a vibrant blue and caused his fingertip to numb upon contact. A chill raced up the length of his arm and forced his shoulder to roll.

He rubbed his finger against his thumb to warm it, all the while contemplating the nature of the substance.

It's as if…the specter exploded, he thought, peering across the room to the other blotches. *But then, why hasn't it put itself back together?*

A high-pitched whistle interrupted his thoughts and signaled the machine was ready.

With the lance in hand and pointed at the blotch, Edgar shifted the lever. Though the rushing steam caused further damage to the floral wallpaper, it dissolved the mysterious fluid as well, erasing it from sight.

"Interesting," he mumbled, surprised at how simple it seemed.

"What?" Mrs. Collins asked, looking desperate for any tidbit of good news with her hands folded together in front of her bosom, and wide, pleading eyes.

"Now, knowing nothing of John's machine," Edgar said, "there seems to be some sort of ghostly mark adorning the walls of this room. And I'll have to check the rest of the house to be certain, too, but I think I can fix this."

"Oh, bless you," she said, a smile finally softening her soured puss.

One by one, Edgar blasted the phantasmal blotches in the living area and once the room was clear, he moved on to the next. The rest of the house was goo free. And though this did not surprise him, what he did find puzzling was that only the rooms adjacent to the ooze-stained walls showed signs of decay. He felt more like a doctor treating an infection than a ghost hunter.

"Strange," Mrs. Collins said, entering the room Edgar was currently in.

"What's that?" he asked.

"I already feel a difference…as if hope has finally returned."

"I'm glad I could have been of assistance, and the Feller family apologizes for any inconvenience—"

"That's an understatement," she said with the wave of a hand, "but, these things can't be helped. It's God's will."

At this, Edgar bit his lip to stifle his tongue. For him, it was a matter of science, not faith.

He had spent the better part of a decade tweaking his formulas and materials to achieve the proper ratio of bitter salts to tincture, deciphering the balance between positive and negative charges and refraction angles to bridge between the spectrums. God and Heaven were irrelevant. Science dictated that energy could not be created nor destroyed, merely transferred from one form to another. Considering how much energy the human body produced just for basic functions, let alone upon exertion, it was only logical to know death was not the end. And from what Edgar had seen of death, peace, and goodwill—two concepts championed by a supposed god—was contrary to reason.

Though he had yet come to an understanding of why only those met with a violent end remained on this plane, he was certain his machine helped their energy transcend to its rightful place.

"If that will be all," he finally said with a tilt of his head.

"I do believe. Thank you," Mrs. Collins said and then added, "and please tell Ellie I'm sorry for her loss."

"I will."

With his machine packed and ready, Edgar left the house's gloomy atmosphere without looking back.

As he walked through the town of Falmouth, back toward Ellie's home, he passed by a few residents, each one offering a warm smile and gracious nod. The people appeared kind and more than happy, and soon Edgar's thoughts drifted to a subject he had not contemplated in years, that of settling down and building a family. Of course, he might broach the subject with Ellie in good time, and even if she weren't interested, her hometown was a fine, suitable place. One worth considering at the least.

The town bordered Casco Bay and had three shipbuilders, the perfect place to pen a possible sequel to his only novel, not to mention completing his lighthouse story. There were plenty of opportunities for future nuggets of inspiration and part time employment with a sawmill, gristmill, and tannery. He could do hard labor or improve upon the business' machinery.

An image of a beaming, curly-blonde haired boy running toward him, arms wide open, flashed in his mind's eye. The boy shared Edgar's extended brow and Ellie's innocence. Before the fantasy boy jumped into Edgar's arms and hugged him in a way he craved, a young man at the corner of Arborside Drive and Johnson Road caught his attention.

He waved a newspaper overhead, shouting, "Rescuers slain in Utah tunnel. Award offered by Union Pacific Railroad Company."

Edgar recalled hearing about the tragic accident that had claimed the lives of nearly fifty railroad workers. A collapse? Or an explosion? If ever a case were ripe for the creation of vengeful spirits, an incident such as that would be prime. He stepped up his pace, pumping his short legs and extending his stride, dragging the Specter Eliminator behind.

By the time he reached the peddler, his chest was tight, and breath labored. Without a word, he fished in his pants pocket for a nickel and then handed it to the young man who looked no older than fifteen.

The boy smiled, handing him a paper. "Thank you."

With the nod of his head, Edgar continued down the street toward Ellie's home.

As he walked, he opened the paper to the designated page referenced in the brief paragraph on the title page. He continued to read, paper held aloft in front of him, and the words simultaneously filled him with dread and excitement.

The Union Pacific Railroad Company reports that during the construction of a railway tunnel through the Wasatch Mountains in the Utah Territory, a dozen workers were trapped by a cave in. The cave in was most likely caused by the use of a new and dangerous nitroglycerine explosive which expedites tunneling but is very unstable. During the rescue attempt, a second explosion killed another two dozen railway workers laboring to rescue their trapped coworkers. The cause of the explosion has still not been identified but it is believed to have resulted from a buildup of natural gases.

Or did the spirits of the first crew sabotage the second? Edgar wondered. He folded the paper, tucked it under his arm, and quickened his pace.

CHAPTER XVIII

Two weeks later, Edgar looked out the coach window and pondered this particular job. The railroad represented a lifeline for the west, a means of delivering food and medicine to curb any emergency. Disconnected from the civilized cities, the western territories were untamed with harsh climates and barren landscapes. Only a few shrubs littered the Great Plains. What plant life existed, the Joshua trees and the creosote bushes with their waxy leaves and yellow flowers, conserved their energy and grew slowly. The surrounding mountains—so enormous and sheer and unforgiving—offered but a few pine trees. The fact that there were people ready and eager to challenge such an environment was a testament to the human spirit. However, lawlessness was all too common; necessity and desperation forced honorable men to do despicable things in order to eke out an existence for their families.

Out of fear, Ellie had petitioned him to purchase a gun before their departure, but he refused. The only weapon he needed was that of his mind. She sat across from him; his mechanical raven perched on her shoulder. She absentmindedly stroked the tin breast plate. The thing had become her friend rather than his as he intended, and though he wanted to be cross, the childish glee in her eyes as she spoke to it quelled his frustration. With her mother and brother buried, Ellie needed something to care for. And he was grateful for the company.

"I think we're here," Ellie said, leaning out the window opposite him.

"Finally."

The moment the carriage stopped, Edgar stood and stretched. His legs stiff and his buttocks numb from the long, arduous train journey and then the jostling coach ride.

"This is it!" the coachman said.

They stepped off the coach and as Ellie worked out her own kinks, the clockwork raven stretched its wings and took flight.

"Don't go too far," Ellie said, keeping a watchful eye.

"That is one mechanical marvel," said the driver as he passed down their belongings from the rooftop to Edgar.

"Thank you, my good man," Edgar said, then held up a one-dollar coin, which the driver happily snatched out of his hands.

"Will there be anything else?" he asked, pocketing the tip.

"Only if you're willing to wait around," Edgar said. "I could make it worth your while."

"There's an awful lot of competition," Ellie said to his ear.

He followed Ellie's gaze and found a rag-tag group of ghost hunters, prospectors, nuns, and tinkerers gathered at the tunnel's entrance. All looked as though they had shirked their mundane lives to lay claim to the generous bounty offered by the Colorado Central Railroad. In Edgar's eyes, they certainly were not competition. He tried not to take offense, but he found Ellie's lack of faith in him and his Eliminator disheartening.

"I'd be willing to wait if the coin is right," said the driver.

Edgar gave Ellie a sideways glance and said, "It will be."

The clockwork raven landed atop the carriage, flapped its copper and feather wings, and squawked as if in protest.

"Everyone's a critic," he mumbled.

"Well then, I best fetch some water for Baron." The old man climbed down from his perch. Edgar offered him a hand, but it was swatted away in defiance.

With his machine trailing behind and Ellie's lightning-rod blade strapped to her back, they left the crotchety driver and brownish black steed to their refreshment.

"What's wrong?" Ellie asked.

"Nothing."

She stopped and grabbed hold of his arm. "Liar. You have that look of deep thought."

"I was just reminded of something a friend said to me once. How earth-bound spirits had always been rare, and now it seems with each new modern advancement to make our lives simpler, pain and tragedy are birthed."

She looked at him sideways. "What are you saying?"

"I'm saying there is a price for luxury." His friends, Andrew, and William came to mind. "Look at the native people, despite the hardships they've faced, they live full, meaningful lives and die with peace and transcend as we all should."

"I'll admit there's been more than enough work to go around to earn a living, but what you're proposing...."

"I know," Edgar said, "it's damn impossible to change the human condition."

With their moods now solemn, Edgar and Ellie approached the encampment. Edgar's gaze fixated on the odd man off on his own with one leg folded and propped against the mountain rock. The brim of his leather hat was pulled down, in an attempt to either block out the sun's harsh rays or to avoid eye contact with the competition. A ribbon of smoke snaked into the air from the cigarette dangling from his bottom lip. A row of silver bullets was strung across his chest with a Colt .44 strapped at his waist.

"I thought silver bullets were for werewolves?" Ellie said, obviously noticing the man as he had.

"Don't tell me you believe in them?" he said.

"What? Ghosts are where you draw the line? Don't you think—?"

"I try not to, actually."

She nodded in understanding. "He may be out of his league," Ellie said, still eyeing the man. "But the same could be said for them." She flicked a finger over to her right.

Edgar stole a glance over at the handful of miners eager for the chance of a better life. Their sweat-stained shirts and patched dungarees were a testament to the hard life they had endured. However, even if their pickaxes and shovels were made of iron, it would only be a temporary disruption of any specter. Just enough time to run away with their lives if they were lucky. "Good point," he said. "We should be prepared to protect them all."

Ellie nodded. "I don't think we need to worry about them." She tilted her head toward the women of the cloth.

"Agreed," he said. The nuns, huddled together in prayer and armed with white candles and bibles, looked ready to excise any spirits lying in wait. "They're smart working together, but the odds are against them here. I hope they have enough time to work their ceremony."

One strong mind focused on a specter can coax it on to the next realm, as Ellie's brother had done. And a nun's life of prayer and self-discipline would certainly strengthen the mind. But the science behind Edgar's Specter Eliminator was quicker and more certain.

Ellie's head lowered and the clockwork raven tipped its head against her cheek.

Edgar took Ellie's hand but said nothing. He knew the guilt of her brother's death would remain with her until the two were reunited in a better place.

The puff of pistons and whir of gears distracted Edgar from Ellie's grieving. The tinkerers stood proud, showing off their inventions to one another. He was impressed by two of them, one with a metallic glove covering his right hand that pulsated with red energy, another with a large glass orb that seemed to spark with an electric charge, like lightning in a bottle, strapped to his back via a brass exoskeleton that encompassed his legs for support. That could work for the Specter Eliminator, but there would still be the problem of a red-hot boiler upon his back.

They eyed him too and he made a mental note to engage the men in conversation, should they survive.

Another man approached the tinkerers with a wide grin, and Edgar figured the man to be looking for recognition. Held out in front of him, a modified, double-barreled shotgun with a large, brass turret system mounted just before the stock and two pressure gauges beside the sights.

Curious, he thought, wondering what kind of ammunition was spooled inside.

Edgar had a mind to venture over and show off his inventions so they may see his true brilliance, but the mechanical bird might malfunction and embarrass him. He looked upon the insubordinate thing on Ellie's shoulder and the clouded eye vexed him still. An image of the bird flying about, then seizing up and plummeting to the ground replaced the one of the men dazzled by Edgar's brilliance. And should the damned bird fall while flying, it would smash into thousands of pieces.

"What's that smile for?" Ellie asked.

"Oh…nothing," he said, but his attention was stolen as an all-too-familiar sound teased his ear. He turned around to see a man rotating a wire-framed hourglass, three dice danced inside, rattling the metal, and calling out to him like a siren's song. Only a few men were gambling, the others had either already lost everything, or had stronger fortitude than he.

"Where are you going?" Ellie asked.

Edgar was already making his way toward the game. He stopped but dared not take his eye off the rolling dice. "I'm just going in for a closer look."

"What kind of game is that?" she asked, stepping up beside him.

"Chuck-a-luck. A carnival game." He continued to make his way to the game table.

"Are they betting money?"

"Yes, Ellie," he said, trying not to lose his patience, "it's a gambling game."

She stopped and took his hand. "You intend to play, don't you?"

He pulled his hand away like a scolded child. "Just a round or two."

"How does it work?" she asked, her tone softening.

"Most wager on a single number appearing and are paid out accordingly if one or all three land on that number. You can also wager on a combination thereof, a range based on the sums of the dice. But that's a sucker's bet."

"And you like this?"

"Yes. Some have said I have a problem, but I don't put much stock in those people."

Ellie followed him to the table.

Since the betting was already underway, Edgar waited for the next roll before placing his bet. When the dealer stopped, a one, and two fives were displayed in the bottom half. Sighs and boos relayed that no one won.

"Place your bets gentleman," said the dealer as he cranked the hourglass's handle.

Edgar unfolded a dollar bill and placed it upon the table while calling out, "Three!"

Once everyone's bets were placed, the birdcage went around several rotations before the dealer stopped.

"Hot damn!" the man beside Edgar exclaimed.

With the dice landing on two, four, and six, Edgar knew the man had only broken even.

Seeing his dollar scooped up along with the others, he reached into his pocket, but Ellie snatched his hand.

"Why don't we go over there, out of the sun?"

"But..." he tried to protest, but her pouty lips and wide eyes won him over.

"The odds are against you."

"Fine."

She smiled and he allowed her to guide him away. Keeping his gaze locked on the tumbler, he mentally placed his bet. *Two.*

The dice rolled over and atop one another as they bounced around until finally stopping. A two and a pair of ones were revealed. Edgar pinched his lower lip between his teeth and turned away from the action.

Ellie escorted him to a shady spot under a Joshua tree as they waited. Despite being the tail end of summer, the desert heat was insufferable. He pushed a twisted, spiny branch aside for her, careful not to prick either of them with a bayonet-shaped leaf.

"Why are we kept waiting?" Ellie asked.

Before Edgar could answer, a man dressed in a black suit stepped out of the large tent and looked around. Edgar could only assume he was the project's foreman. "Excellent," said the man. "So many of you showed. Thank you all. I'm certain you'll have this whole mess sorted by morrow." He gave a gracious grin, but Edgar felt as though it were forced.

"When will you let us get on with it?" someone asked.

The man searched the crowd, obviously looking for a particular person and Edgar couldn't help but wonder if it were James Laurent. He was sure he would find the man here, unwilling to pass up such an opportunity.

"I'm afraid there is still one missing," the man in charge finally said.

"You have more than enough," came from somewhere in the crowd.

"Yeah!" another chimed.

"Patience please, just a little longer." The man turned around and passed through the tent's flap.

"As if we're not good enough," one of the miners grumbled. "I've got a good mind to go home."

"Off with you then," a man replied.

Another was not so kind. "More money for us."

"Why you—" The belligerent miner grabbed the collar of his instigator and slammed a balled fist square into his jaw.

The man dropped to the ground and was immediately pounced on by his assailant. The two men rolled in the dirt, kicking up dust and contaminating the air.

"Knock it off!" a giant of a man with a jeweled scimitar said as he stepped in, grabbing both combatants by the backs of their necks and hoisting them into the air.

The one who had been sucker-punched thrashed with his legs, trying to score a hit, but it was a feeble attempt. With his arms outstretched, the man held them a good five feet apart.

"Let 'em fight!" someone called out. "Less competition!"

"This deplorable heat is bad enough. We don't need you kickin' up a sandstorm to irritate our insides." The hold on the fighters was released and the men stumbled to keep their balance. "So, walk away…now!"

The two men sized up the larger man, who glared down at them ready to pummel the idiocy from their bones, then looked at one another before turning bout face, and walking away.

"So much for the show," Ellie said, surprising Edgar.

"Didn't take you for the violent type," he said with a half-smile.

"I like a good match." She cracked a smile and Edgar couldn't help but find her beautiful. "How many restless spirits you think?" Her question distracted his mind from the desire to kiss her.

"Well, I think we need to assume all of them," he answered. "The miners and the rescuers."

Ellie's eyes went wide as she appeared to be calculating the math.

"Hopefully it's fewer, but it's best to be prepared for the worst."

"Can your machine eliminate that many on a single tank?"

He hadn't thought of that but was reluctant to share. He needed her mind sharp and free from worry. "I'll manage."

"Good," she said with a sigh of relief. "Because I doubt that I could swing this thing fifty times."

"Not to mention any of these fools getting themselves killed in there and joining their ranks."

CHAPTER XIX

The clockwork raven squawked and flapped its wings as if performing a morbid dance to indicate something upon the road.

"What is it?" Ellie asked as she ran her index finger up and down its neck.

Edgar looked out over the horizon while Ellie continued to stroke and coo at the contraption. Off in the distance, he saw a dust cloud swirling and growing larger.

"Someone's coming," he said, then stepped out from underneath the Joshua tree with his hand perched above his brow.

"Maybe we'll finally get started," Ellie said.

"That would be nice," Edgar replied.

Edgar squinted at the rolling cloud. A horse carriage tearing through the barren terrain. He looked for the shapes of stallions but found none. Instead, as it drew closer at its incredible rate of speed, he saw only a driver. His gaze drifted up in search of the tell-tale steam puff, but that, too, was peculiarly missing.

The other so-called hunters stirred also expecting this new arrival to be the one the company was waiting for.

No doubt in my mind. It has to be James Laurent.

His raven let loose a low-pitched chirp, and if Edgar did not know better, he'd swear there was a tang of fear in it.

Ellie stepped beside him, taking his hand in hers.

"What is it?" he asked with a furrowed brow. Their minds needed to be sharp in order to survive the dangers lurking within that pitch dark tunnel. He stole a glance at his creation, the thing had a mind of its own—as unplanned as it was.

"Just a knot in my stomach," Ellie said.

"Well, speaking as a man of science, I'm inclined to rule out clairvoyance. However, as a writer of the macabre, I cannot deny the power of woman's intuition."

Ellie pulled away from him, her face screwed up in confusion. "That makes no sense. Aren't they one in the same?"

"Precisely."

She half-laughed in response. "Oh, to be inside that wondrous mind."

"Careful what you wish for, my dear. The horrors that lie in wait are unfathomable."

"After reading your work, I believe it."

Edgar smirked, but the pleasure of the moment was ripped from him as the coach pulled alongside where he stood, and James Laurent flashed his disingenuous smile out the open window.

"Mister Poe, what a delightful surprise."

"Likewise," he lied, gripping the handle of his machine tighter. He should interrogate James right now for the whereabouts of George's daughter, but that would only answer one immediate question, and he needed to get to the bottom of the whole mess.

Instead, he focused on the powered carriage rather than James. Made from the combination of wood and iron with decorative glass windows, the carriage was a mobile work of art. Though it housed a gear box, the machine lacked a boiler when compared to the steam powered roadster in which he was fortunate enough to ride in Georgia. He saw nothing that could serve as a source of mechanical power.

I need a look inside that box, he thought, eyeing the compartment at the rear of the carriage.

"I see you are intrigued by my mode of transportation," James said, the arrogance in his voice unmistakable. He exited the coach and adorned his pompous top hat.

"I'm curious to know how it runs," Edgar replied, refusing to show deference to James' gentlemanly airs.

"And who is this vision of loveliness?" James stepped past him.

"The name's Miss Ellie Feller," she said, then extended her hand.

Edgar swallowed back bile as James took her hand in his to kiss the backside. The clockwork raven let loose a mechanical *caw*, and for once, it and Edgar seemed to agree.

"What a peculiar bird." James turned toward Edgar. "Yours I presume?"

"Yes," he said, not the least bit ashamed by the smile of pride that stretched across his own face.

James leaned in for a closer look. The raven extended its wings, making itself look larger, and then cawed directly at James.

"You're conscious…" James said as he stepped back, then directly addressed Edgar, "You devil." His perpetual smile now a snarl.

"Come again?" Edgar asked, not quite sure of James's meaning.

"Seems I underestimated you," James said, nostrils flaring. "It won't happen again, I assure you."

Edgar reached out and grabbed hold of James's hand as the man tried to walk away. "Explain to me your disdain for my invention."

James eyed Edgar's hand upon his person. Out of shock of the cold, calculating gaze, Edgar released his hold.

"I just didn't realize how far along you were, that's all."

"Edgar," Ellie said, stretching the word. "Don't be so sensitive."

Edgar smiled and apologized, doing his best to feign flattery. James's eyes relayed malicious intent, and Edgar knew full well his comment was not a compliment. For whatever reason, he intended to find out.

With the cacophony of questions filling the air from the crowd, the man in the black suit stepped out from the tent once more. A wide smile graced his face upon the sight of James, and he walked toward them. "Ah, Mister Laurent, thank you so much for coming."

"I thank you for waiting for me."

"But of course," said the man in charge. "Your reputation is highly regarded." He extended his hand, which James graciously accepted.

Edgar remained silent and still, watching the exchange between the men.

James took a quick glance at the mob circling them and said, "My, they look eager."

"Yes," said the foreman before leaning in closer and whispering, "but I doubt they'll be effective."

At this, Edgar squeezed his balled fist so tightly he drew blood as his fingernails pinched deeply into his soft palm.

James placed his arm around the man's shoulder. "Why don't you let them go on ahead while we discuss the particulars in private?"

"Very well."

"You can't be serious," Edgar interjected. "It's not safe for them."

"Beg your pardon, Mister Poe," the foreman said, "but no one is forcing their hand here."

James glared smugly at Edgar as the foreman addressed the crowd of eager ghost hunters, giving them permission to enter the tunnel and wishing them luck.

"What are we going to do?" Ellie asked.

Torn between following James to the foreman's tent and discovering just exactly what he was up to, and protecting the lives of those entering the tunnel, Edgar took a deep breath in contemplation.

"This is a time for action, not thinking," Ellie reminded him as the last of the crowd vanished into the tunnel's open maw.

"You're right," he said and primed the Specter Eliminator. "Let's go."

CHAPTER XX

Ellie followed him closely, and on their way in, she grabbed a lantern from a cluster of supplies put out by the foreman. They stood at the entrance, both of them trying to peer through the inky darkness. Edgar slipped on his refracting lenses and found no specters lingering at the entrance.

"It's safe," he said, stepping beyond the boundary of sunlight, "for now."

"I imagine not for long, either." She squinted into the darkness, not trying to see her way, but looking for spirits.

"Here," he said, handing her a pair of refracting lenses. "No, wait." He took back the pair he'd offered her and gave her the pair he was wearing.

She slid them on and looked around the entrance, blinking.

"They'll help in there."

As Edgar and Ellie were swallowed by the darkness, Edgar's unease grew. He knew they were a tremor away from death's door. Strategically placed shaft timbers braced against the mountain's weight seemed to be the only protection from a cruel fate. Ellie's lantern provided enough light to illuminate their immediate path.

"Careful!" Edgar grabbed hold of Ellie's arm and stopped her from stepping upon a boarded over passage.

"What's wrong?" she asked, turning to him. "It looks safe."

"Looks can be deceiving. If you're lucky, it's filled with water. Otherwise.... You have no idea how deep that hole goes."

She pulled her arm free, looking as though he had just insulted her. "Those boards are perfectly capable of holding my weight."

"I meant no offense. Just not willing to gamble with your life. Even good timbers can fall at the slightest touch."

A smile flashed on her face, then vanished. Edgar assumed she did not want him to have the satisfaction of knowing the sweetness of his gesture.

From up ahead, a sudden scream broke the awkward silence between them.

"Bloody fools!" Edgar charged forward, his lance leveled and at the ready.

"Wait for me," Ellie said.

Another scream echoed in the dark followed by a wet *thwack*, and then the sound of breaking glass.

They're being killed systematically, he thought, then halted his charge.

"Blazes," Ellie said, bumping into him.

He stumbled forward but caught his balance. The light from her lantern revealed a man face down on the ground just three feet away from him. Blood bubbled up from a hole almost two inches in diameter at the back of his skull.

Up ahead, a bright light flashed, immediately followed by thunder. Two more gun blasts lit up the shadows. Edgar doubted their effectiveness.

"We have to hurry."

"Edgar, no," Ellie protested as he darted forward, but he paid her no mind.

His machine rattled and bounced around behind him. He could picture the uneven terrain wrecking its wheels, but those could be replaced unlike the lives Edgar now found himself responsible for.

With a low, ethereal moan, a translucent man appeared before Edgar, his face twisted into a snarl and a pickaxe perched over his shoulder.

With little time to react, Edgar thumbed the lance's trigger. His raven screeched and flew by him, the breeze from its flapping wings sent ripples of gooseflesh down his spine. Afraid of rusting it, Edgar released the trigger, and the bird passed through the specter as the pickaxe came down. Thousands of bluish-white sparkles burst into the air, then faded to nothing as the ghost was disrupted. A lingering moan all that remained.

His invention flew awkwardly, butterfly-like, after making contact with the spirit. Though it wobbled in the air, it refused to give up, and righted itself before crashing into the rock wall.

"That was close," said Ellie.

"We're not out of the woods yet," said Edgar as he searched for his would-be assailant.

The mechanical bird circled back and landed on Ellie's shoulder.

"And you didn't think he liked you." Ellie smiled.

"I'm not convinced." Edgar stepped deeper into the unfinished tunnel, searching back and forth for threats.

"How do you suppose he did it?" Ellie asked, keeping close to his backside.

"Who?" Edgar asked in return, not bothering to glance in her direction.

"Little Johnny. How do you think he vanquished that ghost?"

"Since when does he have a name?" Hardly the time for such a conversation, but his curiosity was piqued.

"He reminds me of my brother."

Edgar stopped and turned to face her. "How so?"

"I don't know," she said, looking down at the tunnel floor. "His mannerisms, I guess. The way he cocks his head when you say something to him that he's not quite sure he believes." She looked up at Edgar as if the embarrassment of the notion had faded. "And his over-protecting nature."

Edgar studied the collection of springs, sprockets, gears, cogs, metal, and feathers, not ready to buy it.

"Look out!"

Edgar turned around in time to see another spectral miner poised with a pickaxe overhead. Seeing his surprise attack ruined, the ghost wasted no time and swung with his unearthly weapon.

Edgar threw himself to the left in order to avoid the descending blow. The pickaxe whooshed by him and struck his machine. He hit the ground hard, the lance falling out of his hand as a hiss filled the air. A thin stream of hot vapor spurted from the device and Edgar knew at least one of the cylinders had been punctured.

Before he could stand, another specter materialized before him with its pickaxe drawn overhead.

"Edgar!" Ellie warned.

He rolled out of the way and back onto his feet in one fluid motion. A loud *ding* echoed as iron struck rock. Edgar lunged for his machine's firing nozzle, hoping he could eliminate the immediate threats before his machine lost all pressure. He ducked under another wild swing and scooped up the lance, then leveled it on both of his attackers.

"Please," he said as he pulled the trigger.

The nozzle gave a weak spurt of vapor, then nothing. Edgar whacked the lance against the rock wall and a rush of iodized bitter salts blew out the nozzle. He fired it through the malevolent spirits. Their facial features twisted into swirling vortexes as they were forced onto the next realm.

Edgar turned to face Ellie in time to see a ghostly man sneak up on her. "Behind you!"

With absolute trust in him, Ellie whirled her lightning-rod sword around and sliced through the ghost's midsection. As if made of flesh, the spirit's legs toppled over as its torso plummeted, but before the ethereal body contacted the ground, the severed halves burst into a multitude of brilliant specks before fading away.

"We have to go," Edgar said, grabbing her by the hand and pulling her along with his machine.

"What about the others?" she asked.

"We have to assume they're dead, just like we will be if we don't—"

Another scream traveled through the claustrophobic tunnel, then two gunshots. To Edgar's ear, the sound was amplified with a slight ringing. Whether it was due to the tunnel's acoustics or not, he didn't know. Perhaps that was the shotgun he had seen earlier.

Ellie pulled her hand back. "You've assumed wrong," she said, placing her hands on her hips.

He pursed his lips and searched the darkness, wondering just how far it stretched. "Fine. But if I get killed, I'm haunting you."

"Understandable," she said, and though he couldn't see the smile, he could hear it in her voice.

They ventured deeper into the darkness, Edgar doing his best to keep the machine cocked on two wheels in hopes of retaining as much of the fluid as he could. Ellie walked closely behind and slightly off to the side so that the light from her lantern illuminated their path.

A shimmer off the tunnel wall caught Edgar's eye.

"What is it?" Ellie asked as he stepped to the right for a closer look.

"Not sure," he replied. "Shine that light over here."

Ellie stepped beside him and held the lantern up. "Looks like a rail spike."

"Well, I'll be," he said, staring at the cast iron, mushroomed-head nail half embedded in the rock.

"I thought they were supposed to drive these things into the ground," Ellie said, a poor attempt at some kind of joke.

Edgar was too preoccupied to be amused. His mind constructed an image of the large, chisel shaped nail and its flat-edged point. Given its size, he was certain the rail spike was the perfect match for the turret system mounted on that strange shotgun. Though he couldn't be certain without dissecting the device, the idea fascinated him.

As if completely forgetting the danger, he walked away from Ellie in search of the man and his weapon. He fumbled in the darkness, his foot catching on something.

"Are you all right?" Ellie asked as he steadied himself.

"Yeah," he said as the shadows retreated under Ellie's lantern and revealed the man he had seen earlier. The terror of his final moments still etched in his furrowed brow and slack jaw. Edgar's gaze traveled down the length of the man. Blood bubbled forth from a hole in his chest, just above his heart and the shotgun gripped tightly in his death throes.

"Just like the other one," Ellie said, staring at the wound.

"Yeah," he said. "Even in death, they're still putting those damn pickaxes to work."

The pale image of a man stepped out from the rock wall, head lowered but eyes locked on Edgar. He held a pickaxe with both hands in front of his chest.

Edgar's reflexes depressed the lance's trigger, but his machine had run out of pressure. Instead, he dropped the lance and wrenched the shotgun from the corpse's grasp and leveled it on the spirit.

"Two more behind us," Ellie said. "Make it five!"

An additional four spirits appeared in front of Edgar, surrounding them. In his mind, it was proof enough that all of the other hunters were dead, and they were the last two remaining.

"I'm sorry I dragged you into this," he said.

Ellie pressed her back against his. "I don't recall putting up much of a fight."

Edgar fired two shots, one into each approaching apparition. Their ghostly images faded from sight. "Rotate clockwise," he ordered.

In one fluid motion, Edgar and Ellie traded places and he slung the gun over his shoulder by its leather strap. He knelt and wrenched off his machine's housing. Air whooshed behind him as Ellie swung her blade. He hoped she could disrupt the remaining specters long enough.

Edgar uncoupled the pipe and screamed as he gripped the scalding fuel tank. He spun around with the open fuel tank in his hand and splashed iodized bitter salts across the five ghosts Ellie was holding off.

As the malevolent spirits dissipated, a light appeared from up ahead and grew larger. Little Johnny squawked; the mechanical chirp was followed by a high-pitched *ding* Edgar recognized as the tuning forks of James's ghost detecting device.

"It would appear as though you require my help," said James as the warm glow of his lantern kissed Edgar's cheeks.

"If you had come sooner, perhaps we could have saved these poor fools," Edgar replied, not bothering to mask his disdain.

James's machine finished and the forks returned to their resting places. "A simple thank you would suffice." He popped off the fogged crystal and pocketed it, then replaced it with a new, clear crystal.

If Edgar were anything less than a gentleman, he would have grabbed the arrogant man by the lapels and given him a thrashing he would never forget. Instead, he turned his back on James and waited for the re-emergence of the displaced spirits.

"What's wrong with your machine?" James asked.

Edgar took notice of the slight tremble in his voice, but simply answered, "It has a pickaxe hole in it."

"What?" James asked. "Does it still function?"

"Not any longer."

"It's all right," Ellie said. "We're managing without you."

"We have to go," James said, turning to retreat back out the tunnel. "Now."

"I didn't peg you for a coward, James," Edgar said unable to resist a smile.

"Don't mistake intellect for cowardice," he said.

"Pardon me gentlemen," Ellie interrupted them.

All around them, specters appeared, armed with pickaxes and mal intent. Thirty or more.

With a squawk, Little Johnny jumped from Ellie's shoulders and flew away, back to the tunnel's entrance.

"Fine contraption you've got there," James said as the clockwork raven disappeared into the darkness. "That's what you get for not degrading the soul."

"I think I was a fool to argue with your instincts earlier," Ellie said, before Edgar could ask James for clarity.

Edgar peered over his shoulder to see seven specters closing in on them. He whirled around to face them, dropping his machine and retrieving the rail-spike shotgun.

James, Edgar, and Ellie backed up toward each other, forming a defensive triangle.

"Since we're about to die," Edgar said, finger applying slight pressure to the trigger, "I suppose I should tell you that I know what you're up too."

"Come again?" said James.

"I just hope your benefactors return Kimmie safely to her father after you've passed."

"I assure you, Mister Poe, the young lady is alive and well," James said. "No harm will befall her. Kimmie's abduction was simply to persuade her father away from his sanctimonious morality. George Darby failed to see the greater good. He went so far as to accuse me of having a god complex."

Edgar gave James a sideways glance and said, "I wonder what gave him that idea."

"Gentlemen," Ellie cut in. "I don't think this is the time."

A cacophony of grumbles and grunts bombarded Edgar's ears as the encroaching spirits' faces rippled with unbridled rage. Each translucent face in the crowd had dark recesses under their eyes, deep wrinkles in their brows, and trails of blood down the sides of their faces and cheeks. As if of one mind, the mob raised their pickaxes to strike.

"No choice," James uttered to himself.

"What's that?" Edgar said, looking at him.

James turned the dial on his detecting machine and as the gears whirred to life, he placed it down on the ground with outstretched arms and an odd kink in his neck as if he were afraid of the device exploding in his face.

The spirits continued to close in on them, and Ellie buried her head in Edgar's neck, obviously not wanting to see their untimely demise. The tuning forks struck one another, and the spirits flinched as the sound reverberated off the stone walls. Pickaxes fell to the ground as the spirits contorted—flickering in and out of sight.

The closest spirits streamed into the crystal-like metal filings toward a magnet.

The air cackled with energy as James's device sparked. "There's too many," James said. With a resounding *pop*, the crystal cracked and with it, nearly half of the spirits had disappeared.

"You lied," Edgar exclaimed.

James simply smirked at Edgar's revelation.

"What exactly are you up to?"

"You of all people should know," he said, picking up his device.

The remaining spirits recovered and continued toward them with their pickaxes back in hand.

"Well, whatever it is you did, do it again."

James dumped the black fragments of broken crystal onto the ground and loaded a new crystal into the chamber. However, the dial wouldn't turn. He shook the device and smacked it with his palm, but the dial wouldn't budge.

Edgar cradled Ellie close. "Then this is it."

The darkness receded as a beam of sunlight cut through the middle of the tunnel. The spirits did not retreat upon the sight of it, but their ethereal joints stiffened, and their forms faded, slowing their assault. A few more dropped their weapons.

"What is this?" James asked, his hand held into the beam as if it were some miracle from the heavens.

Edgar followed the trail of light, but no matter how hard he strained, he could not see the point of origin.

Ellie lifted her head from Edgar's chest and said, "Little Johnny."

Her words painted a picture for him. An image of his creation standing with its wings outstretched, catching the high noon sun off its polished breast plate, and refracting it through the tunnel flashed in Edgar's mind. "Brilliant."

"Move!" James said. He wasted no more time and weaved in between the spirits, who could do no more than watch with their hate-filled eyes as they passed.

With his machine in one hand, and Ellie's hand in the other, Edgar pulled both of them forward after James. Since the machine was already damaged, he was no longer concerned about it bouncing around on the uneven earth beneath their feet.

He must survive, not just for his and Ellie's sake, but also for the George Darby family. He knew the pain of losing a parent, but he could not fathom the loss of a child. He assumed it was ten-fold. A hundred.

Ellie shrieked.

He turned to see her sea-foam dress caught on the point of a slow-moving pickaxe. Edgar jerked her forward and asked, "Are you cut?"

"I don't think so," she answered.

Though the spirits' movements were slowed by the sunlight, their determination remained unaltered and some of them had plotted a trajectory in anticipation of his and Ellie's approach.

Releasing her hand, he grabbed hold of the shotgun and fired a railroad spike into the ghost's chest. The man's pale image faded from sight and the pickaxe clanked to the floor.

"Let's go!" Edgar said, then fired two more shots off to his left to clear a new path before letting the shotgun fall to his side, the turret system catching him in the rib.

His gaze darting back and forth between spirits, Edgar walked right into the barrel of James's pistol. The metal tip poked him in his already bruised ribs and before he could ask the man what his plan was, an explosion of sound robbed him of his hearing and a red-hot surge of pain filled his abdomen. Edgar's hand instinctively went to the wound as he dropped forward to his knees.

"What have you done?" asked Ellie.

"You know too much, Mister Poe," James said, the gun aimed at his forehead. He reached down and yanked the nozzle out of his hand. "And I can put this to far better use."

"You have your own machine," Edgar said, the coppery tang of blood filling his mouth.

"But it's worthless without yours. I need your machine to degrade the spirits. It's a shame really. We could have made a lot of money working together."

"I don't—" Edgar toppled forward, his face slamming into the ground. James's image blurred at the edges. Edgar's mouth suddenly went dry, and the pain spiked.

"Take it. Just leave us alone!" Ellie dropped beside him and cradled his head in her lap.

"It's not that simple my dear." James leveled the gun at her. "If only you weren't so pig-headed, Mister Poe."

He should push Ellie away, out of the line of fire. Or hoist the shotgun up and blow out James's knee, but he hadn't the strength to do either. He could only lay there in agony and watch as the spirits re-emerged from limbo.

"Run," he said to Ellie's ear.

"I'm not leaving you," she said.

"Touching," James said.

As darkness filled Edgar's vision, the faint smell of burning rosemary and sage wafted across his nose. Upon the ground a thin layer of smoke roiled and the last thing he heard before slipping out of consciousness was a hoarse war cry.

CHAPTER XXI

Edgar awoke from a nightmare. An image of a battalion of men in powered armor marching down the bow of a massive war boat burned in his retinas. The images so vivid, the sounds so close they were still clear in his mind—the metallic army storming a foreign beach; gears, pistons, and cogs moving in tandem with their human pilots, amplifying their strength; bullets ricocheting off their metallic plating; blood staining the land; the American flag waving proudly atop a mountain of corpses and overseeing it all from the ship's bridge, James Laurent, dressed in full captain's regalia.

A gentle hand on his shoulder guided him back to a laying position. "Easy," Ellie cooed.

"Where...?" he asked, staring into her reassuring eyes.

"Safe," she said as she wiped his brow with a dampened cloth. She touched his brow with the back of her hand. "Your fever's broke."

He looked around the unfamiliar room. Short walls made of wooden planks and the ceiling arched canvas. He was laid out on a bench padded with straw, inside an Army wagon. If Ellie had not been with him, surely, he would have panicked. The suitcase he and Ellie shared sat off at one end, his machine nowhere to be found.

"Little Johnny?" he asked.

With the nod of her head, she signaled his location. Edgar turned to see his clockwork raven staring down at him from a perch suspended from one of the wooden bows.

"He's been watching over you since we arrived," she said, then placed the cloth into a ceramic bowl at his bedside. "How are you feeling?"

Though he was pleased to see progress being made in his relationship with his creation, his mind would not release him from the imagery presented to him during his lapse of consciousness. "I had the most vivid dream," he said, ignoring the question. "Armored men with those blasphemous crystals in their backs. I know what James is up to. I've been wrong…so wrong."

Ellie's brow wrinkled as if in doubt. "From a dream?"

"Yes."

"That is amazing."

"Simple ratiocination. Even unconscious, my mind continued to function, aligning the facts in logical order."

He tried to sit up, but Ellie braced her hands against him and locked her elbows. "Don't rush it. You've been out for three days."

"What? Where are we?"

"With friends," she said, her tone dismissive as if his urgency was unwarranted. "Relax."

He grabbed hold of her wrist with a firm hand. A sharp pain flared at his side from the sudden movement.

"See," she said, obviously catching his flinch. "You're not strong enough yet."

"There's no time." He tried to sit up again and this time, Ellie permitted. "James is collecting souls."

"Whatever for?"

"I'm not entirely sure, but I'm ashamed of my part in this."

Ellie crossed her arms. "You've had no part in—"

"But I have." He tried to stand, but the pain would not allow him. With a hand pressed to the wound, he tried again.

"Where are you going?"

"I have to stop him. Don't you see? He's been following me all along, capturing the souls I thought I eliminated."

"I don't follow," she said, head shaking.

"My machine doesn't remove spirits from this plane, it breaks them apart, makes them vulnerable. And James has been collecting the pieces. Imagine the amount of energy the soul must produce to reconstitute itself, but inside the confines of those crystals, it is an unobtainable goal. An infinite struggle. An infinite power source."

"I'm sorry," Ellie said, the science clearly lost on her.

Edgar moved toward the tent flap and as his hand reached outward to push it open, it swung away, and a large man filled the opening. With his long black hair tied back and high cheekbones, the Indian looked formidable. Edgar hoped the man was not here to put him back into bed.

"Chief John Ross wishes to speak with you," he said.

Chief John Ross.

The warriors William and Andrew.

Of the Cherokee.

Who saved Edgar and for whom he had retrieved the type engine for their printing press. Edgar looked over his shoulder at Ellie, who gave him a reassuring nod. *How much did I miss?* he wondered, then said, "I'd be happy to."

"Come."

Edgar followed behind the man, taking in the small Cherokee camp. Pitched tents and old covered Army wagons lined the open field. A few women wove fabric and prepared meals while children played. Chickens roamed freely while pigs bathed in fresh mud inside their small pen. A stark contrast from New Echota in Georgia and a truly pathetic New Home for the Cherokee if this is all the US Government had provided.

"Is this… Indian Territory?" Edgar asked.

"Oh no." The big Cherokee laughed. "This is our camp. Tahlequah is two weeks east of here."

"They happened to be close by when they heard of the collapse," Ellie said.

Edgar looked to the Cherokee warrior and asked, "What were you doing out here?"

"Many of our people have gone west in the prospect of gold, but there is one in particular our Chief wishes to find James Vann, son of old Chief Joseph Vann."

"Does he intend to kill the offspring of a rival chief?" Edgar asked.

The large man laughed heartily, then said, "Nothing of the sort. James Vann was the previous editor of our paper. John Ross hopes to entice him home with a different prospect."

"And why pause the search to help at the railroad?"

"Edgar," Ellie said as a scolding mother would.

"It's quite all right. Honestly, we expected to find some of our people working the track. Though we were here for them, John Ross was more than happy to repay the favor to you."

"I see," said Edgar.

"You had gotten yourself in a lot of trouble," said the large man. "It was fortunate John Ross sought you out."

"I'll be sure to thank him," Edgar said, nodding. "Do you know what happened to the man who shot me?"

"He slipped out amid the commotion. There were a lot of angry spirits to soothe."

Feeling as though he had failed, Edgar looked down at the ground. "I know."

"But I managed to catch you a prize," Ellie said with a self-satisfied smirk.

"Oh?" Edgar asked, not quite ready for games.

From inside her redingote, Ellie pulled out a pair of chemist's goggles with a set of four jeweler's loupes mounted off each side.

Edgar smiled, glad for the game now. "His refracting lenses."

Ellie nodded. "He was in such a fright. I believe he would have left his pantaloons!"

He blew a bit of dirt from the glass and aligned the loops, then tucked James's refracting glasses into his jacket.

"Here we are," the man said, stepping to the side.

One look at the simple tent and Edgar wondered if this was a joke. It was no different or grander than the others. He shifted his gaze to the large man, who nodded as if reading his mind. He shrugged and entered the humble dwelling and found a stout man dressed in a black suit with a bowtie, his starched collar riding halfway up his cheek. A snappy dresser, much like Edgar, however, he sat on the floor behind a fire pit as though he were an unsophisticated brute. The man seemed out of place. With those blue eyes, he must be of white heritage and not Cherokee. How could this Caucasian man be chief of the Cherokee nation?

He glanced around the tent, his shame for thinking such a thing preventing him from looking directly at his host.

"I am grateful for your assistance in retrieving a very important piece of our printing press," John Ross's voice along with his appearance commanded respect.

"Pardon my impertinence, but you seem to be well spoken and educated and you can clearly present yourself as a respectable businessman so how is it you have come to be chief of these—"

"Savages?" John Ross interjected.

"I would not have put it so curtly," Edgar replied. "But yes."

The man leaned his chin against his steepled hands and said, "Perhaps you wouldn't have." He leaned back and smiled. "I am in fact of Cherokee heritage, and it is because of those exact traits you mention that I have become Chief. I assure you, Mr. Poe, there is no higher calling, but that is not what we're here to discuss," John Ross said, his tone serious and scolding. "Sit."

Edgar gave an insincere smile; he could not help but take offense at the tone. He was not some stranger barging in, but an invited guest. With no furniture, he inspected the floor, looking for a sanitary place to sit.

"You look as though you are above sitting at this level."

"I don't think I'm better than you, if that's what you're implying."

John Ross held out his hand, palm up. "Then sit!"

"Fine." Edgar folded one leg over the other, and then lowered himself down to sit cross-legged. His side flared in pain, but he could manage if he sat straight upright.

"Please don't misunderstand me. I am thankful to you and your people for saving—"

"The night Andrew told me of your encounter, I had a vision. One of a family lost to us, and of you assaulting them."

"Assaulting them?"

"With your machine."

With John Ross's stern expression and harsh tone, Edgar could not help but feel cornered. "Where is your gratitude? It seems to me we are even, and with that...." He went to stand.

The man leaned back, nostrils flared, and his bushy brows wrinkled. "Remain seated!"

Lips pursed and eyes narrow, Edgar obeyed.

"My people," he said as he pounded his chest with a balled fist, "the *Ani'-Yun-wiya,* were forced into your wars, to shun our culture, and adopt your ways. And even then, after building farmsteads and developing a written language, we still were not protected by your laws and driven from our homes. We are one with the land that gave birth to us, and she's angered by the white man's greed."

Edgar knew the truth within the words spoken and could not argue against them. All he could do was listen and show respect toward the man who had lost so much.

"Though you helped Andrew and William in their errand, you are no better than those who persecuted my people. You are ignorant of our ways. You continue the white man's desecration of my people beyond the limits of this world."

"I mean no disrespect, and I didn't go to the Trail for trouble," Edgar said. "I only aim to help those who have lingered here on to the next realm."

The man folded his arms across his chest. "You most certainly cannot do it with an infernal machine. Consider the Trail of Tears off limits."

"Give me one good reason," Edgar demanded, irritated by the man's assumption of his incompetence.

"My wife, Quatie, lost her life on that march. She sacrificed herself for a little girl with pneumonia, giving her clothing to the poor child in the sleet. I am telling you my people will handle it in our own way. In due time."

Edgar could relate to the loss, but despite their common pain, his frustration lingered. "Fine, you have my word. But tell me... what is incorrect about my method?"

"You are forcing a natural process," John Ross said. "Your science and your machine are destroying the spirits, not soothing them."

"Though there is not enough evidence to convince me of that fact," Edgar said. "You should be happy to know my machine was stolen from me."

"It does not quench my rage." John Ross released a heavy sigh. "Though misguided, your intentions were true. The enslaver of spirits, however…."

"His name is James Laurent," Edgar said. "I know his intentions and I *have* seen the error in my ways."

"Yes. The spirits are trying to communicate with you. You've already had one vision."

Edgar tensed. He found the idea of another person spying on him unsettling. "How do you know that?"

"My people speak with the spirit world, aid them in their sorrow, and in turn, they enlighten us."

"Did they enlighten you as to how I can get my property back?"

John Ross folded his arms across his chest and said, "Your machine is irrelevant."

"I beg to differ!" With pain and effort, Edgar stood, afraid of saying anything else to incur the wrath of the Cherokee nation.

"Sit down."

Edgar narrowed his eyes upon the man. John Ross's stone gaze and hard features made reading him near impossible. He exhaled softly through his nose and without argument, sat back down.

"If you are to truly help the spirits find peace and pass on, you must learn our ways and stop the enslaver of spirits from capturing more souls. Perhaps you could even use your writings to shed light on the darkness, rather than exploit it."

Edgar leaned in. "You've read my work?"

John Ross nodded. "It seems to me as though you understand people want to believe in the afterlife but are prevented by fear. And you feed that fear to turn a dollar."

"I assure you that is not the case," Edgar said, straightening his back. "I write to understand that fear. To face it."

John Ross unfolded his arms. "People fear death as the worst part of life. Deep down they know the anger, petty jealousy, and resentment they carry will remain with them in the hereafter and bind them to this plane. And that knowledge terrifies them. But rather than change themselves, they rationalize, make excuses for what they see, and turn the other cheek to ignore the truth instead of putting themselves at peace."

Though Edgar held a level of skepticism, he could not rationally comprehend how this man, far from the civilized world could know all of this. He had always thought 'vision quests' were nothing more than starvation induced hallucinations, but the dream he'd had was still vivid in his mind and he could recall the tiniest of details from it.

"We can help you defeat the enslaver of spirits if you are willing learn how to soothe the spirits so they may find peace and pass on. If you do this, you will defeat the enslaver by releasing those he has captured."

Edgar was not completely convinced, but nodded and asked, "Where do we start?"

John Ross's stone face cracked as a smile formed. "First, we must call upon *Yowa,* the great spirit, and request permission. John Ross held out his hand. "Enter the circle."

Edgar looked down and found he was half in the etched pattern. Looking over his shoulder, he scooted inside the circumference and checked to make sure he hadn't broken the boundary.

"This circle of power has been blessed with cedar and sage."

"Why does that matter?" Edgar asked. The information seemed irrelevant.

"In order for us to connect with the spirit world, you must believe."

"Oh, I believe," Edgar said.

"Indeed," John Ross said, "in the science."

At this, Edgar held his tongue and said nothing.

"We do not always know why. We just know what is." John Ross said as he tossed a handful of what looked like sweet grass onto the fire. A light smoke snaked into the air, its aroma soothing.

"Quiet your mind and be open to the spirit's influence. It will come like a whisper. Breathe in deep, hold it, then exhale. Again."

Edgar followed John Ross's lead though he felt rather ridiculous.

Seconds turned to minutes with not a word uttered between the two. Edgar found the task of silencing his thoughts daunting with the gaunt man's short, labored breaths. He opened his eyes and followed John Ross's Adam's apple as it pushed against the constraints of the bowtie with each raspy breath.

"Eyes closed until your mind is empty of all thoughts, Mister Poe," John Ross said without opening his own.

Edgar refrained from arguing and closed his eyes once more. He sat and waited for a vision to strike or for the other man to finally grow bored, but as the minutes turned to hours, his legs trembled with fatigue and his belly roared with hunger.

This is ludicrous, he thought.

As he opened his eyes again, an image of a bear flashed within the fire's flame. He barely had a moment to comprehend whether his mind was deceiving him or if he had truly seen it. John Ross smiled, confirming the vision to be no trick of the eye. The gesture looked unnatural on the man's hardened face.

"Seeing as you cannot seem to help yourself, my spirit guide is here to bridge the gap."

Edgar held his tongue, afraid of saying something unintelligent and insulting. He had basic knowledge of animal totems and their meanings. The bear seemed fitting for the man before him, a symbol of strength, knowledge, and balance amid change.

The small fire burst with life. The flames spiraled up from the pit and licked the roof. As if it were a living, breathing thing, the fire settled down so as not to consume the raw materials of the tent.

"Do you see?" asked John Ross.

Edgar peered deep into the dancing embers. He caught a brief glimpse of a semi-circle with ruffled edges, at its center a red dot, surrounded by alternating blue and white bands.

"What does it mean?" he asked as the image vanished into the flame.

"Your mind is not focused," John Ross berated.

Though he felt he had done no wrong, Edgar apologized.

With a gruff, John Ross's brow relaxed. "We can try again tomorrow. Perhaps then you will take this seriously."

"Again," Edgar said as he uncrossed his legs, "my apologies." He tried to stand, despite the pain and cramping, and stumbled forward, almost planting his hand in the fire for stability before recovering.

"I'm sure you'll find some meat on the spit. However, if you feel uncomfortable dining with us, you may use my horse to travel to town where the company may be more to your liking."

"Thank you, but that won't be necessary." Edgar gave the man a curt nod, then stepped out of the tent.

Outside, Ellie was sitting by her own fire, watching the men and women dance around a roasting pig as two elders played a meandering melody on their flutes and three others pounded their drums. The colors of their attire were as vibrant as the notes emanating from the wood-carved instruments. Though he wanted to sit beside her and watch the festivity, his legs ached at the thought.

Through the dancers, she caught sight of him and gave a warm smile. She patted the earth to her left with one hand and beckoned him with the other. Unable to say no, he breathed heavily through his nose and weaved through the dancers to join her.

"Well?" she asked as he stretched out on the wool blanket.

"Everything's fine," he said as he looked around for his clockwork raven. He had lost one creation and wasn't about to lose another. "Where's Little Johnny?"

"Up there," Ellie said, pointing to a tree branch.

Edgar followed her finger and there he was, perched in an oak tree.

"When we were younger, John loved climbing trees. He would always hide up in one and make me look for him."

"Interesting," Edgar mumbled and when Ellie questioned him, he brushed it off. He had the sneaking suspicion that somehow Ellie's brother's soul wound up in his creation, but all he had to go on was the word of a thief and would-be-murderer. What did James mean when he talked about degrading the soul first? Without absolute proof, Edgar wasn't about to share the information with Ellie in fear of getting her hopes up that her brother was still with her. For now, he would let it go and enjoy the company, dinner, and dancing.

Edgar eagerly waited his turn to be served, despite his stomach's protest. All he could think of now was a carved off hunk of meat from the blackened beast's hind quarters. The pig was served with greens and smoked corn. Edgar found the pork to be the juiciest and most tender meat to ever pass between his lips. Whether it was a testament to the Native American culture or a result of his famine state, he did not know, nor did he, particularly care. The meal was washed down with a spiced juice that held a familiar citrus flavor.

The spectacle before him was one of unity and respect. Each step in tune with the next. Edgar knew what he was witnessing was more than a dance or celebration. From the decorative feathers and jewelry, and precise movements, a complicated incantation was being performed. A proverbial feast of the senses as piñon smoke hung in the air and the rhythmic beat of the drums reverberated in his chest.

He withdrew James Laurent's refracting lenses from his pocket and examined the proceedings. Through the glasses, Edgar noted the group of spectators doubled. Half of the crowd now comprised the deceased miners and ghost hunters. They held pickaxes and the weapons of their trade, but stood peaceably at the perimeter, observing the ritual with the same rapt attention as everyone else. And more strolled into the firelight from the darkness, drawn to it like moths to a flame.

Edgar's spine went cold, and the chill reached all the way to his tailbone. He cautiously glanced behind himself and found he and Ellie were not alone. The specter of a miner stood right behind them, his ax poised lazily, but ready upon his shoulder. The miner's face, and head, was half caved in and his left side singed and blackened. Clearly, he died in the initial blast and cave in. But he paid Edgar and Ellie no mind, watching the fire and dancing as if he was a child watching a circus.

Occasionally, a specter would charge in from the darkness, ax high and ready to strike. He'd penetrate the circle of observers but stop cold before striking the dancers and fall into the same attentive trance as the others. Periodically, the fire flared and emanated an intense, blinding light. When this happened, he was forced to look away and remove the refracting lenses to rub his eyes.

"What is it?" Ellie asked.

Edgar dared a glance back at the fire, but it emanated only the soft warm light of a bonfire. "Nothing," he answered and replaced his lenses. The intense white light still burned from inside the fire, and he could not look directly at it.

It was only during these flare-ups from the fire that the specters reacted. Not all of them, but a few at a time would step forward and walk right into the fire. Once they did, the flare-up subsided.

The specters, their charging and fire walking, all became part of the ritual and Edgar returned to the security of an observer. The chanting and the drumbeats soon lulled him into relaxed reflections from which his path of action became clear and simple.

Well played, Mr. Ross, Edgar thought, realizing this was all a show for his benefit.

The Cherokee Nation held no obligation to a group of white miners and ghost hunters. Nor should they. Though they were indeed helping those who persecuted them, they did so to teach Edgar a lesson in humility.

CHAPTER XXII

With the warm, orange glow of the fire upon his face, Edgar stared at the inside of his eyelids.

John Ross sat opposite him mumbling in his native tongue. "E-Lo-Hi-No-E-Lo-Hi-No."

When Edgar had entered John Ross's tent the second time, he was surprised to find the man waiting for him, as if he'd known Edgar would return, and when.

He had awoken from another vision and though the images witnessed in the dream terrified him, he refused to label it as a simple nightmare. He'd been walking down a deserted street, the gas-lamps hung from patriotic-colored banners. He approached a tavern, its window tops adorned with red, white, and blue semi-circle ribbons. The tavern was empty save for a black skeleton tending bar. The creature held a bottle up for Edgar and poured him a drink of dark liquid. The creature was darker than night as if it had been charred by the fires of Hell, its face hidden beneath the folds of a voluminous cloak that seemed to absorb light. When Edgar tried to pay for the drink, the black skeleton shook its head in refusal and Edgar had the impression the drink had already been paid for.

Unsure of its nature or meaning, he sought out the Cherokee elder for answers.

Without criticism or ridicule, John Ross said, "Be wary of taverns on election day."

Edgar nodded at the simplicity of the interpretation and the faith it implied in dreams. "Well, that shouldn't be a problem. The next general election isn't for another year."

John Ross nodded and invited Edgar to sit. He repeated his instructions from the day before and Edgar paid closer attention. Soon, the sound of the crackling fire and John Ross's labored breathing faded, and the world outside fell silent as his consciousness felt separated from his body.

"Open your eyes," John Ross commanded.

Edgar obeyed.

His gaze locked on the fire. On his peripheral, the edges blurred like ripples in a pool of water. The fire changed, splitting apart, and forming two humanoid shapes. He remained silent, afraid of losing the phenomena to doubt.

As the facial features clarified, the identities of the shapes became clear. James Laurent and George Darby argued over something. Edgar could only presume the argument had to do with either Kimberly or the mechanical man George had tried to hide. The arguing escalated when George shoved his palms into James and James answered the aggression with that toothy grin and the drawing of his pistol.

"I need to hear what they're saying," he said, and the fire went out as if smothered by an unforeseen force.

"What happened?"

"You broke the connection to the spirit world."

"But it wasn't complete. I—"

"Stop looking for all the answers to be given to you," John Ross said, his tone that of a scolding father.

Edgar stood. "I want to thank you for your hospitality."

"Where are you going?" John Ross asked, looking as though he already knew Edgar's response.

"Ellie and I will be taking our leave." He turned toward the door.

"There's still much for you to learn."

"Should I have any questions, I'll return."

"I will not send my men to save you again," John Ross said as Edgar exited the tent.

He didn't bother with a response.

Time was of the essence. With no way of knowing if the vision was of the past, present, or future, Edgar felt the need to revisit George

Darby. If he had any hope of finding out James's next course of action, that was as good a place as any to start.

Outside, the sun's gentle rays broke the horizon. The pinkish-orange glow pushed back the night. A shimmer of light refracted and caught Edgar's attention.

"What are you doing out here?" he asked Little Johnny.

The mechanical bird looked down at him from a low-hanging tree branch.

Edgar's eyes narrowed at his creation, and the truth struck as swift as a gut punch. *The eye!*

The clouded glass eye had slipped his mind until now. A quick pat on his chest and at his waist revealed his refracting lenses were not on his person. *No matter*. He reached up and grabbed the clockwork raven with both hands for a closer look, thinking it would try to flee, but the key had wound down and it was incapable of movement.

"Even though you've possessed my creation," he said, resolved to the idea that Ellie's brother's spirit was indeed inside, "you're limited to the constraints I imposed."

He wound the key and as he did so, wondered if John could hear and understand him. With the tension spring sufficiently wound, the bird came alive. It turned its head, taking in its bearings, then settled down.

"John Feller?" Edgar said, not knowing what else to say.

The familiar *clinkety-clank* sound came as the bird's neck bobbed up and down.

"President Taylor?" he asked as an absurd test wondering if the machine would simply agree to anything.

Little Johnny cocked its head and looked at him with its fogged eye, then rotated its head back and forth in the negative.

"Unbelievable," Edgar said. "I suppose I should thank you for saving us in the tunnel."

Little Johnny bowed his coppery head and rubbed it against Edgar's hand.

"It must be tough for you, not being able to communicate. I promise I'll work on that," he said, his mind already running through the possibilities.

He would need to install a more sophisticated set of bellows, and possibly dissect a parrot in order to have a working understanding of their trachea and syrinx but knew no one who owned such an exotic pet. Popular belief held parrots as having vocal cords, but Edgar knew this to be false. Though the birds could mimic words, they weren't actually talking, rather whistling. If he could recreate that ability using a miniaturized clarinet reed and check valves inside his mechanical bird's throat, Ellie just might have her brother back. The angelic image of the young woman in his mind's eye caused the derailment of his train of thought.

"What about Ellie?"

Little Johnny wriggled his body free from Edgar's grasp. His creation flapped its wings and hovered before him, all the while shaking his head from side-to-side.

"All right," Edgar said, palms up as if in defeat. "I won't tell her, but she has the right to know."

Johnny let loose a mechanical chirp, a sound Edgar figured was created by the sudden stopping and restarting of gears. If he was to create a voice box—for lack of a better word—he would need to find a way to filter out the background noise.

"What are you doing up so early?" asked Ellie as she stepped out of their wagon. She pressed her knuckles to her eyes and rubbed away the weariness.

"I'm sorry if I woke you. I had another vision."

"No," she said, pulling her hands away from her face. "You didn't wake me, but when I saw you were missing from your bed, I worried."

"No need for that," Edgar said with a half-smile. "I just wanted to talk with John Ross. Get his opinion on the vision."

"Oh." Ellie's head hung low.

"What is it?"

"Nothing. It's silly." Ellie lifted her chin and swatted the air. "Whenever someone mentions Mister Ross's first name, I can't help but think of my brother."

The mechanical raven landed on Ellie's shoulder and nuzzled against her cheek. Edgar held his tongue as the kindness brought fresh tears to Ellie's eyes. He knew then, keeping Johnny's secret would torment them all, but it wasn't his place.

"We should probably get back to bed," Edgar said.

Ellie sniffled and mumbled, "Okay."

"We've got a long journey ahead of us tomorrow, we should be well rested."

She nodded, then led the way back inside their wagon.

CHAPTER XXIII

Edgar walked into George's smithy with the rail-spike shotgun strapped to his back and Ellie at his side. Inside, they found George instructing his daughter, Kimberly, on punch pressing nail holes into a hammer-forged horseshoe. Though the young girl's knees trembled with fear of disappointing her papa, her gaze was focused, and her hand true.

They stood patiently and remained quiet as the lesson continued.

Not a minute had passed when George looked up and saw them. "No, no, no." He stepped away from his daughter and approached them, hands waving frantically. "You have to go."

"Please, George," Edgar said. "I need your help."

"Is that...?" George pointed to the shotgun. "Where did you get that?"

"A job in Utah."

"I built it for a friend. Henry Goodrich. He was a good man and you having that could mean only one thing."

"A lot of good men and women were killed because of James's treachery."

George's head slouched as the words obviously rang true in his ear.

Edgar hoisted the strap off his shoulder. "I thought the craftsmanship looked familiar." He held it out for George to take.

George gave a half-laugh, then said, "I didn't take you as one who believed in vampires."

At this, Edgar was unsure of what to say.

"I see," George took the gun and inspected the rotary mounting, "it's been modified to shoot metal spikes instead of wooden stakes."

"You were serious about vampires?"

"No, not me," he shook his head, "Henry. The man claimed a traveler passed through his farm and betrayed his trust. Said the stranger slaughtered his wife and two boys while he was tilling the soil. He found teeth marks on their bodies and believed something wasn't right about the man, so he asked me to make this. Work's work, you know?"

All Edgar could do was fake a smile. A week ago, he would have agreed with that testament whole-heartedly, but today....

George held the gun out at arm's length. "You keep it."

"You sure?"

"Yep. But you have to go."

"Ah-hem," Ellie interrupted and put Edgar back on track for the reason they came.

He nodded, then said, "We cannot, in good faith, go until you help us. So many lives are—"

"I can't. I just got Kimmie back and they—"

"I'm sure they made all sorts of promises they'll break once your services are required again."

"Daddy," Kimmie said, taking her father's hand in hers, "don't be scared."

George looked into his daughter's eyes, then nodded his head. He walked over toward his desk and grabbed a bound booklet, then held it out to Edgar. "This is all I can do for you."

Edgar looked down at the proffered copy of *Scientific American*—the latest issue. On the cover, a detailed sketch of the powered armor he saw in his vision and in bold typeface: *The Future Is Now.*

Edgar took the magazine and turned to Ellie, one finger pressed against the cover. "This is what I saw in my vision."

"Are you sure?" she asked.

"Positive." He turned to face George. "But this isn't what you built for James," he said.

"No. That's an older design. The one he is currently producing."

"So, what exactly did you build for James then?"

"A personal version," George answered, his eyes on the verge of tears. "That's all I can say. Please."

Edgar clinched his fist, but his guilt would not allow him to push any further. George was protecting his loved ones.

"We'll be on our way then." Edgar turned around, and Ellie followed his lead.

"Are you sure?" Ellie asked. "We came all this way."

Edgar nodded.

"Be careful," George said.

"We will. Take care of you and yours."

As Edgar and Ellie left the smithy, Edgar thumbed through the magazine. A whole article was dedicated to James Laurent's revolutionary armor that reportedly would save thousands of soldiers' lives. Edgar continued to read, despite knowing the numbers were grossly inflated. It would not take the opposition long to develop their own powered armor suits.

"Please don't tell me we're getting on another train," Ellie whined. "My backside couldn't handle another ride."

"Well, it says here," Edgar said, gaze still focused on the magazine, "James is giving an exhibition of his technology on the National Mall grounds on the thirteenth. He is competing for Government funds." He turned a few pages until he found the article about the government sponsored event. He scanned it and summarized the gist for Ellie. "It's a week-long event, an exhibition of sorts to debut advancements in the field of mechanical engineering."

Ellie smiled. "Then there's no need to rush off. That gives us a couple of days."

Edgar closed the staple-bound magazine. "What would you like to do?"

"For starters," she crossed her arms in front of her bosom, "you should take me to dinner."

"Do you like seafood?" he asked. "I know a great place on the Freedom Trail."

"Sounds lovely."

"Shall we walk, or would you prefer a carriage?"

Ellie pondered on it for a moment, then said, "I think our legs could use a bit of exercise."

Edgar cocked his elbow outward. "Shall we then?"

She hooked her arm in his and as they walked toward the restaurant, Little Johnny glided above them.

Never having been to the local establishment, Ellie allowed Edgar to order for her. He started the meal with a cup of clam chowder for each of them and an order of the restaurant's signature oysters. The main course consisted of fried seabass, lobster scampi, and hot corn bread.

The chowder was rich, thick, and filled with chunky potatoes and large pieces of clam; the oysters were shucked properly with a slight kick, not overpowering; the sea-bass tender and flaky and the scampi had the perfect balance of garlic and sweetness.

With nothing on their plates save for the cast aside shells, Ellie leaned forward with a devilish grin. "So, what will you be treating me too next, Mister Poe?" Ellie asked in a playful tone.

Whether it was the glass of wine, the oysters, or both, Edgar found himself thoroughly aroused. Of course, it may have just been the soft-tanned leather, steel boned under-bust corset Ellie wore. With the top two buttons of her white blouse provocatively unbuttoned, it was near impossible for Edgar to hold eye contact during the course of the meal. Fortunately for him, her mind was as engaging as her cleavage.

While they dined, Little Johnny perched on the back of the third chair, watching their every move, and Edgar made the mental note to wind him down at the first chance he got. Though he was certainly no prude, the thought of Ellie's older brother watching them unnerved him.

"Since it's probably too late to catch a train, I know of a great hotel that owes me some money."

"Why Mister Poe, are you trying to seduce me?" Ellie asked, her usual pale cheeks flush with a pinkish hue.

"Well," he said with a sly tilt of his head, "now that you mention it."

CHAPTER XXIV

Both Edgar and Ellie giggled like drunken school children as they fumbled through the front entrance of the Rowes Wharf hotel. They spilled into the lobby in a tangle of flesh, and as he steadied himself, Edgar caught sight of the reading area to the right of the front desk. The image of the fine-dressed man sitting in the high-back chair reading the paper flashed in his mind, and a sickening feeling roiled in his stomach.

Had it been James already watching him?

The idea softened his mounting sexual tension.

"Can I help you?" asked the night manager. His stern expression relayed he was not a proponent of young love.

As if sensing this, Ellie stood straight and ran her hands over her corset and down her white-lace dress to smooth out the wrinkles.

"We'd like a room," Edgar said, stepping deeper into the lobby, his voice dull and flat.

The man behind the counter narrowed his eyes, gaze fixated on their left hands as if searching for a wedding ring. "We have two rooms available on—"

Sex outside of wedlock was more commonplace in lower-class venues and was not perpetuated in polite society. "Do you not remember who I am," Edgar said, tone harsh. "One room will do."

"I do. My apologies, Mister Poe. Forgive my rudeness. It's not my place—"

Edgar raised his hand.

"Come now," Ellie said, grabbing hold of his hand and lowering it to his waist. "We, too, are sorry for our behavior. We did not mean to cause a ruckus in your fine establishment."

The night manager gave a curt nod. "I think I have the perfect room for you."

"I'm sure you do," Edgar said, realizing the man intended to give them the room Beauregard Dupuis had been murdered in, and most likely at double the rate as incentive for him to remain quiet on the matter.

"You'll be happy to know, there have been no complaints since you cleared out that nasty pest."

Edgar leaned onto the counter. "And yet you cheated me on the bill."

"Yes, about that," the night manager failed to make eye contact with Edgar, "I can offer the room complimentary for the night."

Edgar straightened his posture, surprised by the gesture, but reluctant to show it. "I expect so."

"Wonderful," Ellie added.

As the night manager filled out his ledger, Ellie leaned in close, placed her hand upon Edgar's chest, and kissed the nape of his neck. Her hot lips followed by the cool air traveling over the moistened spot sent his blood rushing through his veins.

She was eager, that much was evident, and he now knew with absolute certainty that the blossoming feelings he felt for her were reciprocated.

At that moment, Edgar was torn. He didn't want to insult her by taking her hand away, but at the same time, he didn't want the night manager to view her in any way other than as a lady.

He took hold of her hand and whispered, "It won't be much longer."

The night manager turned around, plucked a key off the peg board behind him, and then slid it across the counter. "Here you are. Shall I have your bag sent up?"

"That would be mighty kind of you. Just leave it outside the door, and please, be careful with it," he said, suddenly feeling guilty for stuffing Little Johnny inside.

The moment he and Ellie exited the restaurant, Little Johnny had perched on Ellie's shoulder and stared Edgar down as if daring him to lay a hand upon his sister. Edgar had grabbed hold of the mechanical bird with both hands and wedged it in the crook of his arm as he manually unwound him, rendering the bird powerless.

"I do hope you enjoy your stay," the night manager said as Edgar scooped the key off the counter.

Edgar thanked the man, then led Ellie to the elevator. With no attendant at its helm, Edgar showed his mechanical prowess by operating the levers and once the accordion door closed, Ellie leapt into his arms and kissed him full on the lips. His arms wrapped around her slender frame, and he pressed his palms into the small of her back, drawing her closer to him.

When the elevator doors opened with a *ding*, the two held their embrace and continued to kiss as they nonchalantly checked hotel room numbers for theirs.

Edgar withdrew his lips. "Here we are."

"Make haste," she said, and he went to work on the lock.

With Ellie's hands at his hips, pulling him closer to her, Edgar had trouble opening the door. The key fumbled in his hand as his excitement multiplied. Considering it had been nearly a year since he had a fiancé, let alone been with a woman, Edgar feared the mounting tension would cause him premature release.

"Easy," he said in a soft whisper, removing her inching hands from his waist.

She smiled as if in understanding.

With Ellie's hands at her side, Edgar was finally able to unlock the hotel room door. He stepped to the side and allowed her to enter first.

"Goodness," she said, stretching the word. Her head swiveled on her shoulders as she took in the décor. "Is that an in-room bath?"

As Ellie examined the washroom, Edgar felt pressure around his throat. Though it was just slightly uncomfortable, he found the sensation worrisome. The tightness steadily increased until breathing became difficult, and Edgar withdrew James's refracting lenses, hoping they were strong enough. With a shaky hand, he slipped them on.

Beauregard's pale, bluish-green image stared at him with hate filled eyes and crooked teeth. All that remained of Beauregard was his head, shoulder, and right arm. The rest of his ghostly body was nowhere to be seen, dispersed, or broken down by Edgar's machine. Degraded just as James has said.

On the cusp of unconsciousness, Edgar's mind raced. His thoughts bounced from wishing he hadn't wound down Little Johnny as the mechanical bird would have certainly alerted him to the ghost's presence; to Ellie's warm, plump lips upon his own; to his failure as a supernatural detective, and then....

"I know...what you...need."

The pressure increased as Beauregard's eyes narrowed.

Darkness encroached from the corners of Edgar's eyes; his limbs felt cold—distant—as a weightless sensation washed over him. "Let me...bring her...to you...."

Edgar crumpled to the floor when the stranglehold was released, his refracting lenses slipping off his face. He breathed deep as he managed to get on all fours.

"Are you alright?" Ellie asked, running to his side.

"I'm fine," he managed to say between labored breaths.

"We're not alone, are we?" Ellie looked around the room, but the ghost of Beauregard either didn't want to be seen or was too weak to reveal himself.

"I have to find Mrs. Dupuis."

Ellie stooped down. "Who?"

Edgar scooped up his lenses, then draped his arm over her shoulder. "The widow of the ghost haunting this hotel."

"You want me to go with you?" she asked as she helped him to his feet.

"I certainly don't want you waiting here alone."

"Do you know where to find this, Mrs. Dupuis?"

He shook his head. "But the night manager might."

They walked to the door together, but before leaving the room, Edgar turned back around. "Beauregard, I'm truly sorry," he said and paused, waiting for some sort of reply. He expected a levitating lamp, an etching on the wall, or a punch in the nose for a response, but the silence was unexpected, and weighed heavily on his heart. "I'll make this right, I promise."

When Edgar and Ellie stepped off the elevator into the lobby, the night manager's face screwed up. "Is everything all right with the room?" he asked, his brow still furrowed.

"Yes," Edgar replied.

"Good. I was worried for a moment there. The two of you seemed…eager." A smile broke his confused look.

Edgar stepped up to the counter and got right to the point. "Is there any way you could give me the address of Mrs. Dupuis's residence?"

The night manager scratched his chin. "I don't think that would be wise. She would be none-to-pleased to see you."

"Please," Edgar said, "I wouldn't ask if it wasn't an emergency."

"I don't know." The man looked away, his gaze drifting toward the large chandelier rather than Edgar's eyes. "It's only been recently that she stopped coming."

"Exactly my point," Edgar said, seeing an opportunity. "I feel guilty for my part in her suffering and would just like one last chance to ease her pain."

The night manager's gaze locked on Edgar. A long pause passed as the man seemed to search Edgar for the truth in his statement.

"I've read *The Tell Tale Heart,*" he finally said, "so I have an understanding of your relationship with guilt." A smile formed on the man's face as he grabbed hold of his ledger. He thumbed through the pages until he found what he was after. He jotted down the address on a scrap piece of paper and slid it to Edgar.

"Thank you," Ellie said as Edgar was too preoccupied familiarizing himself with the address.

"Yes, thank you," Edgar added. "Battery Street," he said as he pushed open the door, "just a short walk from the Quincy Market." He stepped to the side, holding the door open for Ellie.

A hard rain fell, and Ellie leaped back inside the open doorway.

"Just my luck," he mumbled, letting the door go. He pulled the lapels of his jacket up and scrunched his neck.

Ellie, still standing in the doorway, opened the door a crack. "I'll wait here."

"Agreed. No sense in both of us getting drenched."

She nodded and he darted off, stepping cautiously to avoid the growing puddles.

When he arrived at the Dupuis manor, Edgar stood, hand on the knocker with no inclination to use it. Fear, guilt, and self-loathing prevented him from doing what he knew in his heart was right. The covered porch protected him from the cascading rain, but the chill of the wind on his dampened skin caused gooseflesh to form.

With a deep breath and a quick prayer, he slammed the knocker's twisted ring three times. He could imagine the thud of the wrought iron resounding through the house and waking Mrs. Dupuis at such a late hour.

The door opened and the lady of the house stood at the entrance in a red quilted robe, her hands working the draw strap into a knot. "You!" Mrs. Dupuis's face contorted into a snarl; her beauty lost to rage.

A crack across Edgar's cheek stole him from his fantasy of the wonders lying beneath the elegant fabric.

"How dare you show yourself at my home."

"Please, Mrs. Dupuis, I need to speak to you about your husband. May I come in?"

"Why?" she asked, hands on her hips. "I think you've done enough—"

"He needs our help," Edgar insisted.

The anger washed away from Mrs. Dupuis, her brow now wrinkled with concern. "But I thought he was gone."

Edgar reached out and took Mrs. Dupuis's hand in his. "I've made a terrible mistake. And I'm here to correct it."

"I must see him at once." She pulled her hand free.

While Mrs. Dupuis went to slip on something more appropriate, Edgar stepped deeper into the spacious living room. Beauregard Dupuis had indeed been a successful businessman, the home appointed with fine paintings and exotic materials. The oversized windows offered incredible views overlooking the harbor. Hardwood floors, marble fireplace, and silk drapes portrayed Beauregard as a man of excess in Edgar's eyes.

A daguerreotype of the couple during happier times caught Edgar's eye. He stepped up to the fireplace mantle for a closer look. The young couple depicted seemed so full of love and hope, their wide smiles and intent gaze upon the other showed a bond rarely seen.

"Times were a lot simpler then," Mrs. Dupuis said, entering the room.

Edgar returned the photo frame. "Forgive me."

"It's quite all right. Now, what has happened to my Beauregard?"

"I failed to help him move on from this world to the next. I need to find out what is keeping him here so that I may ease the transition. I was hoping you would—"

"I know what he needs."

At this, Edgar's posture straightened. "And that would be?"

Mrs. Dupuis approached the fireplace and looked at the photo. After a long pause, she said, "He has asked for my forgiveness."

"I see." Edgar's head hung low as the task now seemed impossible. How could she ever forgive the man for such deceit?

"Don't look so defeated. I forgave him the moment I saw his pale-faced, sorrow-filled eyes."

Edgar felt his jaw go slack, shocked by her statement. "Then why—"

"I never told him that," she said, turning to face him. "Because I love my husband, Mister Poe, and I want him home."

"That's not possible. For reasons unknown to me, spirits are," he searched for the right word, "trapped where they died and refused to move on."

Perhaps if I had stayed with the Cherokee, he pondered.

"Find a way," she said, her tone authoritative and sharp.

The woman before him was smart, strong, and beautiful, and in that second, he wondered what Mr. Dupuis's mistress had looked like. Surely, she must have been angelic for he could not fathom how Beauregard could have sought another companion. He ignored her impossible demand and instead asked, "If you don't mind my asking, why do you think your husband strayed?"

She narrowed her eyes upon him, and he feared he had pressed too far, but then she answered the question, "Because he could. That harlot threw herself at him and he was weak. But that doesn't mean he stopped loving or desiring me."

"That's why she resorted to murder. Her feelings were not reciprocated."

And here I thought the mistress' boyfriend was the murderer, Edgar thought.

Mrs. Dupuis turned away from him and by the nonchalant wave of her arm, Edgar knew she was wiping away a tear. When she turned back around, she said, "I grow tired of this conversation. Take me to my Beauregard this instant."

"Yes ma'am," Edgar said, shrugging his shoulders, "but I don't think you're going to like what you see."

CHAPTER XXV

"Bastard!" Mrs. Dupuis said, slapping Edgar across the face once more after seeing what remained of her beloved husband. "You arrogant…" a hard fist slammed into his chest followed by two more… "uncaring brute."

The fists came fast and hard and Edgar dare not interrupt the assault for fear of incurring the ghost's wrath. And he knew he deserved the abuse.

Ellie made a move to intervene, and Edgar held out a hand, motioning for her to back off. Perched on Ellie's shoulder, Johnny let loose a sympathetic mechanical chirp.

Mrs. Dupuis released a deep sob and her arms dropped to her sides as though she could no longer raise them. She leaned her head forward and pressed into Edgar's chest. "Why?"

The pain in her voice made Edgar's heart ache. Words failed him, a state he was unaccustomed to. He prided himself on his ability to weave the English language into beautifully crafted prose able to touch the heart and shine a light into the darkest corners of the human psyche but seeing Beauregard—his failure—staring back at him with longing, his confidence was replaced with self-doubt and loathing.

What was left of Beauregard simply hovered in the air, his head cocked to the side, eyes wide, and lips pursed. The shame of his beloved seeing him in such a state was apparent.

Mrs. Dupuis turned to her husband and extended a loving hand. She stroked his cheek and said, "I love you. You're forgiven. Please, rest now."

At this, Edgar was surprised not to see Beauregard's demeanor change. The sad, far-away look remained in his eyes as he mouthed the words "Thank you."

The ways of the Cherokee people were not the only course of action. The anger and hatred that had burned in Beauregard's eyes earlier was no longer there and without the aid of incense and chanting. All he needed was to employ his analytical skills and deductive powers and treat each spirit separately. What worked for one might not for another, it was a hard lesson, but one he would never forget.

Despite handing over James's powerful refracting lenses to Mrs. Dupuis, Edgar's strongest pair happened to be enough to allow him to see a radiant white light grow into a large circle behind Beauregard's translucent form. The same light he'd witnessed emerging from the fire in the Cherokee camp. He found the blinding light too intense and turned away with his forearm pressed against his brow for added protection.

Little Johnny cawed, alarming Ellie.

"What's happening?" Ellie asked.

"I don't know," he said, "the light is too bright."

"What light?" she asked in return.

"Beauregard?" He heard Mrs. Dupuis say. "Don't leave me."

Edgar narrowed his eyes and stole a glance. Mrs. Dupuis was on her hands and knees staring directly into the light, weeping, begging for her husband to come back. Wanting to see what she saw, to know what was on the other side of that circle of light, he silently cursed himself for giving her James's refracting lenses. Then, cursed himself a second time for being so selfish. He knew she needed this. There would be other opportunities.

He relaxed as the light faded. Ellie stepped toward Mrs. Dupuis looking as though she were going to give some words of comfort. The woman was still on the floor sobbing so as to spare her the embarrassment; he grabbed Ellie by the hand and pulled her out of the hotel room.

"What are you doing?" she asked once they were in the hall.

"She needs a minute."

"She needs a compassionate hand and a sympathetic ear," Ellie replied.

"What she needs," said Mrs. Dupuis as she opened the door, "is to be taken home."

"Yes, of course," Edgar said, his guilt still evident in his voice.

"Would you like for me to tag along?" Ellie asked wide-eyed.

"Thank you, but that won't be necessary."

Ellie nodded and returned to the room.

Little Johnny craned its mechanical neck a full one-hundred and eighty degrees and stared back at Edgar. The look felt as if it were a challenge to try and wind him down again in order to be intimate with his sister, a challenge Edgar looked forward to accepting on another night. His analytical mind over-ruled his carnal desires.

"Shall we go then?" Edgar asked, pushing the elevator's call button.

Once outside, an awkward silence befell them as Edgar escorted her through the streets. His mind occupied with the endless possibilities the circular doorway brought, and her mind obviously focused on the loss she'd suffered for the third time this night.

"So," he finally said, unable to resist the urge to ask any longer, "what did you see?"

"I saw my husband leaving," she said, her voice dull and flat. "The end of happiness."

Edgar bit his lower lip. He knew exactly how heavy the woman's heart must be and decided not to press the issue. She hadn't simply lost a husband—cheating or not—she'd lost a friend and confidant, she'd lost the hopes and dreams they shared, and the promise they had made the day they'd said, "I do." A piece of herself had stepped into that circle and Edgar needed to respect that.

Once they arrived at her home, Edgar wondered how she managed alone in the manor, but dared not ask. His chest still sore and probably bruised from her last outrage at him.

"Again," he said as they climbed the stone steps to the front door, "I'm sorry for your loss."

"Thank you, Mister Poe, for everything you've tried to do for my Beauregard."

Edgar stood there on her front steps for several minutes after Mrs. Dupuis stepped inside and closed the door on him, contemplating the meaning of her words. He hadn't simply *tried*, he succeeded. For the first time in years, Edgar had successfully relocated an earthbound spirit to the afterlife. The circular doorway was proof enough.

"Should have just asked her what she saw in that door, feelings be damned," he mumbled as he turned away.

Walking back toward the hotel, the moon casting its soft celestial light upon him, but the thought of Virginia waiting for him on the other side twisted his insides. How long would they have to wait in order to be reunited?

Jealousy boiled his temper, his fingers pressed into the palms of his hands. The love shared by the Dupuis' proved strong enough to transcend death and his had not. Despite his transgressions, Beauregard condemned himself to remain with his beloved.

Had Virginia not loved him enough to remain earthbound?

"Poppy cock," he told himself. "She simply spared me the heartache."

Deep down he knew he was lying to himself. Though their bond was stronger than most, even he classified the love he shared with Virginia as spiritual, and not earthly. In that regard, it only made sense to think she would transcend, as was expected, and wait for his natural passing.

Shaking away the self-doubt, Edgar recalled happier times before his beloved wife was struck ill. The nights she had spent beside him as his pen feverishly worked. When he had leaned back in exhaustion, the words failing him, she would kiss his brow and whisper inspiration in his ear.

Edgar's head tilted back to gaze into the clear, starry night. As he wondered which one shone for her, a gentle wind nuzzled his neck, and he was reminded of the valentine poem she had penned for him:

Ever with thee I wish to roam —
Dearest my life is thine.
Give me a cottage for my home

And a rich old cypress vine,
Removed from the world with its sin and care
And the tattling of many tongues.
Love alone shall guide us when we are there –
Love shall heal my weakened lungs;
And Oh, the tranquil hours we'll spend,
Never wishing that others may see!
Perfect ease we'll enjoy, without thinking to lend
Ourselves to the world and its glee –
Ever peaceful and blissful we'll be.

"Forgive me for doubting you," he said, still staring into the heavens.

When Edgar entered his hotel room, he found Ellie sitting on the bed—fully clothed—with Little Johnny perched on her shoulder. He found the sight more than a little creepy and wondered if Ellie would still have that childish grin on her face if she knew the truth.

"Thought for sure you'd be in bed by the time I got back," he said, slipping off his jacket.

"Didn't seem right." Her smile faded. "Tonight turned out differently than I had imagined."

Unsure if her words were an invitation to pick up where they left off or not, Edgar simply nodded in agreement.

"Were there any more outbursts from the widow?"

Edgar shook his head and said, "No, but she couldn't get rid of me fast enough."

"Too bad she blames you."

Edgar lowered his head, the shame and humiliation of his failure returning.

"So," Ellie stroked the back of Little Johnny's head, "what do you want to do?"

Where was she trying to take the conversation?

As if sensing his awkward reluctance, she continued, "Perhaps we should just head out to DC. Maybe we can get a sleeper car on the train."

Edgar nodded. "Perhaps that's best."

CHAPTER XXVI

The aged artist, Thomas Sully, painted his beloved's portrait with a steady hand. Though Edgar hovered over the man, he remained as quiet as a field mouse, doing his best not to interfere. As an author and tinkerer, he knew the solitude creation demanded.

He averted his gaze from the canvas to his dark-eyed beauty. Virginia, exuding graceful patience, slouched forward in her high back chair, left hand tucked under her chin and an opened book in her right. She held the pose with dignity and sophistication, he almost felt ashamed for keeping her modeling a secret, but in some social circles, a model was regarded just a mere step above a prostitute.

As Thomas mixed a new color from his six-color palette, a soft, raspy wheeze escaped Virginia's lips.

"Darling?" Edgar said, taking a step toward her.

The wheeze grew deeper, hoarser. Virginia's rose-tinted cheeks lost their luster as her skin turned a pale shade of gray.

"I don't believe I have that color," Thomas said with little concern.

"Virginia, hold on." Edgar's next step caused the floorboard beneath him to crack and split. He stumbled forward, falling onto the wood.

He looked up to see Virginia's skin wither and shrink to her bones as if all the fluids in her body simply evaporated. Her brown irises fogged, and she looked upon him with soulless eyes, her face contorted in confusion.

"For Pete's sake, will you hold the pose?"

"Mister Sully, mind your tongue," Edgar said, appalled by the man's lack of action. He just sat there, brush in hand.

"Edgar, what's happening?"

He didn't have an answer for her. This trip to Philadelphia was to have immortalized his love's beauty, not create a future book cover for an unpenned tale of macabre.

Virginia's hair fell in clumps to the floor and her bottom jaw dropped out of place. This was it; this was goodbye, and Edgar was powerless to say the words.

Thomas stood abruptly, tossing his paints across the room in a tantrum. "Worst corpse I've ever worked with!"

Edgar's body floated weightless between dream and waking consciousness. The sound of screeching metal filled his ears. In that second of time, he had no recollection of where he was or what he was doing there. His chest tightened with panic as the floor drew closer. Breathing labored, he took a deep, soothing breath. He remembered the purchase of a train ticket for him and Ellie to DC. A party. Succumbing to sleep. But why was he falling out of bed? With an Umph! He hit the floor.

"Oh!" Ellie fell out after him, landing atop his chest.

In the brief moment where their eyes met, and the prior awkwardness dissolved, Edgar's heart went a flutter at her natural beauty. He opened his mouth to say something poetic, but screams from panicked passengers filled the air, coming from all directions, as the train car slammed into the one in front of it and jumped off the track. Edgar managed to pull Ellie close in hopes of using his own body to protect her before they were thrown about. Their bodies twisted and tangled together as the car tumbled over. Glass shattered and rained in upon them, lacerating their skin. Ellie's heart thundered against Edgar's chest as she screamed.

Little Johnny flapped and rolled in the air so as not to crash into the walls and Edgar could almost hear the concern in his mechanical chirps and whistles.

"Hold onto me," he said.

A sharp blow to his head blurred his vision. Whether he had hit his head on the roof or if a piece of luggage slammed into him, he did not know. The pain lingered and his cheek moistened as tears mixed with blood. Uncertain if they were going to survive, he pleaded for a swift demise if this was to be the end.

As if in answer, the jerking stopped, and the train car settled on its side. What lasted for all of ten seconds felt like an eternity.

Edgar checked Ellie over. A few minor cuts on her brow and forearms. "Are you all right? Anything broken?"

She shook her head. "I don't think so."

"Get dressed, quick. We have to get out of here."

She nodded and obeyed. Tossing her dress over her night gown, she stood and slipped on her shoes. Little Johnny landed upon her shoulder. "I've never been so frightened before," Ellie said, hand pressed to her chest. "And the ride had been going so nice with you raising all that money for your magazine."

Edgar had raised nearly fifteen-hundred dollars for *The Stylus* during the trip. The train had been filled with social hob-knobs walking the corridors in silk robes and gowns, a flute of champagne in each hand. Easy marks for a charismatic, misunderstood poet such as himself.

With his pants around his ankles, Edgar tried to stand, but his right leg buckled under the weight, and he stumbled to one knee.

Ellie reached out to stop him from falling face first. "You okay?"

"Yes," he said, attempting to stand again. Pain surged as the knee bent, but he remained upright, pulling his pants up in the process. "I must have banged it pretty hard." He slipped on his jacket, then added, "Nothing feels broken though."

"That's good." Ellie stepped right up beside him with her arm out. "Lean on me if you have to."

He shook his head, then added, "Thank you, my dear."

She nodded and backed away.

With his hand pressed against his thigh, just above the knee, he took his first step toward the door.

"Go easy," Ellie said.

Edgar took her words to heart as he reached for the door handle. Outside their room, the screams of terror from neighboring cars had turned to cries for help. He turned the knob and pushed on the door but felt resistance.

"What's wrong?" Ellie asked.

"Something's in the way."

"You don't think it's someone, do you? A body?"

"One way to find out." Putting his shoulder into it, Edgar tried again. The door opened, pushing the blockage aside.

Peeking out, refuse and luggage littered the floor.

"Well?" Ellie asked, hands steepled.

"No body, come on."

Jagged metal from the wreckage threatened to rip into their flesh. Ellie remained on his heels as he led her through the narrowed train. Fortunately, most of their sleeper car was empty. The station had been desolate when they'd purchased their tickets, and they had passed nary a soul as they were ushered to their car. The social elites had remained toward the rear of the train.

Up ahead, Edgar saw a figure moving ahead, but before he could call out to him and ask if he was all right, the man disappeared into the shadows. Edgar took hold of Ellie's hand and moved to follow.

"Someone. Anyone. Help me!"

The fear-filled voice came from an adjacent room. Edgar stepped over a luggage bag and shattered a large shard of glass underfoot.

He pressed against the door and said, "Help is here."

"Oh, thank God! Please help me. I'm trapped!"

Edgar tried the door handle, but it was locked. "Can you unlock the door?" he asked.

"If I could, I wouldn't need help, now, would I?"

"A simple no would have sufficed," Edgar mumbled. Turning to Ellie, he said, "Stand back."

Once Ellie stepped off to the side, Edgar hoisted his injured leg and drove it into the door beside the knob. The wood splintered and gave way as pain coursed up his leg and spine. Gently, he placed his foot down and limped inside.

"Thank you," said the man inside.

With little moonlight filtering into the room, Edgar could barely make out the man pinned between the mattress and crumpled ceiling.

"Dear Lord," Ellie said, stepping into the room behind him.

"Please, don't leave me," pleaded the man.

"No one's going to leave you," Edgar said. He stepped closer, looking for any injuries that could prevent him from dislodging him.

"Get me out of here," the man said.

"Excuse me, sir, but I am not one to jump in feet first. Perhaps you could help me by showing a little patience as I decipher the best course of action."

The man extended his arm and said, "Pull on it!"

Seeing the futility of reasoning with the man, Edgar grabbed hold of his hand and pulled with all his might.

"Owe! Okay. Stop!"

"What's wrong?" Ellie asked. "Do you need me to pull, too?"

"No more pulling," said the man. "The metal is digging into my leg."

Edgar let go of the man's hand and crossed his arms. "That is precisely why I was reluctant."

"Please," the man's voice sympathetic as if he assumed Edgar would leave out of frustration.

"Don't worry," Edgar said, "we *will* get you out of here. What's your name?"

"Holden. David Holden."

"Nice to meet you, David." Edgar looked around the room for a lantern or match. "If only I had more light."

Little Johnny squawked, drawing Edgar's attention, he then glided to David's side. A sparkle of light illuminated at the center of his creation's eyes and grew until the glass orbs could no longer contain the energy emitted. Two beams of red light sliced through the darkness, revealing the jagged metal folded between David's thighs. Fortune had smiled upon him, another inch to the right would have certainly castrated him.

"What is that?" David asked.

"A Specter Detector," Edgar said, nodding proudly to Little Johnny.

"A what?"

"A pet raven of sorts…"

"KAW," Little Johnny objected.

Edgar tried to calculate the precise angle at which he could pull the man to safety without cutting the femoral artery in his right leg, and if he did, how much time he would have before David bled out. Of course, Edgar did not feel failure was an option. The man, on the other hand, proved an incalculable proponent. Everything hinged on whether or not David could remain calm and not squirm.

"Well?" the man asked, his impatience returning.

"I can see what was cutting into you when I pulled."

"Can you—"

"Sir," Edgar stood straight, "I am weighing my options."

"Deliberate faster, would you?"

"Is there anything I can do?" Ellie asked, looking none too pleased with either of them.

He might as well have been standing erect, chin up and chest out as if he were some Neanderthal.

"No, I think I can manage," Edgar finally said. He stepped to his right. "All right, suck in your gut as much as you can, and I'm going to pull you this way."

David nodded and extended his arm once more.

"Ready?" Edgar asked.

"Aye."

With every ounce of strength he could muster, Edgar pulled. The force more than enough to dislodge David, and both fell to the floor.

"Everyone all right?" Ellie stepped toward Edgar and helped him back on his feet.

He nodded, then turned to the man who remained on his backside, clutching his chest.

"I'm bleeding," David said without even looking at his hand for confirmation.

Edgar dropped to his knees. "How bad?"

"Not sure."

"Let me see." Edgar took David's hand by the wrist and lifted it off his chest. A long, jagged slash ran from his solar plexus to his belly button. "I thought I told you to suck it in?"

"I thought I had." David cracked a smile.

Edgar turned to Ellie and said, "We have to get him out of here, now."

Together, Edgar and Ellie helped him to his feet and guided him out of the sleeping car and through the wreckage, using Little Johnny's illuminated eyes to guide the way.

Once they had reached the car-end door, Edgar took David's full weight upon his shoulders as Ellie tried to open the door. She pushed, pulled, then pushed again with her shoulder, but the door would not give.

"I think it's jammed," she said.

"Let me try," Edgar replied. "Take him."

Ellie slipped under David's arm, then leaned against the wall for support.

Edgar tested the door, uncertain if it was lodged or if Ellie's petite frame was not capable of mustering enough strength to overcome the distorted metal. With a grunt, he found it to indeed be stuck. A cool breeze brushed the nape of his neck. He turned around to see the nearby window had been broken and figured it to be large enough for them to escape through. The question was if doing so would increase David's injuries.

As if reading his mind, Ellie said, "You're not suggesting we climb through that, are you?"

Edgar balled his fist and scrunched it up into his sleeve. "Why not?" With his hand protected, he knocked away the remaining shards of glass.

"Just get me out of here," said David.

Even in the dim light, the man was losing his color. Edgar turned to Ellie and asked, "Would it be easier for you to lift him up, or help him down?"

"I can barely hold him now," she said, her brow wrinkled in frustration.

"All right." Edgar moved toward her and helped ease the burden. "Can you manage to climb out on your own?"

Ellie's frustrated look was replaced by one of scorn as her brow relaxed and her gaze turned hard.

"I'm sorry, I meant no offense," Edgar said, too afraid to look her in the eye as he spoke.

"Once I'm outside, give me a minute, I'll look for help."

"Done," he said.

As Ellie climbed out of the broken window, and vanished from sight, Edgar felt David's weight intensify as if he were no longer helping to keep himself upright. "Hang on a little longer."

"Huh! What?" David jolted awake.

"Easy," Edgar said, then guided him closer to the window.

"Everything all right?" Ellie asked from outside.

"Do you see anyone?" he asked, not bothering to answer her question as he did not feel he could truthfully. Everything was far from all right.

"Yes," she called, "there's a group of people. I'll be right back."

Before Edgar could protest, Little Johnny zoomed out the window after his sister.

"Help is on the way." Edgar took David's left hand and pressed it to the wound in his stomach. "Keep the pressure on."

David nodded weakly.

Seconds felt like minutes as he waited there, the man's burden growing exponentially with each passing one.

"Ellie?" he called.

No reply.

"I don't...feel very well," said David. "Did the train start up again?"

"No," Edgar said, his legs seized by cramps.

"Then why are we moving?"

Edgar straightened his arching back and jerked the man up. "Stay with me."

David's eyes rolled upward as the burden on Edgar doubled.

"We're here," came Ellie's voice.

"Thank you," Edgar said as he looked upward.

"Can you ease him through the window?" someone asked, voice deep with a commanding undertone.

"I will most certainly try," Edgar said, then positioned his hands around David's waist.

Taking a deep breath, Edgar bent his knees and lifted him up. Slow and steady, Edgar used the wall for leverage and slid the dead weight up toward the window. Though he feared the possibility of exposed glass cutting the stranger, there was nothing he could do to prevent it. Feeling alone and claustrophobic, his muscles screamed with pain. Memories of physical training at West Point danced in his mind as he dug deeper within himself. The intense exercise from the early morning runs to the late afternoon marches where a single misstep meant more running had conditioned his body. He only needed to tap into the muscle memory.

"Just a little further," he encouraged himself.

"That's good," said the man on the other side, and suddenly Edgar felt the weight dissipate.

He slouched forward; a sigh of relief whooshed over his lips.

"Are you coming?" Ellie asked.

"Just a minute," he replied, then took a deep breath, held it, and released. "All right, I'm coming."

With his hands tucked into the sleeves of his jacket, Edgar grabbed onto the window frame and pulled his tired body up and out. Two men reached up for him and grabbed him by the shoulders, easing some of his weight.

"Thank you," he said to them as they helped him out of the wreck.

"Are there any others trapped inside?" someone asked.

"Not in this car," he said as his feet touched solid ground.

Ellie ran up to him and threw her arms around his neck. She squeezed him tight for the briefest of seconds, then let go and stepped back.

A train derailment was not a common sight. The locomotive and five coaches had jumped the track. The engine and the first coach lay on their side, with four of the cars zigzagged off the track.

He turned toward the crowd of injured passengers, some laying on the ground, others standing about with befuddled looks, all moaning in misery, and asked, "Does anyone know what caused this?"

"It must have been a damaged rail," one of the men who had helped him replied.

Edgar was not much of a train aficionado, but he knew the contact point between the steel wheel and track was no larger than a dime. If indeed a damaged rail was the cause, then there would be no finite way to determine if it were an accident, negligence, or sabotage. Any number of things could have made impact with the exposed metal, hindering the delicate balance.

Edgar searched the injured for the unmistakable denim, white-striped bib overalls, but the train's engineer was nowhere to be found. Spotting a conductor dressing the head wound of an elderly woman, Edgar approached with Ellie in toe.

"Excuse me, but have you seen the engineer?"

"I'm sorry, no," said the man, "but I have not made my way to the engine yet."

"Allow me," Edgar said, then turned away from the conductor.

"I'm coming with you," Ellie said as he passed her. "Do you suspect they need help?"

"No, my dear, I suspect they're already dead."

"Edgar!" she said, stretching his name with that scolding motherly tone.

Admittedly, his tone had been emotionless, but his mind was too preoccupied with the plausibility of the situation and tact had been pushed aside by logic.

"My apologies," he said as they continued to walk toward the front of the wreck, "I meant no disrespect."

As they drew closer to the overturned locomotive, a sudden aroma—one of a sweet, acrid charcoal—passed through his nasal cavity and caused his tongue to fold against the roof of his mouth.

Edgar recognized the smell and knew immediately what they would discover inside the twisted metal.

Ellie's arm shot upward to cover her nose and mouth. "What is that?" she asked, voice almost muffled.

"You should turn back. I'll—"

"Nonsense," she said, lowering her arm briefly.

Unsure if Ellie could handle seeing a body burned beyond all recognition, he tried again, "You're not going to like what we find."

"I'm not leaving your side," she said, still walking.

Without wasting another word, Edgar nodded his head and continued toward what he assumed to be a grisly scene. He overtook her with his longer stride in hopes of sheltering her, but she matched his pace, and they walked side-by-side.

Smoke billowed from the open window and the cab door swung loose in its frame. He caught the door and with great effort, pushed it aside. The odor nearly unbearable. Just as he expected, they found the engineer and fireman underneath a pile of hot coals, a blackened, blistered arm jutted out. Edgar could only suspect it had been a last-ditch effort for help.

Upon seeing the mountain of reddened coal atop the dead bodies, Ellie pressed the back of her hand to her lips and muffled a gag. In one fluid motion, she turned on her heels and ran.

Edgar stepped deeper inside and let the door go. Minding his steps, he walked across steel rather than wood flooring, and stomped out several small fires eating away at the wooden panels. He checked over the instruments but lacked the necessary training to decipher any foul play.

"Need any help in here?" asked a man who had poked his head inside the open window.

He turned and replied, "There's nothing that can be done here."

At the sight of Edgar's face, the man flinched and recoiled as if Edgar was the dead and burned engineer.

"Pardon me," Edgar apologized for his appearance and tried to wipe any soot or blood from his face with his hand.

"Hey…you're him."

Here we go, Edgar thought, in no mood to entertain a fan.

"Edgar Poe!"

"In the flesh," he said, then made a move to walk around the man, but was blocked.

"We're looking for you."

Edgar halted and looked the man over, double checking if he recognized him from anywhere. He was dressed as a tradesman, probably a factory man, a plug-ugly. No one Edgar would know.

The man saw Edgar's doubt and suspicion and stammered as he explained himself, "George Darby.... He sent us to find you."

"In the locomotive's cab?" Edgar asked.

"No," the man said, stumbling. "We meant to meet your train. But when we heard of the derailment, we came down the line to assist."

"We?" Edgar asked.

"My friends and me. The others are assisting...." He motioned down the line.

"Quite right. Of course," Edgar conceded, embarrassed at his own suspicious nature. "Very good of you."

A devilish grin stretched across the man's face as he slapped his hands together. "Old George sent word that you were in a spot of trouble and could use some assistance." The man stepped back and allowed Edgar to exit the cab.

"I didn't catch your name," said Edgar.

"My apologies, you must think I'm a twit."

"Not at all," Edgar said.

The stranger extended his hand. "Name's August Harrison."

Edgar accepted the gesture and as they shook hands, he said, "Nice to meet you."

"The pleasure is *all* mine, Mister Poe. Been a big fan since *The Man That Was Used Up*." August led Edgar away from the overturned locomotive. "I'd love to buy you a drink and get your take on the Penny Dreadfuls currently in circulation. I mean, before you, they all seemed to lack art and style. Cheap sensationalism to say the least, but you changed that."

"My good sir, I'd love to accompany you for a drink and discuss the history and future of the gothic tale, but now is not the best time."

August laughed. "Can't think of a better time for a strong drink, myself."

"Yes," Edgar chuckled, "Put in that light, I have to agree with you. But first I must inform my traveling companion else she worry herself to death."

August helped them gather their belongings and secure a room at a hotel he recommended. Ellie was none too pleased with the idea of him leaving her to drink with August and his friends, but he went ahead and left her alone anyway. He was certain he would hear an ear full later, but if brushing elbows with death did not warrant a stiff drink, what did? Besides, he doubted Little Johnny would allow any sort of intimacy this or any other night.

As Edgar and August walked, the conversation remained on the dark recesses of Edgar's mind, the trappings of guilt, and the loss of loved ones that permeated his writings. The same questions that were presented to him by fans and critics alike since penning "Metzengerstein," but they seemed fresh and less intrusive coming from this friend of George's.

He was just starting to feel comfortable around this kindred spirit when a sudden wave of apprehension crashed down upon his psyche like waves breaking on the rocks. Sweat beaded his brow as a dream flooded back upon him: Red, white, and blue banners hung from the gaslights along the main street.

Edgar stopped. The image instilled the sense of dread he had always hoped his words provided to his readers.

"Ryan's Tavern is just over there," the man said in response to Edgar's abrupt stop. He pointed at a red brick building off to the right. Red, white, and blue pleated fans adorned window tops.

Edgar's heart raced, hands trembled, and while trying to suppress the quiver in his throat, he asked, "What's going on around here?"

"There's a special election, for sheriff I think."

Edgar hadn't had any intention of catching the night train. Ellie and he did so on account of the Dupuis. So, George could not possibly have known he was on it. Something was amiss. "On second thought," Edgar told August, "It's getting late. I appreciate the offer, but I should—"

August grabbed hold of Edgar's arm and squeezed. "I'm afraid I have to insist."

The mounting fear in Edgar's heart gave way to outrage. After wrenching his arm free, he said, "How dare you touch me."

August reached around his back and withdrew a straight-backed fighting knife. A six-inch long blade and without a hand guard. Before August could raise the weapon to threaten Edgar, Edgar grabbed hold of the man's wrist with one hand and unsheathed his own blade. Holding August's weapon at bay, he then pressed his to August's Adam's apple.

"If you truly are a fan of my work, then you know what I'm capable of." Edgar applied more pressure and only eased up when a single droplet of blood rolled over the blade's polished edge.

"My friends are inside, and they'll come the moment I call."

Edgar narrowed his eyes upon the man. "You'll choke on your own blood before they can offer any assistance. Tell me," he applied more pressure, "what were your intentions?"

August swallowed hard, the blade cutting deeper into the throbbing lump of his throat. "Some guy paid us handsomely to stop you from leaving town. Said we could use any means necessary."

"What was his name?"

"No names were exchanged."

Edgar pulled his knife back but kept his grip tight on August's wrist. It was obvious to him now the train wreck was staged. "And were you paid up front?"

August nodded.

"Will an extra fifteen-hundred dollars lining your pocket buy your cooperation?"

At this, the man's eyes went wide, and Edgar released his hold upon him.

August returned the knife to his backside and asked, "You have it now?"

"I do." Edgar sheathed his knife and reached for the wad of money he had managed to raise for *The Stylus*.

Either way he looked at it, Edgar knew he'd have to put his dream on hold a little longer. It was a gamble, even after handing the money over, August could betray him, but without knowing how many lay in wait, he didn't like his odds of walking away. Chances were, he could kill this man before him, and die at the hands of his vengeful friends here on the street, or at the hotel August had recommended. The odds were against him making it to Ellie and getting out of town, and that would only endanger Ellie.

No.

His best course of action was to appeal to August's greed.

He held up the wad of greenbacks and said, "You can take this money and keep it all for yourself. All you have to do is tell your friends you had to kill me at the wreck, or on the way here. We'll be out of town in the morning."

With spring-like reflexes, August swiped the cash from Edgar's hand and tallied the bills. August's eyes remained wide, and his head bobbed as he said, "That's a really good idea."

"Then we have a deal?"

"Aye."

Edgar turned his back on the man and came face to face with a rearing horse. The beast whinnied as its front legs kicked out. He managed to jump back before the hooves made contact with his chest but fell to his backside.

"Whoa," the coach driver commanded as he pulled on the reigns.

The horse planted its feet safely in front of Edgar and let loose a neigh, then stamped its hoof against the brick a few times. With its nostrils flared and ears stiffened, Edgar could tell the beast was angry with him. How he failed to hear the animal's approach was beyond him.

"You all right there?" asked the driver.

Before answering, Edgar stood and checked around for August. The man had slinked away into the shadows. Hoping the hired thug would stay there, he turned and gave the driver his full attention. "I'm fine. My apologies for spooking your horse."

"I don't know what got into her, but you should have been minding your step."

"Again, my apologies," Edgar said, still eyeing the uneasy steed. "Good night, sir."

"Is there somewhere I can take you?" asked the man.

"That's very kind of you," he said. "I guess it's my lucky night."

CHAPTER XXVII

"Hello," Edgar called, but the streets were barren.

Unfamiliar with the buildings around him, he found himself lost. The streets seemed to be never ending, the alleyways engulfed in shadow so thick he could not see his hand in front of his face.

How long had he searched? "Ellie! Anyone!"

A thunderous sound broke the eerie silence, that of a hundred horses galloping straight for him. The constant thump drummed in his head, racking his nerves. He covered his ears, but it did not dampen the noise. His rational mind told him to look away, as if somehow knowing the only horror capable of such a deafening roar, but his curiosity prevailed, and he waited with unblinking eyes for the beast to reveal itself.

Countless, feathery, leg-like appendages moved in unison with a sinuous grace toward him. Frozen with fear, Edgar's body stood rigid as the reddish-brown beast marched ever closer. Legs trembling, he commanded his limbs to obey, but nothing responded. The monstrosity stopped a few feet away from him and reared up. Face to face with the beast, he made eye contact with two of its four eyes. The fleshy lobes on either side of its segmented head wriggled in the air and gave Edgar the impression of a snake's tongue gathering miniscule chemical particles of its adversary. The mouth opened to reveal a proboscis with hook-like jaws ready to ensnare his head and draw it in.

Like greased lightning, the worm-like creature lashed out and wrapped its body around Edgar's legs, then up his body, encompassing him in a hold tighter than a lover's embrace. He tried to scream, but no sound came as the pressure increased upon his chest. Lifted off his feet, his body was pulled into the open jaws. The pinchers closed in around him and darkness swallowed him.

Gasping for breath, Edgar sat up in bed. His heart pounded as he gathered his bearings. Ellie lay in the bed next to him undisturbed by his sudden movements.

"Just another dream," he said. He swung his legs out from under the covers and stood, knowing he would not be able to sleep any further this night.

He poured himself a glass of water from a pitcher. Though he would have to be mindful of Ellie's sleeping, he distracted his mind with work. Finally ready to act on inspiration brought on from the mechanical raven's possession.

With the deafening silence encompassing the room, he whittled away. Careful not to slice his finger, he worked the knife into the African Blackwood. He found the dark material pliable and both light and strong so as not to hinder the bird's flight capabilities.

Edgar planned to carve tiny keyholes to place inside Johnny's neck, assuming he could fit three. He based his concept off the clarinet's key system, though admittedly, he knew Johnny's voice would come across monotone with so few tone holes. In theory, Johnny could breathe in air and mechanically open and close the keys to form sounds using violin strings coated in whale oil to transfer vibrations. Once fitted inside the mechanical bird, Edgar planned on stuffing long-hair wool into the space in order to minimize resonance from internal reflections caused by the gears, cogs, and springs. All this in the hopes of creating harmonic alchemy and providing Johnny with a clear, concise way to speak.

Edgar looked up from the painstaking work, blinked, then pressed his fingers into the corners of his eyes. Ellie still lay asleep, her slender left leg protruding out from the covers, enticing him. He should cover her to protect her modesty, but the intimidating stare from Johnny—

who sat perched on the bedpost above her—left him with the impression, "I'll poke your eyes out."

Instead, he returned his focus to the carving.

As he worked, he lost track of time and his mind forgot about the worm-like creature haunting his sleep. Once all three keys were done to his satisfaction, Edgar fitted them with wafer springs, matched them with felt pads and fitting the whole with a miniature bellows.

Ellie stirred, attracting his attention.

"What are you doing?" she asked as she sat up. The sudden movement caused the loose flap around her gown to slip and reveal more than Edgar could have asked for. Hand pressing the top sheet against her bosom, she said with a playful smile, "Well."

"Just some…improvements to little Johnny."

"I do say, Mister Poe, you are never one to be satisfied. Always tinkering."

Edgar could not argue the point and returned to the delicate task.

Ellie took the robe draped over the footboard and tossed it over her shoulders. "Your contraption can already fly, has proven itself in battle, what could possibly be left to improve upon?"

"How about the ability to speak?"

The playful smile faded as a look of seriousness washed over her face. "Wouldn't it need some sort of intelligence for that?"

Edgar could not refuse the chuckle that escaped, and Ellie narrowed her eyes and pursed her lips in return, unaware of the joke.

"I'm sorry, it's just that, I find it amusing you would think that flying and coming to our rescue didn't take some semblance of intelligence."

"Well, no, isn't that what you designed him to do?"

"Not exactly. I designed him to grasp my shoulder or other perch and maintain his balance there. He was to let out a caw and extend his wings in the presence of a specter or phantom. That's it. Little more than a self-righting warning bell." Edgar paused and scratched his chin in contemplation. "However, there's something you should know."

Edgar pulled another chair out from the table where he was working and motioned for Ellie to sit. As she approached, Little Johnny let loose a mechanical chirp, then leapt into the air.

"She has a right to know," he said as Little Johnny landed beside him.

Ellie looked upon him with an arched eyebrow. "What are you talking about? What haven't you told me?"

"Before you ask me to explain myself," he said with his hands up in defense, "I don't know how or why, but somehow, your brother's spirit has landed inside my machine."

"What!" In a flash, Ellie's hands shot out and grabbed the mechanical bird. She brought it close to her face, twisted and turned it in all directions to look it over, and then said, "Johnny?"

His creation remained motionless; Johnny gave no response to Ellie's question.

Tears swelled at the base of Ellie's eyes. "Is this a joke?" she asked, placing the bird down on the table.

He shook his head. "I assure you, if it is, it's on me."

"How could you be so cruel?" Ellie stood up, turned away from him, and released a deep, pain-filled sob.

"Ellie, I—"

Caw!

Ellie turned back around, and as she did, she wiped a tear away with her index finger.

Little Johnny hopped to the table's edge and nodded his head.

"Johnny?"

The collection of cold springs and gears nodded vigorously.

Ellie stepped to the table and dropped to her knees. "But how?"

Johnny shook his head and Ellie turned to Edgar for the answer.

"I honestly don't know. That night at the lighthouse, your brother's spirit entered my machine. He did not reveal himself to me most likely out of fear."

Ellie looked away from him, her face puzzled with thought. "James looked right into Johnny's eye. He knew."

Edgar stood and approached her. With a hand on her shoulder, he said, "It really doesn't matter how or why. He's here. That's all that matters. Isn't it?"

Her smile returned when she looked at him. "You're right." With both hands, she reached out and grabbed Johnny. She stood as she brought his cold, metallic body to her bosom. No words were spoken as the embrace carried on.

Just as Edgar was going to excuse himself from what he deemed an awkward family moment, Ellie asked, "So can you do it?"

"What?"

"Give him the ability to talk to me?"

"I think so. I have everything I need—"

"Do it," she said, then placed Johnny back on the table.

With Ellie's curious eye over his shoulder, Edgar carried out his plan with meticulous attention to the tiniest of details. He would have preferred to have attempted the installation without her knowledge on the off chance he was wrong, but there was an odd peace in having her present and acting as his assistant. Not since Virginia's death had he felt such a sense of companionship, and he could only hope his success with Johnny would strengthen that bond.

Once the final spring was attached from the lever in Johnny's narrow neck to the tone hole, and the wool was stuffed inside encompassing all the pieces, Edgar closed the metal flap. He then released the breath he hadn't realized he was holding.

"Is it done?" Ellie asked as he leaned back in his chair.

Edgar wiped the bead of sweat from his brow and said, "I think so. It's up to him now."

"Go ahead, Johnny," Ellie said, eager to hear her brother's voice once more. She had a wide smile and an unmistakable gleam in her eye, Edgar hadn't the heart to tell her it wouldn't be the same.

Johnny opened and closed his whale-bone beak, but only a less harsh, more natural caw came forth, accompanied by the tinging of metal gears.

"What's wrong?" Ellie asked, leaning in closer to her brother.

"He just needs to work it out." Edgar moved to Ellie's side and slouched, "Johnny, channel your energies on the bellows. It will force air through the violin strings, make them vibrate."

He had so many questions to ask Johnny. Had he seen the circle of light upon his death? Was it still available to him? Did he glimpse

Heaven or Hell? How did Johnny bond with his creation? Which should he ask first?

The beak worked up and down, but still no words came forth. Johnny's head slumped forward as if in defeat.

Ellie stepped back and said, "It didn't work."

"Give him a chance."

"You've done something wrong. Made some error."

"No!" Edgar stood up straight. "I didn't fail. He failed. If a pea-brained bird can figure out how to mimic words, he should be able to, too."

"Where are you going?" Ellie asked as he grabbed his coat.

"For a walk. I need to clear my head."

"When will you be back?" she asked.

"Does it really matter?"

Without waiting for a reply, he opened the door and exited their room. He stormed out as if he were a child and though his frustration demanded he slam the door behind him, his courtesy for his fellow man over-ruled. The hour was late, and his fellow patrons of the hotel were surely asleep.

CHAPTER XXVIII

Outside, the air was crisp, the moon high, and the stars bright. Not a soul around, just as Edgar liked it. With his hands in his jacket pockets, and his neck scrunched in his shoulders, he walked down the desolate street without a destination in mind. Though he didn't want to entertain the idea of failure, his thoughts lingered on what he could have possibly done wrong, or different to correct the error.

Bluish-white lightning streaked across the heavens followed by a thunderous crack. A sudden chill in the night brushed his cheek. He stopped for a moment and looked around; the sense of someone watching him unshakable. His gaze searched the neighboring trees, the stone wall lining the cobblestone streets, and in between the corniced houses. All was quiet. Eerily so. He wondered if August and the other hired thugs skulked in the shadows waiting for their chance to strike.

Edgar slid his right hand out of his pocket and into the fold of his jacket for the small, silver knife he kept there. With no immediate threat, he left it where it was and pressed on, confirming it was there. He could circle the block back to the hotel where they stayed.

Before he could hook the first right, the streetlamp's light diminished, the tiny flames flickering in an unfelt breeze. The shadows toyed with the fleeting light; a morbid dance transpired as the two forces struggled against one another. He searched his surroundings again, wishing he had brought his refracting lenses.

Realizing it was more than a trick of the eye, Edgar bounded to the closest light source. Something tugged at the cuff of his pants as he moved, but his momentum pulled him free. Once basked in light, Edgar searched the ground and saw nothing but shadow. As if it were a stain upon the earth, Edgar could not see the ground beneath the murky surface. Dark as pitch, it gave the illusion of substance, and flowed like water around the light's edges.

With his scientific curiosity overpowering his mounting fear, Edgar bent at the knees and touched the gelatinous liquid. His hand recoiled immediately; the fluid was so cold it burned to the touch.

The ripples he created bubbled up, and the puddle took on a defined shape. Edgar stood and stepped back from the rising mass. Before his eyes, the shadow formed into a walking skeleton darker than night, its skull hidden beneath the folds of a voluminous cloak.

No doubting or denying it. The creature was the bartender from his dream, which must now certainly be considered a vision.

The bones created a melodic tone as they rattled and bumped against one another with each unnatural step.

Edgar withdrew the knife and unsheathed the blade. "Stay back."

Click-clack, it stepped closer.

Feeling foolish after his empty threat, Edgar lunged with the knife—a small attempt to regain his manhood.

His assault was halted when the thing caught him by the wrist and wrenched his arm, bending it to the side. Without any muscle mass, the strength exuded from the creature was beyond Edgar's comprehension and he felt as though his elbow were about to pop and break.

Was this his punishment for failing all those souls?

"Please," he managed to say as the pain reached a new plateau.

With the flick of its head, the hood flew back. Eyes of fire burned through him, terrifying him, and once more Edgar felt like the scared little boy with the sheets pulled over his head.

The skeleton's jaw bones separated, and Edgar took notice of the sharp incisors and for the first time he considered the actual existence of vampires.

"No," he demanded as the creature lowered its head to bite.

Edgar suppressed his paralyzing fear and slammed his free hand against the top of its skull. He pushed back with everything he could muster, but it was not enough. A high-pitched scream escaped his lips as the fangs broke through the skin on his forearm. Burning pain filled his arm as if fire were being pumped into his veins like venom.

"Nevermore!"

The monotone voice broke the silence, and Edgar looked up to see his creation in a free-fall dive, the moonlight refracting off its copper body. Thrilled to know he was right, Edgar momentarily forgot about his attacker.

Johnny slammed his new body into the middle vertebrae of the skeleton creature. Whatever unnatural glue was holding the bones together fell apart upon impact. The cloak fell loosely to the ground and the bones toppled over like a house of cards, each one melting back into the shadows upon impact.

"Edgar!" Ellie shrieked as she ran toward him.

"I'm all right," he said, the burning sensation in his arm already subsiding.

Edgar rolled up his jacket sleeve to investigate the wound. Oddly, little blood could be seen around the crater-like puncture marks. Instead, a black, viscous fluid leeched from the holes.

"Oh, my heavens," Ellie said, seeing the mark. She took him by the arm and pulled him. "We have to treat that *now*."

He stumbled forward. "Ellie, wait."

"I know we passed by a church earlier," she said, ignoring him.

"Stop." Edgar yanked back his arm.

"What's the matter with you?" she asked.

"Me? You're the one acting paranoid."

"Mister Poe," she said with her hands on her hips, "for all we know that was a vampire and now that you've been bitten, you could become a creature of the night." She stepped closer to him, the bridges of their noses almost touching. "Unless you're already turning."

"Don't be silly," he said.

"Don't be dismissive," she replied.

"Fine, though I doubt we'll find a chapel open at this ungodly hour."

Without another word, Ellie grabbed him by the hand and pulled after her.

Edgar did not resist but matched her stride. He looked over his shoulder to see little Johnny soaring overhead, keeping a watchful eye on the two of them. Why on earth would his first words be a quote from one of his poems? Was it some poor attempt at humor? *Perhaps it was a mistake to give him speech.*

To Edgar's surprise, the chapel was open without access to the main church. Ellie guided him to the Holy Water Urn, then dunked his arm into its basin. She watched intently, as if for his skin to melt away beneath the shallow pool. No such thing occurred.

"Are you satisfied that it was not a vampire that attacked me?" he asked, smiling.

She drew a deep breath through her nose and released his arm before replying, "For now, but I'll be watching you."

Edgar withdrew his arm from the water and rolled down his sleeve. "My dear, I would not have it any other way."

"If that…thing…wasn't a vampire, then what was it?" she asked.

"No idea." He shook his head. "Perhaps a Lich? Or a Harbinger?"

She looked upon him, mouth agape in fear and incomprehension.

"I've been doing wrong. A lot of wrong. I'm sure I've made enemies on the other side of that circular doorway."

"So, what do we do now?" she asked with a sound of defeat.

Edgar drew a deep breath and straightened himself. "We continue our journey to Washington," he said, then, with a shake of his head, added, "Hopefully, without further incident."

CHAPTER XXIX

Edgar and Ellie made their train without further incident. Though Edgar remained vigilant, August had been true to his word, and the supernatural forces that had assaulted him, kept their distance. The pain in his injured arm had ebbed but left a gnawing itch that took every ounce of his strength to not claw through his skin for some sense of relief.

During their travel, Edgar interrogated Johnny about his spectral condition and how he came to possess Edgar's creation. Johnny's voice was monotone and there were few illuminating explanations. Upon his death, Johnny had indeed seen a circle of blinding light, but the lighthouse specter which had taken his life chased him away from it, preventing him from crossing over to whatever plane awaited him. Ellie had broken down in tears and excused herself upon hearing how her brother had been hiding in the shadows until Edgar arrived. When it came to how Johnny had become trapped in his "mechanical contraption" he simply responded that the crystal had lured him in.

And as far as Johnny was concerned, this was Hell.

"Stop. Stop it." Ellie interrupted, crying again. "Please."

Edgar saw how upset she had become, and his curiosity was not that cruel. "Another time," he told Johnny.

"Remove the key," Johnny answered.

"What was that?" Edgar asked.

"The key. Remove it. I don't need winding."

Edgar couldn't comprehend his meaning. Without his key, the mainspring would wind down and lock all his drive wheels and spindles. He'd be immobile.

"But then you couldn't move."

"Could."

"The mainspring will lock your workings..." Edgar stopped. "Lock the workings..." he repeated to himself.

"Johnny," Edgar called to him formally and waited for the bird to nod in acknowledgement. "I'd like to disconnect something as an experiment." Edgar felt foolish asking permission of something he built, but while it was a creation of his, it was clearly no longer his creation in the possessive sense.

Johnny looked upon him for a moment and then extended his left wing.

Edgar held up his long nose pliers for Johnny to see. "I am going to disconnect your wing from your main drive but leave the wing mechanism intact."

Johnny nodded in understanding, or maybe approval. Ellie was silent as Edgar inserted the long-nose pliers under Johnny's wing and worked a pin free.

Edgar released the wing and it fell limp and extended at Johnny's side like the arm of a paralysis victim.

Johnny spun his head ninety-degrees as if in surprise.

"Now," Edgar instructed, "attempt to retract your wing."

Johnny straightened his head and fidgeted his talons in a short two-step, then went still as if concentrating.

The wing twitched once, causing both Ellie and Edgar to gasp, then retracted fully.

"Interesting," Edgar said. "Now.... Can you raise it?"

Johnny's talons did another two-step, his body went still again, but nothing happened. The raven seemed to shiver as if fluffing itself and Edgar heard its inner workings whirring futilely. Then Johnny shook his lowered head and said, "Damn."

"Johnny," Ellie scolded.

"Amazing," Edgar said. "Not your fault Johnny. It appears you're able to actuate your mechanical components without a power source, but only if they are connected to some sort of drive system."

"Meaning?" Ellie asked.

"He doesn't need the mainspring to power his movements. If I remove it, he'll never need winding again and be able to move freely under his own power." Excited by this revelation, Edgar turned to Johnny, "You are more than in control, Johnny. You are the power source."

Ellie clapped and let out a short cheer.

Johnny bobbed his head up and down and said, "Yes. Yes. Yes. Yes."

But Edgar fell still and melancholy. Johnny was in control because he was a new and intact spirit. But what of the spirits Edgar had weakened and degraded with his machine? How much power did they contain? And how much control did they have?

"Oh dear," Edgar said, "I think I fully understand what James is doing now."

"What?"

"I think Johnny's spirit willingly entered the crystal, which explains why he was capable of maintaining his free will. James forced the others while in a weakened state."

"Where are you going with this?" she asked.

"I've inadvertently helped create a new slave labor force. And I think I'm going to be ill."

CHAPTER XXX

Upon arriving in Washington, DC, Ellie asked, "So what's first on the agenda?"

Edgar pulled the copy of *Scientific American* out of his jacket pocket and opened it, "We've arrived in time to see the troop transport ship which uses a new Corliss Steam Engine invented by a Mister G.H. Corliss."

"What makes this engine different than any other?"

Edgar could tell by the way Ellie was looking past him that she had only asked the question to entertain him, so he kept his response brief. "This concept uses a wrist-plate to convey the valve motion from a single eccentric to four gears to increase thermal efficiency."

"Right," she said with a half-smile.

"You know," he said, taking her free hand, "I appreciate the effort."

Her smile widened. "Why don't I get us a nice room while you go see this exhibition?"

Edgar's head cocked to the side as if he couldn't believe what he heard. Surely this was some sort of test? He hesitated with his response.

"I'm serious," she added, shaking her hand free.

"All right, if you're certain."

"I am."

He kissed her cheek. "Where shall I find you?"

"I don't know, any recommendations?"

"There's the Willard Hotel on Pennsylvania Ave. You can see the White House from most of the rooms."

She smiled wide like an adolescent girl attending her first ball. "That sounds wonderful. I've never seen the Capitol before."

Edgar looked at the bags. "I should come with you first."

Ellie touched his shoulder and said with a smile, "Nonsense. I'll get a coach and use my feminine wiles to make the driver load our bags for me."

"Why Miss Feller, such language is not befitting a lady." Edgar couldn't help but snicker. "If he seems unsure of the name, ask him for the old City Hotel. It's changed names recently."

"Okay, I will."

"Thank you again. I promise to make it up to you."

"Well, Mister Poe, I look forward to that."

With that, he tipped his head and bid her ado.

"Be careful," called Johnny, his voice hitting two notes, although stressing the *Be* instead of the *Careful*. He'd get the hang of it soon enough.

"I will! Keep an eye on your sister for me," he added.

After talking to a few local residents, Edgar found the exhibition was being held about a quarter of a mile downstream, on the bank of the Potomac River. Deciding to hold onto the last few coins he had, he walked. The sun arched high, and a cool breeze prevented him from working up a sweat.

When he arrived, there was no mistaking he was in the right place. A large crowd had gathered on the grassy knoll, some sitting on blankets, most standing, all waiting patiently. Men in uniform, standing at attention, lined the dock.

Barely able to see the water's edge, Edgar weaved in between the crowd and excused himself as he bumped and jostled individuals.

"Ladies and gentlemen, there it is," said a well-dressed man through a speaking trumpet, perched above the crowd on a scaffold, "The Burleson."

From downstream, an ironclad vessel plowed through the still waters as the onlookers gawked. She was three decks high with two smokestacks forward of amidships, standard for a riverboat. Her sides had been pushed to the outer edges of the hull, so it appeared as if a city block of row houses had been built upon a dock and set adrift. The only portholes appeared to be along the upper deck and the only entrance, a large gate and bridge at the bow. The unfortunate vessel had then been hung with iron sheets and left black as tar. Only the US

Navy could build something so ugly. An ecstatic murmur of praise and of revulsion filled the air.

"She is 270 feet in length, is powered by six boilers," the well-dressed man on the scaffold gave his pitch, "and can transport one-thousand tons of equipment, supplies, and men upriver at ten knots! Twice as fast as the best paddleboat.

"Built of the strongest oak timber and protected by one-and-a-half-inch thick iron panels, The Burleson can safely transport troops and equipment anywhere in the western territories! It's a movable fortress!"

The stranger next to him bumped his elbow into Edgar's side as if they were friends and said, "It can carry an entire battalion, horses and all."

Edgar faked a smile. "Impressive." But from what he saw, this new naval transport ship was nothing more than a common riverboat with iron sides and without the fixed paddlewheel at the stern. Edgar assumed the ship to be using a two-bladed, spiral propeller. He had read about the screw drive application and seen working drawings but had yet to witness the technology implemented. That in of itself was not enough to keep him rooted in the ever-growing crowd.

His time was better spent searching for James Laurent, so he pushed his way through the spectators trying to get a glimpse of everyone wearing a top hat. Most allowed him passage without complaint, but there were a few who begrudgingly stepped aside.

When Edgar finally broke free of the sea of people, his arm ignited in pain at the sight of the hooded skeleton. He clutched his arm and pressed his thumb deep into the wound Ellie had lovingly bandaged.

"Here?" he mumbled, "not now."

The world fell silent as fear strangled his heart. Chest tight, pulse quickening, Edgar swallowed hard and steeled his nerves. He survived his first encounter with the unholy creature, and he would survive this one, though he wished he had more than his knife upon his person.

The creature stood ten feet away from him and raised its bony arm to point behind Edgar. Sure, it was a trick, his gaze remained locked on the hell spawn until a terror-filled scream broke the silence. He turned around to see the transport ship had veered toward the peer at a velocity too great to allow adequate stopping time.

Edgar dared a glance over his shoulder, afraid of the skeletal monstrosity sneaking up on him, and finishing what it started. The creature was no longer there, he looked left and right, but there was no sign of it. The pain ebbed and he eased up on the pressure he was applying. Surprisingly, the gauze was still free of blood. He knew then, the wound was unnatural.

Screams filled the air. Bumped between several spectators as they ran away, Edgar dodged left, then right as the crowd dispersed in a frenzy.

He shoved his way through the panicked crowd with disregard for his own safety and it took every ounce of strength he had to remain upright.

Wood snapped and buckled beneath the crushing inertia of iron. The peer collapsed beneath the transport ship's hull, its blunt bow riding up the damp riverbank and crushing helpless spectators who thought the shore protection enough. An explosion rocked the ground and sent the remains of the peer into the air. Fire and splinters rained down, most of it splashing into the water, some onto the fleeing crowd. Whether the explosion was from the boiler or stock-piled munitions on the craft was irrelevant, the carnage was the same.

Edgar stumbled and fell as many others toppled over. Someone who managed to stay on his feet stomped on his hand in their haste to get away. He tucked it against his chest and regained his footing.

"Help me. Help me!"

To his right, a woman lay on the ground clawing at the massive log and burning debris atop her legs. The scaffolding erected for the announcer had crashed down upon her, pinning her under its weight.

Edgar dashed to her side and immediately tossed the loose boards aside before the creeping flames could cinder her flesh.

"Thank you," the woman said with tear-filled eyes.

"Please relax, Madame," he said in the most calming tone he could muster with his labored breath.

When he attempted to move the crossbeam, the bones in his shoulder blades and back creaked in protest, the sound eliciting a reflexive flinch.

"Are you all right?" asked the woman as Edgar removed his hand from the log.

"Don't worry about me," he said, then looked around for any able bodies to help. Most of the crowd had vanished; those who remained were either injured or already aiding another less fortunate soul. A few stood around idly, either in shock, or gawking at the carnage. The moans of the injured like a symphony of pain and anguish to his morbid ear.

As Edgar used one of the loose boards as a brace against the log, he saw a soldier crawling through the mud on the riverbank. Though his uniform looked ripped, he appeared uninjured other than the bleeding gash from his forehead.

"You there," he called to the man, "can you help us?"

The soldier, a Private, stopped and stood, then after a brief glance around at the carnage, nodded and approached them.

"We need to lift this log off her leg," he said to the Private.

The man nodded and bent at the knees, and though his refusal to speak was odd, Edgar assumed it was shock and said nothing.

Edgar turned to the woman and said, "On three, we're going to lift. Think you can slide yourself out?"

"Yes."

"Good." Edgar then looked to the Private. "You ready?"

Again, the Private merely nodded.

Edgar dug his feet into the ground and grabbed hold of the log, "One…two…three…"

The two men worked together and managed to hoist the beam high enough for the woman to scuttle out from underneath.

"Thank you," she said as she massaged her injured leg.

Edgar's gaze locked on the large, abrasion across her calf. He saw no obvious splinters. As he turned to face the Private to thank him for his assistance, the man swayed.

"Private, are you alright?" Edgar made a move to steady the man.

Before he could offer support, the Private's right hand shot toward his temple and his eyes lolled upward until Edgar could only see the whites. He fell to the ground, face-first. Edgar's first impression of the man had been wrong.

A sliver of iron protruded out from the back of his skull and was the cause of the blood trickle.

"Is he," the woman asked as Edgar bent down beside him but dared not finish her question.

He pressed his fingers on the carotid artery, just below the man's jaw line, and took his eyes off the Private only to look upon the woman as he spoke. "No, but his pulse is weak."

"You have to help him," she pleaded, obviously no longer caring about herself, but this stranger who stepped up and put her needs above his own.

"Madame, I'll do everything I can."

Edgar slipped off his blazer and he searched the horizon for any Emergency Teams. He could only hope those too cowardly to remain and offer help had at least alerted the authorities.

A lone horse whinnied as it waded through the water, distracting Edgar's attention from the task at hand. He found himself lost in the moment as the animal exited the water and strutted toward the grass. Though he knew the creature was merely looking for a place to dry off, he could not look away as the beast sniffed and pawed the ground. As if finding the optimum spot, the horse bent his front knees, leaned to the left, and flopped to the ground. It rolled to one side, stood up, then did it all again, this time to the other side.

Though it pleased him to see the animal alive and well, it also reminded him of the twenty or so still trapped inside the doomed vessel.

"Aren't you going to do something?" said the woman.

Not bothering to reply, Edgar ripped one of his sleeves off his shirt to use as a make-shift bandage. He wrapped the man's head all the while wondering if he should remove the shrapnel. Blood seeped through the thinning material and Edgar could imagine the non-stop torrent that would flow once the iron sliver was removed. The decision was made. He was ill-equipped to face such a scenario.

From the water's surface, a light gleamed, and for a moment, thinking the boat had been some sort of submersible, and the woman's prayer answered, Edgar was filled with hope. The possibility that all was not lost inspired confidence within him. The light grew in intensity, and Edgar waited for the ship to break the surface and all aboard to disembark safely, but then another light emerged, followed by two more, then ten.

Dozens of circular doorways to the afterlife presented themselves. Edgar was a fool. The people standing around idly were not spectators gawking at the gore, but the specters of the dead themselves. Gooseflesh rippled across his body and a slight twinge of pain irradiated from his arm. An overwhelming feeling of dread crept over him. The fact that he could see these circles and apparitions clearly without the aid of his refracting lenses frightened him.

"Why are you stopping?" asked the woman.

"I've done all I can," he said, trying to mask his fear and wondering how many of those circles of lights were going to go unused.

Her nostrils flared as she breathed deeply. "Nonsense."

"All I can do is apply pressure to stop the bleeding, anything else could kill him."

"We can pray," she said, matter-of-factly.

Edgar looked off, hoping to see an emergency team, but they had yet to arrive. "I suppose," he finally said.

The woman gave a smile, nodded, and then began.

CHAPTER XXXI

Though it had felt like an eternity sitting beside the injured man, keeping pressure around the metal splinter to ebb the blood flow, and listening to the dozens of injured all around moan and beg for help, it had only taken a military unit ten minutes to arrive on the scene. They were followed by two groups of volunteers who seemed too preoccupied with who was going to get paid what to provide any sort of relief. As if being considered first on scene paid more. Lives were at stake, and he aimed to write a column to emasculate each and every one of those supposed volunteers.

Fortunately, the men of the Army were more concerned with providing aid than monetary gain. Edgar released the wounded Private in his care to more experienced men. Though their immediate diagnosis was not promising, they assured him they would do anything and everything to save the man's life.

Edgar passed several disembodied spirits as he walked the burned and bloody grounds. He kept his head down, trying not to let on that he could see them and despite their violent end, none were aggressive toward him. Their faces wore confused looks as the rescue teams worked on the living while others hauled their soulless husks away. People did not instantly turn into hostile spirits. It was a slow process, a deterioration of will and moral fiber, he rationed. When he made the conscious decision to approach and interact with one of them, he noticed several shadowy cloaked figures guiding disoriented spirits into the bright circular doorways.

Fear overrode his curiosity, and he made his way straight for the road, not stopping for a moment to help any of the injured. But coming toward him, a few men escorted a man in a top hat toward the shoreline.

Couldn't be, he thought, but then saw the Specter Eliminator trailing behind.

His first instinct was to storm up to him, jam the tip of James's nose deep into his cranium, and reclaim what was his, but instead he ducked into a cropping of black mulberry bushes. He edged a few blunt-toothed leaves to the side as James walked to the center of the devastation, raised the lance, and let loose a cloud of iodized bitter salts. He wore a genuine grin now, like a child making soap bubbles.

When James put down the lance and pulled out his own mechanical device—the damned spirit collector with a fresh crystal—Edgar's mind worked in double-time deciphering James's ultimate plan.

Was it possible foul play was the cause of this tragedy? Could James be so scrupulous as to sabotage his competitors and endanger the lives of so many? And to what gain?

Hearing the symphonic ting of the colliding tines on James's machine, Edgar had his answer. From this distance, he could not hear what the men were saying, so by all rights he should not have heard the reverberating vibrations. He searched his surrounding area to discover another similar device to James's portable one, this one mounted on the tree the mulberry bushes encircled, and in that moment, Edgar was certain if he searched the area, he'd find more collecting devices.

How did you do it? How could you do it? Edgar wondered. Clearly James sabotaged the boiler. Was it a simple fouling of the works, or an actual bomb? But no, the ship only exploded when it struck the pier. It had veered off course before the explosion. Did he sabotage the rudder or steering? Simply intending for the ship to appear uncontrollable and thereby securing more federal funds for his own endeavors? But then why the concealed spirit collectors? And why be ready with the Specter Eliminator? No, however he did it, James had clearly meant to kill as many people as possible.

As the man swapped the crystal on his machine for a fresh one, Edgar abandoned his hiding spot and made a mad rush toward his enemy. James was preoccupied with his device, and the accompanying soldiers were looking off, surveying the damage.

Getting right up on James, Edgar snatched the new crystal from its housing, shocking all of the men. Before James could react, Edgar chucked the crystal into the river. Two of James's men hooked Edgar by the arms and restrained him before he could grab the Specter Eliminator's lance.

"Get your hands off me," he demanded as he struggled to break free.

"I am surprised to see you here, Mister Poe," James said, stepping closer.

"No doubt," Edgar said, leaning forward so that the two were nearly nose to nose. "Did you receive a wire telling you otherwise?"

James smiled wide. "Why I'm certain I have no idea of what you speak."

"Just as I'm sure these men have no clue as to what you are really doing." Edgar gave another jerk of his arms, but the men's grip was firm and steadfast. Their countenances uncaring and unchanging, and Edgar doubted they would believe him at this point if he laid the truth out for them. "I'd like my property back."

"Is everything all right over here?" someone asked.

Edgar turned to see who was speaking and was more than relieved to see an officer of the law dressed in a starched, navy-blue overcoat. The afternoon sun refracting off his gold-plated badge.

"Arrest this man!" Edgar demanded.

"Pardon me," James replied with an indignant, quizzical look.

The officer slapped his Billy-bat into his open palm and said, "Unhand this man immediately."

Though the two men obeyed the command, Edgar was sent stumbling as they released him with authority. He caught himself and gave them a stern look as he straightened his jacket.

"Explain," the officer said, looking directly at Edgar.

Edgar could speak of every dishonorable thing he believed James guilty of, but without sufficient evidence, they would be nothing more than unfounded accusations. Instead, he remained with the facts. "This man shot me and stole my property." Edgar indicated his machine.

"And you wish to press charges?" asked the patrolman.

Edgar looked James in the eye and said, "Absolutely."

James smiled that wide, toothy grin, the smug look only infuriating Edgar more. "Officer, I assure you I've stolen nothing."

"I have witnesses!"

The officer's gaze searched Edgar and James for any tell-tale signs that one of them might be lying, but Edgar had already seen James's poker face. The man was as hard to read as a stone. There was no sweat beading on his brow, no shifting of the eyes, and no mumbling of words as he searched for just the right thing to say. Just that damned smile. He remained calm and collective, the consummate professional.

The officer reached out for the machine and said, "I'll be confiscating this, and we'll all have to go down to the station until this is sorted."

"That won't be necessary officer," James said, reaching into his jacket. "I have what you need to settle this dispute right here."

James unfolded a document and held it upright. Edgar's jaw went slack at the sight of the gold embossed eagle insignia with red ribbon. He knew what it was before he read a single line, but how it came to be was beyond his comprehension.

Can't be, he thought as he read the words *United States Patent*. But it was, right there in the second paragraph. That document granted James the right to exclude him from his own device for the next fourteen years.

This had to be a joke. How could this fraud get a patent for his invention? And so quickly?

"It's a lie," he said, "a sham of the system."

The officer puffed his chest and released a nasal sigh. "Looks legal and proper to me. Afraid there's nothing I can do here. But you two," the officer leveled his Billy-bat at the two thugs, "keep your hands off this man."

The thugs nodded, but Edgar's thirst for justice was not satiated. He stepped right up to James, not caring about the men or the officer. With the bridges of their noses just millimeters apart he asked, "Just how far does your reach go?"

James cracked that same smile Edgar was beginning to loath but said nothing.

Infuriated, Edgar grabbed James's lapels. "Answer me!"

The officer grabbed Edgar by the wrist and wrestled his hand free. "That's enough from you. Let's go." The officer pulled Edgar's arm, tugging him away from James.

"This isn't over," Edgar said as he was escorted away. "Not by a long shot."

CHAPTER XXXII

Once the officer released Edgar to his own, personal recognizance, he sought out Ellie, and filled her in. He then went on to explain his doubts that any of the works presented by James Laurent in their earlier dealings were of the man's own design. The man was likely a talentless fraud who made his mark in the world by stealing the hopes and dreams of others he had the gall to deem beneath him. Despite these feelings, the crowd that gathered to witness James' exhibition was larger than Edgar could have imagined.

Edgar and Ellie worked their way through the crowd, vying for a good vantage point. Johnny perched on Edgar's shoulder gave him the appearance of someone important, or at least someone of prominence, and they had little trouble reaching the front of the roped off spectators' area.

A stage had been erected on one side of the National Mall, and bleachers on the opposite. To the right of the stage, a squad of soldiers stood at the ready. With his bodyguards in tow, President Taylor made his way up onto the stage. The moment *Old Rough and Ready* took to the stage, Edgar knew this exhibition was an exercise in formality; the grant money was as good as James's, even if the troop transport ship hadn't been destroyed.

President Taylor was a Major General who had defied the odds by living through four wars. He was credited for the victories of two major battles during the Mexican American War and defeated the Seminole Indians in Florida. The amount of bloodshed he had endured would send a weaker man scurrying into a hole never to see the light of day again, but Zachary Taylor had become President of the United States. He would certainly see the value of powered armor.

"Ladies and gentleman, Mister President," the announcer called everyone's attention. "It is my distinct honor to present to you, James Laurent, and his PA-6." The President cocked his head to the left and put his hands together in applause, the crowd followed.

Edgar traced his line of sight to see a dozen men marching in tandem across the open field, the sun glistening off the copper plating of their metallic suits nearly blinding. He estimated each suit to be seven feet tall and probably three-and-a-half to four feet wide at the elbows. The suits resembled the plate-armor of a medieval knight, each section over—or underlapping the other to completely cover the fragile body inside. The cylindrical helmets should have reminded him of smokestacks, but all he thought of was James' pompous top hat. *The vanity of the man.* He wondered how well the men could see through the narrow eye-slits.

Though they marched in formation, there was something too mechanical about the movements, a far cry from the fluid grace Edgar had been taught all those years ago in the academy. There was just no way for the external single-axis hinges to duplicate the flexibility of the human joints.

Hands raised to shield their eyes from the brilliant, reflected light, the crowd cheered as James stepped out from behind his creations. He smiled in triumph as he approached the stage. Edgar gnawed on a loose piece of skin from his lower lip as James and the President shook hands, Taylor encompassing James's hands with both of his as if they were the best of friends reuniting for the first time in years.

James took the podium and put on his disingenuous face. "It is an honor to stand here before you today and present to you the soldier of the future. Imagine soldiers impervious to swords, bullets, and artillery. Imagine soldiers who are faster and stronger than any enemy they could face. Imagine an army protected from the hazards of war."

The crowd interrupted his spiel with applause.

"Well, you don't have to imagine it any longer. Enjoy this exhibition of Laurent's Powered Armor Suits," James smiled, sure he'd hooked them all. "And I'd like you to imagine a war fought without the loss of your sons."

Ellie leaned close to him and whispered, "They are impressive."

Rather than chastise her for voicing her uneducated opinion, he remained silent. Instead, he dissected each movement. There was no denying the ingeniousness of the design, no matter who's it was, but for Edgar, the price to power such a thing was too great.

"It has taken us years of testing and prototyping to bring the PA-6 to you today," James continued. "True, a few men have given their lives to the cause as we ironed out the faults, but I assure you, here and now, this is perfection."

Spoken like a true politician, the truth within the lie, Edgar thought. Disgusted by the sight of James, Edgar turned his attention back to the armored soldiers.

From his vantage point, Edgar could not see a single scrap of flesh exposed and he could only imagine the sheer weight of all those overlapping plates. Gears, cogs, and cables were fashioned at the elbow coup, with rods mounted on their shins connected to a large gear located at the small of their backs. If a weakness existed, it would be there. One could possibly cram a wedge into the toothed gear and gum the whole system up, if one could manage to sneak up on such a thing. Smaller, clock gears were fastened at the temples of the helmets and Edgar assumed their function was to extend and retract the magnifying eye lenses. Acting parallel to the wearer's movements were artificial ligaments attached along each appendage and though the invention sickened him, Edgar couldn't help the anticipation of seeing the physical enhancements to speed and strength they produced.

The dozen armor-clad men stopped in a line at the far end of the field.

The formation of soldiers across from the spectator area filed onto the field. As they established a defensive firing line four rows deep, it was clear they were part of the exhibition. There had to be a hundred of them.

The unit of PA-6s advanced at a walking pace toward the unarmored soldiers. Their movements' mechanical but intimidating. The hundred soldiers leveled their guns at the advancing men inside the metallic armaments.

James stepped to the side of the podium. "Mister President, would you give the order?"

"With pleasure," President Taylor said. He stood and stepped forward, "Fire!"

The first row of guns fired in unison. Smoke plumed from the barrels as bullets ricocheted off the metallic exoskeletons, kicking up chunks of dirt and grass after veering off course.

The PA-6s continued to advance.

The second row fired, but not one of the dozen PA-6s fell or even slowed.

The third row fired, then the fourth. But the PA-6s kept advancing. Three quarters of the distance already closed.

"Hold your line," President Taylor commanded to steady the nervous soldiers.

The PA-6s were so close when the first row fired again that the ricochet threatened to kill them with their own bullets. The line broke and scattered. The armor-clad soldiers in the PA-6s marched calmly and steadily over the hundred soldiers' position without even firing a shot.

The crowd applauded wildly. President Taylor shook his head, frustrated by the retreat of his men, but also in admiration. James Laurent looked swollen with pride.

Five soldiers wheeled a cannon through the ranks, their screwed up faces a sign of the exertion on their bodies from pushing it. A lone, armor-clad soldier stepped out of line from his group and approached the cannon while the five soldiers scurried back to their unit. Obviously afraid of what was about to transpire.

The mechanized soldier hoisted the cannon, mount, and all with ease, and held it under his arm. A mule brayed at the edge of the field and pulled a cart across the open space. The soldiers who had spurred the animal took cover.

A member of the artillery squad stepped forward, a torch in hand. He ignited the powder in the vent, then rushed back into the ranks, and as the short fuse burned, cinders danced on the breeze.

The cannoneer took aim at the moving cart and when the cannon roared, the cart exploded, throwing the mule a good twenty yards.

As the crowd applauded, the cannoneer dropped his spent weapon and took up another. As he did, one of the other armored soldiers stepped out of the group and made himself an easy target. The cannoneer took aim at his brethren.

"Oh," Ellie exclaimed before raising her hand to her mouth.

Several others in the crowd gasped as well, all sharing the same frightening image of springs, gears, cogs, flesh, and bone erupting in a plume of blood from the cannonball's impact.

The torch bearer touched off the powder in the vent.

The boom of the gun powder left a ringing in Edgar's ears and the wind carried an aromatic combination of burnt paper and chalk from the cloud of smoke.

The brave soldier caught the iron ball before it could make contact with his chest. As the crowd roared with excitement, he playfully tossed the ball up into the air, then hurled it back at the soldier who fired it with the same intensity caused by the cannon's combustion.

To demonstrate the suit's protective abilities, the soldier allowed the cannonball to strike him, knocking him off his feet and onto his backside. When he stood, there was merely a small dent in the chest plating.

Edgar knew then the copper hue was a rouse, perhaps done to give opposing armies a false sense of hope. If iron had struck copper with such force, the damage would be irreparable. *Bronze perhaps,* he wondered.

"Amazing," someone in the stand said.

"Truly remarkable."

"No one will disrespect this great country again."

Edgar could only shake his head. Their blind acceptance of James's PA-6 only showed their ignorance. Should war erupt, other countries may fall to America's new militia, but it would only be a matter of time before their own mechanical monstrosities were birthed. Unless that was James' plan all along? To create an arms race where he was the sole supplier. He leaned to his left and said to Ellie's ear, "Something needs to be done. James needs to be stopped."

"How?" she asked, eyes still on the show of strength.

"I should challenge him to a duel right here on this open field."

"And you would be an honorable man facing a dishonorable adversary."

"Not enough to kill him," Johnny said in his monotone voice Edgar had yet to adjust to. "Abolish the idea."

Though it pained him to admit it, Edgar could not argue either point. A man courting death as James had was not to be trusted to remain civil with everything on the table. He would stoop to depths Edgar could never imagine. And even if he did manage to defeat James, there were no guarantees someone else wouldn't come along and pick up his mantle.

"What are you thinking?" Ellie asked, breaking the sudden silence between them.

"We need to find his workshop and destroy all traces of this profane process. And make the suits appear unstable so no one would dream of copying James's design."

"There's no way to ensure that," Johnny argued.

"What other course of action do we have?" Edgar asked, voice dull and flat.

Neither Johnny nor Ellie responded, and Edgar took their silence as agreement. His mind drifted from the show of strength and resilience playing out on the field and went to work formulating a plan. Given the armored troops had marched to the exhibition rather than being delivered, Edgar deduced James's workshop to be somewhere in Washington DC. Somewhere close. His gaze drifted toward James, and he couldn't help but wonder if his enemy had seen him, expected him, or even if he cared at this point. Every step Edgar made, James seemed to be two ahead. Would he anticipate such a move?

Even from across the field, Edgar could clearly see the smug look on James's face as he conversed with President Taylor. It was evident the project was about to be fast-tracked and Edgar would need to make his move tonight.

"Ellie, I want you and Johnny to go back to the hotel."

Ellie's back straightened. "What for?" she asked, her voice high-pitched and offended.

Several people turned their heads and narrowed their eyes, but she paid them no mind.

"It's too dangerous," Edgar said in a quiet whisper. "I don't want anything to happen to you. I couldn't bear it."

"And I don't want anything to happen to you. We're in this together."

"Yes," Johnny chimed in.

The level of camaraderie between the three of them excited and frightened Edgar. It had been so long since he had any one of value in his life. Sure, he had colleagues and acquaintances, but they were people who preferred to be on his good side to avoid receiving his criticisms. Definitely not people he would define as friends.

"Johnny, could you fly over there and eavesdrop for us?"

"Yes," came the reply.

"Really?" Ellie asked Johnny. "You are very conspicuous."

Edgar scowled, partly because he wasn't, but mostly because she was correct. He had not built the bird with covert surveillance in mind.

"Quite right," he told Johnny. "Fly high. Circle around behind them."

Johnny spread his wings and took flight from Edgar's shoulder.

An announcement was made, and the crowd erupted into applause. Edgar wasn't sure of what he'd missed but deemed it irrelevant since the armored men still threw cannon balls at each other on the field.

With all eyes on the exhibition, Johnny managed to circle around the left unnoticed and perch on a large oak tree providing the stage with shelter from the midday sun.

The mechanized soldiers performed a drill routine that highlighted the powered armors' speed and strength. They pulled carts loaded with munitions, raced horses the length of the mall, and leapt over the grandstand like giant copper toads. The circus performance made Edgar wish he knew more about the PA-6's inner workings. What kind of shock absorbers were in the joints? Hydraulic or pneumatic? What was the composition of the suit's metal?

After more applause, James took the podium. "That concludes our exhibition. Thank you all for coming." The arrogant scalawag went so far as to take his top hat off and bow to the crowd.

President Taylor patted James on the back and James turned around with his hand extended. All smiles, the two shook hands as if they were best of friends.

"What do we do?" Ellie asked as the people around them stood to leave.

Not wanting to lose any more of the element of surprise, Edgar said, "Keep hidden in the crowd and hope Johnny comes through."

Both Ellie and Edgar turned slightly before standing, keeping their faces to the side to avoid being seen head on.

They moved with the crowd, remaining in its center until they were able to duck behind a large pine tree. Edgar took Ellie by the arm and pulled her over to it. The people shuffled on, lost in their individual conversations about what they had seen and future possibilities.

Edgar peeked around the pine, hoping the PA-6 suits were still within sight and found James giving President Taylor a closer look at them.

"Do you see Johnny?" Ellie asked.

"No," he said, not bothering to look for the mechanical raven. His gaze locked on President Taylor who was running his fingers down the metal plating, looking like a love-struck schoolboy.

"There he is!"

Edgar couldn't help but turn to see, the level of excitement in Ellie's voice demanded attention.

Johnny landed on Ellie's shoulder, and she immediately stroked a finger against his chest plate. For a moment Edgar wondered if the gesture was wasted or not, but then Johnny spoke, and Edgar's mind went to work.

"Whitehouse for dinner."

"Perfect," Edgar mumbled, then turned back to see James and President Taylor still conversing. "We should have ample time to do what we need to do."

"If James's workshop is relatively close," Ellie said.

Edgar pursed his lips before saying, "Now's not the time for pessimism." Then addressed Johnny, "Follow the armor. We need to know where his workshop is."

CHAPTER XXXIII

Edgar and Ellie ducked into a cropping of bushes as the mechanized soldiers passed single file through a barn-style door into a large brick building. The sun had set as they followed Little Johnny nearly a quarter mile past the newly finished East Wing of the Castle to be known as The Smithsonian Institute. Edgar had made the mental note of returning to see the completed effort, already recognizing medieval Gothic architecture and Romanesque motifs. The building would be a perfect backdrop for a new, deliciously twisted tale of the macabre.

Johnny circled high above, keeping watch over the workshop, and them.

"What are we going to do?" Ellie asked.

No guards stood watch, but it was safe to assume everyone was inside by the black smoke billowing from the chimney. Wishing they had had a chance to arm themselves better, Edgar suggested, "Let's search the perimeter."

They found no guards and no other entrances, so they crossed the street to wait in the dark alley. As they entered, their footsteps on the gravel alerted someone deeper down the alley. Edgar halted Ellie with his left arm and drew his knife.

"Whoa," George Darby said, hands up in surrender.

"What are you—?" Before he could finish, two more familiar faces stepped out from the dark.

Andrew, the Cherokee said, "Osiyo."

"To hi tsu," William added.

Though he knew the gentlemen capable of speaking English, Edgar refused to insult his friends by asking for them to speak it. If they felt comfortable enough to say hello to him in their native tongue, he would respond in kind. "Osiyo."

"Osiyo," Ellie answered too.

George whistled in surprise and William looked upon him like he was an idiot. George nodded and put his hand over his mouth.

"What are you doing here?" Edgar asked.

"Waiting for you," George answered. "I want to help."

"What about Kimberly? Is she safe?" Edgar asked.

"She's with her grandfather," George said. "And God help anyone who tries to take that little girl from that bull of a man."

Edgar recalled meeting Arlene's father at her and George's wedding. Given Kimberly was the only earthly connection the man had to his beloved daughter, *God help them indeed.*

"And how did you find us?" Edgar asked Andrew and William.

"When you left, Chief John Ross asked us to gather information on this James Laurent," Andrew said.

"We've been tracking him and scouting this shop for days," said William.

"And they accosted me before I got too close," George added, crossing his arms in front of his chest in defiance.

Under lighter circumstances, Edgar would have found amusement in George's over-reacting. Knowing Andrew and William on a personal level, he knew accosted was too strong a word.

"Andrew and William, I have to ask," Edgar said, "we're about to do more than scout. Are you certain you want to be involved?"

"We saw what happened at the exhibition and could do nothing to help," William said. "The enslaver of souls must be stopped."

Edgar nodded in understating. Their help would not have been appreciated.

"John Ross may get angry with us—"

"But we like you," William finished for Andrew.

"Can't say that about many white men," Andrew added.

"I appreciate it, both of you. As for you, George, it is good you came. They performed a demonstration of the suits and for the life of me I could not find the crystals powering them. I thought they would be exposed."

"They're behind the hypoid gear."

"The large ones mounted on the back?" Edgar asked.

George nodded and said, "Yes."

"We must reclaim these crystals," Andrew said. "It is the will of *Yowa*."

Realizing the only reason the great spirit of the Cherokee nation would want the crystals, he asked, "Has he trapped some of your people's gho... Souls?"

George rolled his eyes, and Edgar knew then and there that the man had not changed his position and was only looking for vengeance.

William and Andrew ignored George and nodded in response to Edgar's question. "But this is a crime against all spirits," Andrew nodded.

"Can the spirits be set free?" Ellie asked.

Andrew nodded. "Chief John Ross is a great man capable of many things."

"Oh," Ellie gasped and then turned to Edgar. "Johnny?"

Edgar nodded, but then shook his head, and then finally settled on a shrug of the shoulders. "I suppose it will be up to him."

Ellie steadied herself against the alley wall and nodded.

"How much longer?" William asked.

Edgar's brow wrinkled as to the meaning of his question. "For what?"

"Men inside to leave."

"We don't know," Ellie answered.

William crossed his arms in front of his chest, gaze locked on the building as if attempting to will the men out.

Edgar, realizing they may be waiting for a while, turned to George, and said, "I know it must have been difficult to leave your daughter."

"It was, but I could learn a thing or two from my eight-year-old. She has her mother's strength. She damn near demanded I fix what I've done. I took her to Paul's after you left my shop."

Edgar smiled. The resilience of children was truly remarkable. He wondered at what turning point in his life he had lost his, and whether it was reasonably the same for all children. Everyone lost that sense of wonder and innocence, whether it was a natural progression of age and maturity, or something ripped away by jealous adults. The idea fascinated him, and Edgar knew there was a story somewhere in there. He would just have to explore it, but now was not the time.

"They're leaving," Ellie said, ducking down.

Everyone followed her lead, though Edgar doubted the men would see them under the cover of darkness and thick underbrush.

The unarmored men spilled out of the workshop all smiles and jocularity, obviously proud of themselves and the exhibition they had performed. Edgar could not blame them; it was not their fault. For a moment he wondered if he could convince them to help if he told them the truth, but with Ellie, George, Andrew, and William by his side, he didn't need to take such a risk.

The small platoon was barely out of sight when Johnny swooped down into the alley and perched on Ellie's shoulder.

"Was that the lot of them," Edgar asked.

"Yes," Johnny answered.

William, Andrew, and George recoiled from the mechanical bird. "What the hell?" George asked.

"This is Mister Johnathan Feller," Edgar said. "Recently deceased."

"Pleased," Johnny said, raising his wings and bowing his head.

"This," he pointed at Johnny's clouded, crystal eye, "is what happens when my infernal machine doesn't degrade the souls before it enters a crystal."

"Astonishing," George said, attempting to touch the crystal, but settling for watching Johnny track his finger back and forth.

"Enough of this," William said and strode confidently out of the alley, recklessly crossing the street directly for the workshop doors.

Edgar gave Andrew a sideways glance. The native shrugged and moved to follow.

Johnny's gears whirred as the mechanical bird flew past him and soared into the air, following James's men.

Edgar said, "Where's Johnny going?"

"He'll be back. He's just making sure no one doubles back," Ellie said.

Edgar nodded, then took up the rear.

William walked straight up to the nearest window and peeked inside. After a brief pause, he waved his arm, signaling them all to move forward.

George immediately went to the door and tried to open it. "Locked," he mumbled, before fidgeting in his pants pocket. He pulled out a set of long, thin tools with hooks on the ends, then bent at the knees, and inserted one into the lock. After just a few moments of twiddling and twirling, a mechanical click echoed and George stood, saying, "Let's go." He opened the door and was the first inside.

Andrew and William followed George's lead, it was obvious to Edgar that his friend had been there before, but as he moved to enter, Ellie grabbed him by the arm.

"What is it?" he asked.

"I'm going to wait for Johnny," Ellie said. "My charms will distract anyone who returns."

"Of course." He kissed her cheek and the look of concern upon her face vanished and was replaced with a wide grin.

"Be careful in there."

Edgar nodded, then entered.

CHAPTER XXXIV

Inside, Edgar was taken aback. At the far end of the shop was a boiler with a large hammerhead mounted on a piston rod by various cylinders and linkages. He drifted toward it, to mentally discern its purpose. He followed a rail used to transfer materials throughout the shop via a miner's cart. The legs of the massive structure were bolted to plates embedded in the masonry floor in an A-frame design. Steam leaked from the connecting pipes and Edgar could not fathom the pressure it took to drive the cylinders in order to raise the mighty ram off the worktable. Scattered on the floor were intricately shaped dies and tups. Off to the left and the right were four more boilers, each attached to a swan-necked crane. All of the equipment appeared to be top of the line, and suddenly, Edgar felt inadequate. There was no denying James held the superior intellect and deeper pockets.

A firm hand grabbed hold of his shoulder; he turned to find George standing behind him. "There's no time for this," he said.

"It's a shame," Edgar said. "The possibilities for good are endless."

George removed his hand. "In James's mind, he *is* doing good."

"I know," Edgar said, then fell silent.

"Let's stick to the plan," George added. "I'll show you what you need to do to remove the crystals, then I've got to find the suit I made."

"Where do you think it is?"

Edgar followed George's gaze to a catwalk leading toward a second-floor room off in the corner. "That's his office," George said, voice dull and flat and Edgar wondered if that's where George suspected James of keeping his daughter.

He dared not ask.

"We must hurry," William said as he approached.

"Right," George replied, snapping out of his apparent self-loathing.

They followed George over to the nearest suit of armor.

George squeezed his hand in between the gear spokes and tapped on a metal plate with his fingertip, the sound hollow. "This is what you're looking for," he said before tugging on the latch. The plate swung away and revealed six crystals clipped onto a rectangular plate.

Six?! Edgar thought. Six crystals to power each suit. That was seventy-two souls enslaved just for the exhibition that day. How many souls would it take to power an army of suits? And what would James do to get them? How many more tunnel cave ins? How many more riverboat accidents? Had James actually sabotaged Edgar's train? It offered a double enticement; James could kill Edgar and, in the process, capture the souls of everyone else killed in the accident.

Where had James gotten these six? Who were they?

"Is it safe to remove them?" Edgar asked, fearing a static shock, or damaging the crystals and causing unnecessary pain to the spirits.

George nodded, as if he would know, and pulled a crystal free.

"All right," George said, handing the crystal to Andrew, "You know where I'll be if you need me."

Edgar nodded, and George darted off.

"Does he need help?" Andrew asked.

"No," Edgar said. "Start gathering the crystals."

They, too, nodded in response and went to the next suit in line. Once the last crystal was pulled free from the suit, the suit sagged and settled as if the tension had been released from its cables and gears.

Edgar dropped the lot in Andrew's bag and moved to the next suit. The two Indian warriors were already two suits ahead of him.

A gun shot rang in the air outside. Andrew and William turned, eyes narrowed, gaze piercing as if they could see through the brick wall.

"Ellie?" Edgar said to himself.

William tapped Andrew on the back and said, "We'll investigate."

"I'll come, too," Edgar nodded.

Before they could reach the workshop door, it opened, and Ellie came in.

"Edgar," she called before seeing him.

Upon hearing her frightened voice, he knew something had gone afoul. Her soft tone carried an unspoken apology. Before he could answer, a metallic ball was lobbed into the workshop and landed with a loud *cur-clunk*.

William and Andrew crouched, one ready to go right, the other left. But it wasn't a bomb. It was Johnny's lifeless raven body — uncoiled springs stuck out at odd angles from a blackened, jagged hole.

"No sudden movements, Mister Poe," James said, pressing the barrel of his pistol against Ellie's temple for emphasis.

William and Andrew raised their hands and stepped to flank Edgar, but stopped when five men adorned in black entered, each armed with a truncheon. One look at the braves and Edgar was sure they would take action at the first opportunity, but until then, they'd let him negotiate with this evil white man.

Edgar looked into Ellie's blue eyes and saw her fear and regret in the pool of tears threatening to cascade down her cheeks. "It's going to be all right," he said, and in his heart, he was not lying.

"Now how can you say that with any certainty?" James asked.

Edgar recognized the gun as the one James had shot him with before, a double-barreled Howdah pistol, loaded with either buckshot, a single slug, or the often-lethal combination of both referred to as "buck and ball." With one disengaged lock plate, James had not reloaded before capturing Ellie and would not be able to take them all down, but certainly he was aware of that. Edgar stole a quick glance at his creation and determined it was indeed a single slug. The question now pondering Edgar's mind was whether or not James would save that final round for him or not.

"Let her go. We both know if you pull that trigger, you're a dead man."

"And who says I'm afraid of death?" James pushed Ellie forward, bringing her one step closer to Edgar. "Tell me, how much loss can one man withstand?"

Edgar had his answer. James had already tried to kill him on two occasions and failed; now he sought a more indirect approach.

James leaned into Ellie's neck and breathed deep, taking in her scent. "She's quite lovely. I'd wager even more so than your dearest Virginia."

Edgar's hands balled into fists, his fingernails digging deep into the soft flesh of his palm. One look in Ellie's fearful eyes and he knew he had to remain calm for her sake no matter what tactics James used.

"You don't have to do this," Edgar said, keeping his hands in the open, palms up.

James shook his head. "You can be so naïve. If not me, then someone else. This is bigger than you and me."

"And where does it stop, James? Are your suits of war going to be fixed with my Spector Eliminator and your Soul Collector to gather spirits on the battlefield? Is that how you will power the next generation? And why wait for war? Why not wipe out the savages once and for all and enslave their heathen souls?"

William tensed and Edgar was unsure if he planned to attack James or himself, but Andrew calmed him and nothing unfortunate occurred.

"Mister Poe, you truly are a genius." James's eyes grew wide as the idea percolated in his mind. "Are you sure you won't work for me?"

Edgar paused, realizing this to be the perfect chance to buy some time.

"How much money did you earn on what is clearly your greatest work?"

"Art is subjective, James," Edgar replied. "You'll have to be more specific."

"Don't worry, I already know the answer. You earned a paltry nine dollars from the sale of *The Raven*, and yet the publishers raked in hundreds, perhaps even thousands on your blood, sweat and tears. I've watched countless others grow fat on my labors as well. Isn't it time we made our fortune on their blood? Their tears?"

Edgar pinched his lower lip with his teeth, the truth in James's words was undeniable, but that was the nature of the business. A contract was placed before him and in the end, he had signed it.

"I had a choice," Edgar finally said. "As do you. Look at this place. Imagine the good you could do for the world."

"None of this is mine, save for the vision," James replied with a sour grin. "But it will be."

"And at what cost?" Edgar shifted his gaze to steal a glance at the two brave warriors anxiously awaiting their moment to strike.

"That's irrelevant," James said, drawing Edgar's attention back.

Disgusted by his adversary's blatant disregard, Edgar said, "Your evil knows no bounds."

"It's not evil to want this nation to stand above all others and turning a profit in doing so. That *is* the American way after all. And I ask you, how can saving lives be considered evil?"

Edgar's gaze remained fixated on the pistol, and the space between its bore and Ellie's temple. In their debate, James was allowing slack. "You're not saving lives; you're trading one for another."

"Souls," James said, that devilish grin causing Edgar's stomach to roil. "We could debate the semantics all night, but that doesn't sound like fun to me."

"It's not here!" George called down from the second floor.

James turned to see who was up in his office, the gun following his gaze and giving Ellie the necessary moment to stomp her heel into James's foot and drive her elbow against his abdomen.

One of the braves let loose a high-pitched battle cry and it was followed by George with, "For Kimmie!" as he ran down the stairs two at a time.

Before James could reposition the gun, Edgar dashed forward, grabbing him by the wrist and keeping the gun pointed in the air, away from Ellie.

"Run," Edgar told Ellie.

In his peripheral, Edgar saw George rush forward to support her arms and move her out of harm's way.

"But—" she tried to argue.

"Now!"

"Always the gentleman," James teased as he struggled against Edgar.

The two were equally matched; neither could gain an advantage over the other.

With Ellie clear of the melee, George came to Edgar's aid.

"No," Edgar told him. "This is between us."

"Edgar, no," Ellie called.

George stepped back, and in Edgar's peripheral he saw William and Andrew engage the henchmen, one already lay unconscious.

In their morbid dance to prove which was Alpha, James's pistol waved wildly in the air. As Edgar pressed his weight forward, hoping to twist James's wrist, forcing him to drop the pistol, an uncontrollable itch emanated from his wound and spread throughout his arm.

"Not now," he mumbled, knowing it meant only one thing. The skeletal figure was near. Death approached. But for who?

"What are you on about?" James asked.

His question went unanswered as Edgar searched the workshop. The distraction was all James needed. He released his hold on Edgar's right arm and slammed a hard fist square against Edgar's jaw. Edgar's head rocked, but his grip on James's pistol arm remained.

"Edgar!" Ellie's voice held a mad-panic and Edgar feared she would do something rash.

"Hold on!" George said. "I'm coming."

Deep down, Edgar knew neither of them could make it to his side in time to prevent the looming barrel of James's pistol from rounding on him. The struggle had shifted to the point of no return, James's weight was bearing down on him, his footing was slipping, and his adversary's grin was widening.

Edgar stole a final glance at Ellie. Even with the terrified look in her eyes, she remained beautiful. Light refracted off a brass lever to Ellie's right and instantly, hope returned.

"Ellie. The lever!"

Her head craned to the right and without thought, she threw her weight onto it. A mechanical arm came to life and travelled on its fixed axis.

James chuckled at him and his pathetic effort.

Edgar's arm burned with an infernal itch, his muscles trembled with fatigue, and his heart thundered in his chest. The mechanical arm came within inches of them and looked as though it was going to fall short of taking James. Knowing this was his only chance, he dug down deep to muster every ounce of strength he had. With a roar, he shoved James back, taking him off his feet and guiding him into the snapping jaws of the crane.

"What the—" James gasped as he was hoisted into the air.

The pistol clanged to the floor without discharging as James threw his hands above his head in hopes of freeing himself. Another crane arm came round; this one operated by George and grabbed James by the legs.

James was slammed against the worktable, legs dangling off the edge. He writhed against his bonds as Edgar made a move toward the operating controls of the massive steam-powered die-press.

"I wouldn't if I was you!" James said, staring straight at Edgar.

Edgar stood there; hand on the final lever, contemplating his action. He had killed many a fictional character in his lifetime but had never taken an actual life before. Though he was a connoisseur of the dark and macabre, he was no killer, but the man before him was a danger to all. There was no denying that. He turned to Ellie and then George for confirmation, both anxiously awaiting his next move, neither betraying their emotions.

With the decision made, he fixed his gaze on the helpless James and pulled the lever.

The press hissed as steam vented from boiler to cylinder.

"You're all going to pay!" James managed to say before the inevitable.

With a reverberating *ping*, his upper half was pulverized beneath the ram head's crushing blow. James's arms rose to welcome the ram, but it was only the counteraction of his chest cavity collapsing. His legs swung limp and thudded to the floor, severed upon impact. Blood jettisoned in all directions, splashing across Edgar's face and chest, the sudden strike causing his body to flinch. Edgar's tongue instinctively rolled over his moistened lips, the coppery tang igniting his taste buds.

Goopy strings of flesh and blood stretched and popped as the hammer rose back into its inert position.

"Ergh!" Ellie turned around and spilled her stomach's contents.

Edgar remained still, James's blood running down his face and dripping from his chin, waiting, watching.

William, Andrew, and George walked up to him, one putting their hand upon his shoulder. "Does that constitute a tragic end?" George asked, the back of his hand pressed against his pursed lips.

"George, you surprise me, I thought you didn't believe," Edgar said.

The slight man pursed his lips and shrugged his shoulders.

There were too many variables for him to answer honestly. Edgar looked around, hoping to see a circle of light. Then a sickening thought crossed his mind. If one was destined for Hell, would an elegant circular doorway present itself?

He doubted it.

The room darkened, although Edgar was the only one who reacted.

"What?" Ellie asked.

Lost for words, Edgar managed to say, "This isn't over."

Andrew and William tensed and searched for danger, but were searching blind.

A black orb hovered at the back wall and grew. Seeping outward like a shadow growing at dusk.

James's spirit cackled, everyone hearing it.

The specter flew from behind the steam press and swooped at Edgar. He fell to the ground and James's malevolent spirit swooped at the group once more before spiraling upward and through the roof, cackling all the way.

The group rose to their feet and waited, but James did not return.

Edgar broke the tense silence by asking, "What kind of suit did you make for him, George?"

"*The* suit," George said, "a more efficient, compact, designed to run off one crystal. But it's not here. So that's good, right?"

Edgar stepped closer to the table's edge, his gaze traveling over the crimson stain. Could James have wanted this? Somehow planned for it? He spotted James's right hand but could not see what he was looking for from his current angle. Edgar hopped on top of the work surface and rummaged through the gore, minding his footing so as not to slip and crack his skull open on the metal.

"What are you looking for?" George asked.

"His ring is missing," Edgar replied.

"What ring," Ellie asked.

"He wore a very distinct ring," Edgar said.

"His mother's ring?" George asked.

"Yes," Edgar said, knowing that if James had the forethought of mounting that family heirloom on George's creation it would be like a homing beacon for his soul.

"What do we do?" Ellie asked.

Edgar slouched as the words failed him. In time, the answer may come to him, but for now, he had to deal with the situation at hand. The danger was too great for Andrew and William to linger around a dead white man. Surely, they would be hung at the gallows without a proper trial.

He turned to them and said, "You two must leave now. It's not safe for you here."

They nodded in agreement, but William held out his hand shortly thereafter.

"I think it would be best if I held onto the crystals for now. Should you be detained, and these found in your possession, the Lord knows what would happen. Ellie and I will safely deliver these to John Ross. You have my word."

Andrew placed his hand upon William's shoulder and nodded. William gave no protest and with a gentleman's handshake, the two Indian braves set course for home.

During the goodbyes, George had checked on the five thugs James had brought with him. Though they had the snot kicked out of them, they were alive, and George relayed the information to Edgar with a nod.

Edgar turned to Ellie and found her knelt down beside the lifeless, mechanical body of her brother. She was gathering the pieces into a neat pile.

"Ellie," he said.

She looked up at him, tears swelling in her eyes. "Can you fix him?"

"Of course," he said, doing his best to muster enough enthusiasm to feign confidence and appease her broken heart, if only for a few moments.

"This would be a lot easier if those savages had killed these men," George said as he sneered down at the five unconscious men.

Edgar, surprised to hear the racist comment, replied, "The fact that they refrained proves them to not be savages, George."

George shrugged his shoulders. "I suppose. Still, it would be easier to sell this as an accident if they had."

With a sniffle, Ellie said, "No one else needs to die today."

"Exactly right," said Edgar. "And given how much of a scoundrel James was, these men might not be a problem at all. Either way, you should head home as well. You have a daughter to think about. If this goes south, I'll be the only one taking the fall for it."

Ellie stood straight, her fire returning. "To hell you will."

"I'm going to let the two of you hatch this out and get while the getting is good."

When his friend moved to leave, Edgar said, "George…"

"Yeah?"

"Thank you for being here," Edgar said.

"Yes, George, thank you," Ellie added.

"You're welcome. Good luck."

As George left, Ellie wasted no time in asking," So what's the plan?"

"I guess we have to wait for these guys to wake up. Everything hinges on them," he said.

"Fine," Ellie said, folding her arms across her bosom. "In the meantime, how about you fix my brother?"

Edgar couldn't help but chuckle. He found Ellie's assertiveness charming. "How about we do it together?"

A smile stretched across her cheeks and the way she looked at him with those hope-filled eyes empowered him. In that moment he knew, with her by his side, he could accomplish anything.

CHAPTER XXXV

Edgar paused on the porch of John Ross's grand home in Tahlequah, the Cherokee capital, and turned to face Ellie. With her brow wrinkled and lips pursed, her worry unnerved him. The question and the fear of its answer danced in her eyes. He shifted his gaze to Little Johnny and asked, "Are you sure about this?"

"Stay with Ellie." Johnny's answer was hard and fast, no time given to thinking it over.

"I respect that," Edgar said, then looked Ellie in the eyes. "What about you?"

A single tear streaked down her rosy cheek. It was obvious to him that she had been giving this a lot of thought. She turned to face her brother, who was in his usual spot upon her shoulder and said, "My only fear is that you'll resent me for this decision."

"Never," Johnny replied.

Another tear broke free from Ellie's eyes. "And when the decision is placed before me to stay or pass through the doorway? What then?"

"Yours to make," Johnny said. "I'll respect it either way."

"Oh Johnny." Ellie looked away from him and Edgar as the tears spilled forth.

"It's settled then," Edgar said. "These souls have waited long enough." He held up the bag of crystals and rang the bell.

"If you behave yourself," Ellie said, "maybe they'll invite you to work on the Cherokee Advocate."

"Why Miss Feller, I am never less than a proper gentleman."

With a chuckle, Ellie said, "Go on, then."

Everything had been working in Edgar's favor as if the cosmos recognized his new righteous path and whole-heartedly approved. He and Ellie had successfully restored Johnny's body. The crystal housing Johnny's spirit remained unscathed, and it was a simple matter of reassembling the mechanical body. Also, it had taken little convincing to persuade James's goons to go along with Edgar's story of a tragic industrial accident claiming the life of James Laurent. The mere promise of them being allowed to close the deal for the armored power suits in James's stead was all it took. They had been ill-informed on the inner workings of the suits and by the time they realized they had been duped it would be too late. They had already corroborated Edgar's story, putting him and Ellie in the clear.

All that remained was to set the imprisoned souls free and then he and Ellie would be allowed to explore their relationship.

John Ross sat in a high-backed chair before a roaring fire; his eyes fixated on the flames and penetrating beyond the veil.

"You've done well, Mister Poe. *Yowa* is pleased."

"Thank you," Edgar said, then held out the bag of crystals. "How will you free them?"

"We will send them on a forced march halfway across the… "John Ross stopped when his gaze fell on Edgar's forearm. With the reflexes of a coiled snake, the bear of a man lashed out and grabbed hold of Edgar's wrist. The bag fell from his grasp, the crystals spilling across the floor.

Edgar saw a black line peeking out from his bandage as if someone had pumped ink into his veins.

With no regard to Edgar, John Ross pulled Edgar's sleeve higher and then ripped off the bandage.

"Easy," Edgar said.

Black trailed outward, up his forearm and down to his wrist from the puncture mark.

John Ross released his hold on Edgar, nearly throwing his arm back at him. "You must leave."

"What?" Edgar tried to protest.

"You are marked by death. It follows you. I will not have you endanger my people."

Edgar stood, rooted to the spot, John Ross's fearful stare unnerving him.

John Ross stood, chest puffed, fists balled and ready to strike. "I will not ask again."

Uneasy, Edgar simply nodded. Before turning to leave, Edgar pulled down his shirt sleeve so as not to alarm anyone else in the tribe. He exited the grand house and was greeted by Ellie's warm smile, but that soon faded as she looked upon his solemn face.

Ellie took his hand in hers and asked, "What's wrong?"

He wasn't sure of the answer, but one thing was certain. "I'm in trouble, Ellie."

ABOUT THE AUTHORS

Keith Gouveia is an accomplished horror and dark fantasy writer and fierce advocate of independent and artisanal publishers. His other recent releases are *The Screaming Field,* a tale of scarecrow terror, and *The Black Cat and the Ghoul,* a continuation of Edgar Poe's tale. He is also editor and contributor of the horror anthology, *The Snuff Syndicate.*

Matt Peters holds an MFA in Creative Writing from the University of New Orleans. He teaches in the Creative Writing Program at Full Sail University and runs Beating Windward Press. His fiction has been published in the journals *580 Split, Burrow Press Review*, the *Burlesque Press Variety Show*; and in the anthologies *Voices Rising: Stories from the Katrina Narrative Project, Bits of the Dead, Keeping Track, Forget How You Found Us, Gutters and Alleyways*, and *Crossing Lines*.

CROSSROAD
PRESS

Made in the USA
Las Vegas, NV
17 September 2024

95321804R00152